THE LEGEND OF THE THIRTEENTH PILGRIM

Also by Jessica North

THE HIGH VALLEY
RIVER RISING

The Legend of the Thirteenth Pilgrim

Jessica North

Coward, McCann & Geoghegan, Inc.
New York

Library of Congress Cataloging in Publication Data

North, Jessica.
  The legend of the thirteenth pilgrim.

  I. Title.
PZ4.N8579Le 1979 [PS3564.0763] 813'.5'4
ISBN 0-698-10944-9   78-10281

Printed in the United States of America

THE LEGEND OF THE THIRTEENTH PILGRIM

Chapter One

This morning, walking on the quay, I thought I saw Pandora's ghost.

She stood in the shadow of the customshouse, a motionless silhouette against the pale sky, head lifted proudly as she gazed toward the sea. A cloud of gulls wheeled overhead, circling and crying; a storm petrel skimmed through the flock to land at her feet—but she paid no attention, standing transfixed, seeming to search the distance for some sign or omen.

Pandora come to life again—and, oh, but she was beautiful!

For an instant I expected her to turn and speak my name; to say, with her faintly mocking smile and tone, "Good morning, Catherine."

The whole impression lasted no longer than it takes to draw one quick breath—to gasp—and even in that paralyzing second I did not really believe I'd encountered a specter. Pandora was dead, sealed forever in a huge marble vault hundreds of miles from here, in Venice. While my emotions shouted, "Pandora!" reason quietly told me that the girl was merely a stranger who resembled my sister.

She was only a few steps from me, half turned away, thick hair falling in a tawny cascade over the green leather jerkin I gave her three Christmases ago—long before our terrible and final quarrel. Her face was hidden, but I knew from the set of her shoulders she wore a mask of arrogance—that impertinent smile that marred her astonishing beauty, but successfully disguised her fear.

My heart hammered as she turned toward me.

Then the illusion vanished instantly. This girl was broad-featured and freckled, Pandora's very opposite.

"Do you speak English?" she asked.

"Yes."

Looking at her, I was amazed to have imagined the least resemblance to my sister. Pandora had been tall—as tall as I am—while this girl was of only average height. And her hair, much darker than mine, had not been brown but brown-gold. Now that my bewilderment had evaporated, I felt irritated with myself. I do not ordinarily harbor even brief illusions; I do not imagine I see ghosts in broad daylight, my sense of make-believe does not run riot. Those excesses had been Pandora's specialties, not mine.

"They told me there was an early steamer to Piraeus," the girl said. "But no one's here. Do you know the schedule?"

"I'm sorry, I don't. We only arrived here yesterday. I'm sure they can tell you at the hotel."

"Oh. Well, thanks anyway."

She strode off, seeking a better informant, and I turned to make my way slowly back to the hotel—a flood of memories welling up in me, pouring over the defenses I'd built against them.

Hours later, I still cannot dispel a sense of Pandora's presence. She seems strangely close tonight; in the rustle of the vine leaves outside the window, the echo of footfalls in the tiled corridor, a murmuring voice that passes the door. And looming in my mind is the picture of a sailboat, a tiny craft tossed helplessly by the storm waves on a lake in northern Italy. I see Pandora struggling in the water, then sinking below the wind-whipped surface. I always imagine it that way, even though I know there was no struggle; she had not known she was dying.

I understand, of course, the cause of these memories and the reason for this morning's illusion. It was a dream I had last night—a dream I've had many times before, and one in which Pandora plays a part. Perhaps I shouldn't call it a dream, for it is really the reliving of a scene from childhood, a memory of what happened on a crisp September day twenty years ago.

I had celebrated my fifth birthday early the previous summer, and my sister Dorrie (it was later she began calling herself Pandora) had just turned four.

In the dream—or in my memory—I saw our two small figures descending the steps of the front porch of our house on King William Square—a proper and solid New England residence that had belonged to the Andrews family for four generations. In our starchy blue skirts, white blouses, and navy blue sweaters, Dorrie and I might have been twins but for my greater height. I proudly carried a great yellow chrysanthemum, newly opened. A gift for my teacher? For a game of show and tell? I cannot remember.

Trailing us came the much larger figure of Miss Fuller, one of the series of elderly women who looked after us in our motherless household.

"Just a minute!" called a sharp voice from the doorway, and Mrs. Thornton, who was in charge of the house and of our whole world, stepped out to hold a quick, whispered conversation with Miss Fuller.

"Professor Andrews—" He was our father. "—is worried that—" Her voice faded, then she said, ". . . It might even happen today."

Then I could hear no more, but both women gave us such strange looks that I felt sure we were suspected of some atrocious misconduct. At last Miss Fuller nodded firmly and we were on our way.

"Don't go so fast, Catherine. Take nice little steps like Dorrie. Why are you always so headstrong?" Miss Fuller, hindered by rheumatism, stumped behind us as we moved toward the corner of College Avenue.

"Step on a crack, break your mother's back," Dorrie chanted, and I deliberately trod hard on the next crack in the sidewalk, wondering if the magic would work—hoping to give our runaway mother the punishment she fully deserved for leaving us.

I held Dorrie's small hand tightly in mine. She was the baby; I had been taught to guard her against unspecified, mysterious but terrible hazards.

Morley Day School, where I spent the mornings in kindergarten while Dorrie played in nursery, was only two blocks away, and there were no streets to cross. Usually, Miss Fuller walked us only to the corner and then watched, shading her eyes with her hand, until we safely reached the playground entrance. I loved the adventure of walking the long block alone, and the responsibility of being in full charge of Dorrie filled me with pride.

But today, Miss Fuller turned the corner with us and followed. Insulted by this lack of confidence and feeling cheated of my freedom, I whispered to Dorrie, "Race you!"

We were off pell-mell down the sidewalk—not quite racing, for I clung to my sister's hand—but in seconds we had left Miss Fuller behind us.

Then the dream always shifted, became confused and frightening. There was a long sedan . . . black? Dark blue? It swept by the curb to halt abruptly just ahead, huge and threatening. Two men leaped from it, leaving the doors agape. The larger man had a flushed face and a bristling moustache; his companion, vague and featureless, wore some kind of uniform.

"Come quickly, little ones! Quickly!" the big man said. Hands, not rough, but terrifying in their strength and purpose, seized both my arms. Dorrie was snatched from me, and above her hysterical cries I could hear Miss Fuller screaming for help.

And, as if by magic, help came instantly. Before I could be thrust into the waiting sedan, other men were racing toward us—men who must have been hiding nearby, for they seemed to appear from nowhere.

The dream ended as it always did; a confusing blur of struggles and shouts, a police siren wailing in my ears. Then my father knelt beside me, comforting me while I wept—not only from fright, but because the yellow chrysanthemum had been trampled and crushed.

In many ways, that morning shaped and changed our lives, and led to all that followed. Remembering it, I see Pandora in a hundred swiftly changing scenes and poses—the heart-shaped face with its elfin and faintly mischievous smile, the luminous gray eyes that showed the first promise of a cool beauty. And even then her thick, tawny hair always had a sheen of gold. Yet she was not a beautiful child anymore than I was.

Sometimes, working up my courage, I inspected myself in the big mirror that hung in the upstairs hall; it was always a painful experience. I was too tall, too bony, all points and angles; my straw-colored hair, no matter how faithfully I brushed it, hung lifeless and frighteningly skimpy. Would it all fall out before the year was over? Would I have to wear a wig like old Mrs. Sassman who ran the student boarding house next door? It seemed a real and terrible possibility.

Dorrie's troubles were the opposite of mine. I remember her standing helpless in the school playground, tears streaming down her plump cheeks while a circle of girls taunted her.

"Fatty Dorrie," they chanted. "Fatty Dorrie! Fatty, fatty!" And one girl strutted back and forth, shouting, "Tub a' lard, tub a' lard! Can't run across the yard!"

I charged them, my hard fists flailing, and with squeals and shrieks they fled. Strong and wiry, I was able to battle for my honor, but Dorrie had no defense except tears.

I remember Mrs. Thornton, the housekeeper, saying to Mrs. Sassman, "It's a shame about Dorrie. She'd be a pretty child, but you can't keep her out of the refrigerator." Mrs. Thornton's eyes narrowed and she lowered her voice. "The poor thing eats like that because she misses her mother. I read about such cases in a magazine article by a doctor. It has to do with a craving for affection."

I didn't quite believe this because Dorrie was too young; our mother had run away and left us when Dorrie was hardly more than a baby. How could you miss someone you never knew? Even I, a year and a half older, could hardly remember. But I hoped Mrs. Thornton was right. I wanted to blame our mother for Dorrie's troubles—for any troubles. It would be another crime she had committed against us.

Dorrie's astonishing transformation took place when she turned fourteen and became stage struck. She pored over every stage and screen magazine she could lay her hands on, and suddenly revealed an iron determination. She dieted, exercised, and climbed and descended the stairs over and over again with *Webster's Collegiate Dictionary* balanced on her head.

"I'm going to be a star, Catherine," she announced, and indeed there were stars in her eyes. "And you'll be a famous artist. We'll be wildly rich and everybody will love us!"

"Sure, Dorrie," I said, and continued working on my sketch. "Our fairy godmother will touch us with her magic wand."

"I don't need magic! I can make myself into anything I choose!" The unaccustomed fierceness in her voice startled me. "And I won't be called Dorrie anymore. I've always hated my name, it's so ordinary, so ugly. I'm going to be . . ." She paused, then announced dramatically, "Pandora! Pandora Andrews! How do you like that?"

I frowned, but still did not take her seriously. "I don't think Matthew will be pleased," I replied. Matthew Andrews was our father, but we never called him anything but Matthew.

She tossed her head, imitating some actress she'd studied. "Who cares what Matthew thinks? I'm asking your opinion."

I sighed, then said, "Pandora's a glamorous stage name, but it might be unlucky."

"Why unlucky?"

"Oh, Dorrie, don't you remember anything from school? Pandora was the girl in the Greek legend who opened a chest and let loose all the troubles in the world."

"Why did she do that?"

I shrugged. "Just curiosity, she had to see what was inside the chest. And I think the story's also supposed to show that if a woman's too beautiful, trouble comes."

"How perfect!" Dorrie whirled, executing an awkward but vigorous pirouette. "Everything you've said is a sign that Pandora's the right name for me. I'd love to be so beautiful that I made trouble for everybody. And the curiosity part, too—I'm always desperate to find things out. Remember how furious you were when I read your diary? And when you caught me steaming open your letters?"

"Yes, I remember! And don't you dare snoop in my room again, Dorrie."

"Not Dorrie. Pandora," she corrected me, and her gray eyes widened as she looked dreamily into the future. But fortunately she could not see what lay ahead—could not know that part of her dream would come true with a bitter irony.

Two years later I watched her on stage when she was star of a school play—slender and lovely in a pale lavender gown. The audience, captured by her beauty, forgave her everything; the voice that often failed to carry, the missed cues. And I brimmed with a kind of maternal pride for my little sister, my special charge.

Later, I forced back tears as Pandora, a bride at nineteen in a cloud of white lace, floated down the aisle of St. Paul's Church to marry Ralph Harper, a handsome but unstable man she had met at drama school in New York. We did not know then that Ralph had divorced a wife in order to marry my sister.

Pandora's marriage hardly survived a year, which didn't

surprise me. But I was astonished and shocked when news came that she had married again—a quick, impulsive marriage to Gordon Carr, an instructor in my father's department at the college, who then gave up his promising career to follow Pandora to New York. Again, I concealed my emotions; this time for a different reason.

But by far my most vivid and painful memories are of the last time we saw each other—on a cold, glittering November day in New England; a Thanksgiving that for both of us proved utterly thankless, when Pandora, angry and defiant, stormed out of the house forever on a course that led to violence and death.

It was only three months earlier that our father, Matthew Andrews, had suffered a brief illness and had died. I was living alone in the big brick house on King William Square; it now belonged to me.

Matthew in death had been as even-handed with his daughters as he had been while living. I was given the house and a small amount of cash and income—not quite enough to live on, but I had my salary from the Audiovisual Department of the college where I worked as a designer and illustrator. Pandora inherited bonds and insurance money of equal value. I did not question Matthew's fairness, but I wondered why he had arranged things this way. Did he think I would never leave the house where I had spent my life? At times I wondered about this myself, but always pushed the thought from my mind.

Pandora was to arrive on the ten o'clock train from New York that morning, and I was eager to see her—not that we had been close in recent years, but because today was the first holiday since Matthew's death.

I felt oppressed and bothered by the emptiness of the house, which on most days scarcely affected me. But today, the silence of the rooms was almost palpable, and I retreated to a chair near the bay windows in the living room to wait for Pandora.

Across the street, the college campus stretched deserted. Its elms, after last night's storm, had turned to glistening silver and crystal. Oldham Hall, where Matthew had taught history for more than thirty years, sparkled like a fairy-tale ice palace, and beyond it rose the turrets of other crystal castles. When Pandora at last arrived, emerging regally from the taxi, I thought of the Snow Queen.

In her long white coat with its mink-trimmed hood and cuffs, she looked a medieval princess; an imperial, slender figure against the background of snow—white on white with a single slash of color, the sheaf of vermillion roses she carried in her arms. Even the taxi driver recognized royalty—behaving like an old-fashioned coachman as he scurried to bring her overnight case to the front door—homage Pandora rewarded with a ravishing smile and tip that was probably too generous.

We embraced in the hall. "Catherine, darling, you look marvelous! And that blue dress is lovely, just the color of your eyes. Surely you didn't find it in this town!" She whirled into the living room, the full sleeves of her coat billowing. "What heaven to be home again, even if it's only for one night."

"Can't you stay the weekend?" I asked, disappointed but not surprised.

"I have to dash back tomorrow morning. Besides, with this snow, you'll probably be off to some ski resort."

"No. Everyone I know is with their families, and I don't enjoy going alone. Maybe next weekend."

"Really, Catherine!" She gave me the wry, knowing smile I'd seen her use several times on television. "The only way to go to a ski resort is alone. How else can you meet those gorgeous skiers?"

She presented me with the roses. "Happy Thanksgiving!" Taking off her coat and long gloves, she shivered. "I'd forgotten how drafty this house is. Do you have the makings of a hot toddy?"

"Give me two minutes in the kitchen," I told her.

"Angel!"

When I returned with her drink and a vase for the roses, Pandora was standing near the fireplace, hands behind her back.

"I've brought you the most fabulous present," she said. "Guess!"

"I've already had my present. The roses."

"No, no. This is something special."

Pandora never appeared anywhere empty-handed. She greeted hostesses with the finest wines and most expensive bonbons, while surprised hosts were showered with everything from cigars to fishing lures. Her lavishness often exceeded her income, but few people suspected, as I did, that Pandora was trying to buy approval; that she paid bribes for the affection she craved and could not believe would be freely given.

Behind the perfectly gowned, perfectly coiffured, perfectly enameled figure she presented to the world lurked the chubby little girl who'd been taunted in the playground. A lovely woman had emerged, but the frightened, helpless child had only gone into hiding.

"Guess, Catherine!" she repeated, eyes twinkling.

I remembered a childhood game. "Animal, vegetable, or mineral?"

"Mineral! All mineral!" she exclaimed. "Oh, I can't wait for you to guess. Here!" She handed me a small but heavy package.

I undid the china paper, opened a carved wooden box, and found myself gasping.

"The opals! Oh, Pandora!" Australian fire opals that had once belonged to our grandmother shone against the cream velvet of the case. The stones, set in thick old gold, had a flame like the light of winter stars—flashing earrings, a necklace, and a fingering cut as a shimmering crescent.

"They're yours now, Catherine. I want you to have them."

Matthew had given his mother's opals to Pandora at the time of her marriage to Ralph Harper. "Think of them as a

gift from your grandmother who died before you were born,"
he had said. "After all, you carry her name, Dorrie."

Did the words carry a quiet reproach? He'd said nothing
when Dorrie began calling herself Pandora; he simply never
spoke the new name.

Gazing at the opals, I shook my head. "No, Pandora.
They're too valuable for you to give away."

"But you have to accept! I never wear them and it wouldn't
be right to sell a gift from Matthew." She sipped her drink. "I
admit if they were diamonds or jewels worth a real fortune,
I'd snatch the money in a minute, but they're not so expensive
that I can't be sentimental and give them to my sister."

"Do you have any idea what they're worth?" I asked.

"I ought to know. I had to pawn them three times when I
was down on my luck. Take them, Catherine, before they're
lost in a pawnshop forever."

I don't know which astonished me more—that she had
pawned a family heirloom or that she now admitted doing it,
but her admission ended my qualms about accepting.

"Thank you, dear," I said. "I love them. Remember,
though, they'll always belong to both of us."

"Fine," she said, smiling. "As long as you're the one who
pays the insurance." She kissed me quickly on the cheek.

"Whatever made you think of giving me the opals?"

"Well, I wanted to bring you something special and I
couldn't think what. Then last week there came a sign."

Pandora had always claimed a firm belief in what she called
"signs." The superstition had come from Mrs. Ginori, an Italian widow who looked after us for almost three years. Mrs.
Ginori saw omens everywhere; in shooting stars, flights of
birds, even in double-yolked eggs. Pandora eagerly adopted
all of Mrs. Ginori's magical auguries and invented hundreds
of her own—such as counting the cars of a passing train to
learn how many years of happiness she would enjoy. But if
the answer disappointed her, she cheerfully multiplied by
two.

"What was the sign?" I asked.

"As I said, I was absolutely baffled about a gift for you, and then my agent sent me to audition for a part in a television film. It turned out that the character I was reading was named Catherine Anderson, so close to Catherine Andrews that I kept thinking of you. The story took place in Australia during the gold rush and the very first lines were about Catherine being given some fire opals. Isn't that amazing? It was a sure sign of what I should do."

"Yes, amazing," I said dryly, wondering if there were a word of truth in this. Probably not; she was dramatizing what was undoubtedly a simple decision. Feeling uncomfortable, I changed the subject. "How did the audition go? Did you get the job?"

"It went beautifully, especially a scene where I played the guitar and sang 'Waltzing Mathilda.' I've been studying the guitar, you know. But I turned the role down—the character was too vapid, sickeningly sweet."

She spoke with the careless assurance she always assumed when telling lies. Pandora simply couldn't admit to any failure or limitation, however unimportant. When we were children, her glib disregard for the truth angered and frustrated me, for she not only invented excuses but sometimes manufactured completely unnecessary falsehoods, like the time at summer camp when she boasted about how expertly she played the piano—Dorrie, who had never taken a lesson and could not even tap out a scale.

Now, as she chatted airily about the various offers she'd rejected, I listened with sinking spirits. She had not changed— had not even grown more subtle—and this pretense of success, like her pretense of so many accomplishments, struck me as pitiable. I longed for her to accept herself for what she was: a beautiful young woman, admired and envied. Although her career had not been spectacular, she had every reason to be proud of the limited success she had won—several appearances on television, two good off-Broadway roles, and jobs in summer stock every year. But reality could never be enough for Pandora; still a child crying for attention, she had to appear perfect and unexcelled. Listening to her, I silently blamed our mother, whose desertion had made Pandora what she was. Had I, too, been marked in some different way? I could not tell, could not see myself as I saw my sister.

"The best money is in television commercials," she was saying, "but it's boring work."

"You do them very well." Pandora, I now realized, was tense and somehow apprehensive. No stranger could have detected this, but I knew the symptoms; the quick gestures, the tilting of her head. I glanced again at the opals, suddenly suspecting they were a bribe—payment for something Pandora had done or planned to do shortly. I knew my sister thoroughly, and her motives were not always what they seemed.

By the time we sat down to dinner in the late afternoon, Pandora's mood had changed from gaiety to an almost sullen silence.

On the table, candles burned in silver holders, flanking a centerpiece I had arranged; a wreath of late autumn leaves with the last purple asters from the garden, a hopeless attempt to lend a festive touch to the meal. But everything, I realized, was wrong; the pretense that the two of us somehow made a family only emphasized the fact that we were lone survivors.

Glancing at the candles, Pandora arched a delicate eyebrow, then her gaze traveled to the asters and back to her plate of turkey with oyster dressing I'd bought at a carry-out food shop.

"Really, Catherine, it's mawkish," she said.

I agreed completely. "I'm obviously too sentimental about holidays. We should have gone to a restaurant."

"The two of us rattling around in this barn of a house. How do you stand it alone?"

"Mrs. Thornton still comes in three mornings a week."

"What fascinating company!"

"You forget I'm at work five days a week. And in the evenings I have classes at the Art Center."

"You spend eight hours a day drawing charts and illustrations and then go to an art school at night?" Her tone was incredulous. "You must be mad, Catherine."

"I've been studying jewelry design. Silverwork and lost wax casting."

"Jewlry? But you hardly ever wear any!"

"Wearing it has nothing to do with making it."

She drained her wineglass, refilled it. "I propose a toast," she said. "To my divorce—it became final last week. I'm no longer Mrs. Gordon Carr. But I suppose you knew that already."

"Yes," I said, meeting her strangely intent gaze. "Gordon telephoned last Monday."

"Well, he certainly didn't waste any time. Did you congratulate him?"

"Were congratulations in order?" My tone was sharper than I'd intended.

"Of course." She drew a cigarette from an enameled case and flicked her lighter. "You're the one Gordon should have married, Catherine. I've always thought that."

"Not quite *always*," I corrected her. "Now may we talk about something else?"

Pandora ignored me. "Who knows what happiness the future has in store? Gordon's coming back here to teach next year, after he finishes some dull book he's writing."

"What's that to me? Gordon and I were friends, nothing more." This was the truth, but not quite all of it. At one time I had believed our friendship would change, would become love. I had recovered from this illusion, and I could think of Gordon with no feeling of hurt or loss. But it was different when Pandora spoke of him; the anger and bitterness I had long since buried threatened to spring to life again.

"I'm thinking of selling the house," I said, shifting the subject abruptly. "It's the only residence left in a line of rooming houses and it's too big, too expensive to keep up."

"A ghastly white elephant," she agreed quickly.

I suppressed a retort, determined not to let her goad me to anger, which for some mysterious reason she seemed bent upon doing. "And I'm thinking of taking a long vacation as soon as the college semester's over in February, a leave of absence for several months. Perhaps I'll go to an art school in Arizona."

"Yes, we both need a change. I have some plans of my own." She hesitated, gave me a shrewd, hard look, and said quietly, "You've never forgiven me for marrying Gordon, have you, Catherine?"

The abruptness of her remark caught me unprepared. "Will you stop harping on that subject?" I felt blood rush to my face. "There's nothing to forgive."

"But there is! He was in love with you—he just hadn't quite realized it." Rising from her chair, she moved to the window, pacing. "I think the main reason I married him was because he loved you and I was jealous. I had to prove he'd choose me."

"Jealous of me! What utter nonsense!"

She turned toward me, her eyes and voice suddenly listless. "I always have been. Everyone always loved you best, especially Matthew. Oh, I understand why. You're strong and sensible and calm—all the things I can't be. You never make a mess of your own life or anyone else's."

"Stop it, Dorrie!"

She smiled thinly. "Not Dorrie. Pandora. I chose the right name for myself, didn't I? Pandora who let evil loose, Pandora the troublemaker." She crushed out her cigarette with a vicious gesture and I watched her, confused and alarmed. I had learned long ago to expect anything from Pandora; but never this, never self-accusation.

"I'm only twenty-three but I've already had two miserable marriages and several rotten love affairs you can't even imagine." She reached for another cigarette, her hand trembling. "I came between Ralph Harper and his wife, and I didn't even love him. I wrecked everything for you and Gordon just out of spite. Everywhere I go, I cause trouble. It's a gift I have, my one talent."

I rose from my chair, feeling helpless, unable to deal with

any of this. I could calm Pandora when she was in a tantrum, I could quiet her outbursts of dramatics, but this was different; she spoke in a hopeless monotone that seemed beyond despair.

"I was lying to you about that television job," she said. "I didn't turn it down. The truth is they didn't want me. Nobody does; I haven't worked for months, haven't even come close."

I took a step toward her, wanting to give comfort. Then something halted me where I stood. Her eyes, which had been expressionless in the taut, chalky face, suddenly stared at me with such malice that I drew back.

"I'm going to have a new life," she said, her voice dropping to a whisper. "A new life! And there's no way you can stop me, Catherine."

I forced myself to remain calm. "Have I ever stopped you from doing anything, Pandora? Have I ever interfered?"

"Yes! In your own sweet, quiet way, you've made me feel guilty for years. You've always stood between me and the one thing I needed."

"Dorrie, get hold of yourself!" My patience had come to an end. "You're not making sense, you don't realize what you're saying."

She lifted her head defiantly, seeming to gather strength. "I'm going to Italy."

"Fine, go to Italy," I said. "Who's objecting? I told you, I'm going on a trip myself."

"You don't understand, Catherine. I'm going to . . ." She hesitated, then delivered the blow—spoke the words she'd been building toward all day. "I'm going to Italy to live with Mother."

"Mother?" I heard the words, but did not comprehend them. "What do you mean?"

"I mean *Mother*! My mother, Althea Hoffman!" Her voice rose, hard and shrill. "A woman who happened to be your mother, too, much as you'd like to forget it!"

I stared at her, speechless. Althea Hoffman . . . a name

never spoken in this house, a name to be banished from memory. I felt as though Pandora had struck me in the face, and I turned away from her. "You can't do this."

She blazed defiance. "I can and I will! We've been writing to each other for nearly a year. Why shouldn't I go to her? Now that Matthew's dead—"

"Thank you for that," I said. "At least you waited that long, so I suppose you must have some trace of loyalty in you."

"You don't understand loyalty, Catherine, you only understand hate."

Suddenly my numbness and shock vanished; sheer anger carried me toward her. "Yes, I understand hate. I hate her for ruining Matthew's life, I hate her for abandoning us. You can't remember her, but I can." Face to face, Pandora flinched, stepped backward, and I followed, pressing her. "Sometimes I used to remember in a dream. She was sitting beside my bed, holding my hand and singing a song I'll never forget as long as I live. Then she was gone. Gone forever."

"But she wanted us, she tried to have us with her."

"You mean she tried to steal us away! She hadn't hurt Matthew enough, she even wanted to take his children from him!" My rage seemed to feed upon itself, rekindled by its own heat, and I felt my fists clenching and unclenching. "Don't you remember the look on his face when someone who didn't know she'd been his wife mentioned her name?"

"Of course people mentioned her name. She's famous."

"Famous? A second-rate celebrity and a tenth-rate singer."

Pandora moved past me, going to the table to pour herself another glass of wine. When at last she spoke, her voice was quieter but still trembled. "I was proud of being Althea Hoffman's daughter, but I never dared say so. I used to slip off to the public library to hunt for magazine articles about her. There was one with a beautiful picture of her taken backstage after a concert in Paris, and when the librarian wasn't watching, I tore it out and brought it home. It showed her with her husband, Victor Donato."

"He wasn't her husband," I said harshly. "He was just a rich man who kept her."

Pandora seemed not to hear me. "I'd look at the picture when no one else was upstairs—I had it almost a year, then I burned it because I knew how angry you and Matthew would be if you found it."

"Angry?" I exclaimed, incredulous. "Are you completely insensitive? Can't you understand how it would have hurt Matthew? Didn't you care?"

"You and Matthew kept us apart!" The words seemed wrenched from her. "I needed her, she loved me, but I couldn't be with her. Later on she didn't seem so important to me—I forgot her, almost. Then about a year ago I read in the paper that Victor Donato had died. I wrote her a note saying how sorry I was, and she answered with a long letter explaining everything. That was the beginning." Pandora took a sip of wine, seemed to summon her courage. "Matthew's dead now, but I'm not. I'm going to have a new life, a wonderful life, and nothing you say or do makes any difference!"

Perhaps that would not have been the end, perhaps I could have controlled my hurt and anger, if only she hadn't smiled at me—a triumphant smile, mocking and false. The pent-up resentment and pain of years seethed in me, then exploded. "Go to Italy then, and the sooner the better! As far as I'm concerned, it isn't far enough away. Go live with this wonderful woman who explains all she did to us in a nice letter! She caused you to suffer too, Pandora, caused your spite and your selfishness and your lying. She made you into what I see today and, believe me, it's not a pretty picture!"

Pandora blanched with fury. Lifting the wineglass, she dashed its contents into my face, then hurled the glass against the wall to shatter. Turning with a cry, she ran toward the hall. I heard her stumble up the stairs to her room, and the door slammed violently.

I wiped the wine from my face, then stared dully at the blood-colored stains on the linen. Moving to the window seat, I let my eyes wander over the familiar room which now seemed alien, its atmosphere laden with the hostility of our quarrel. The heat of my anger had given way to a chill feeling as cold as the ice-locked garden beyond the glass. Wind had heaped the snow into mounds; there were drifts near the privet hedge. I thought of Matthew on a summer day kneeling to cultivate the beds of phlox and gentians, gentle Matthew who had been hurt beyond recovery by Althea Hoffman.

I thought of the day long ago when, hidden by the lilac bush, I had listened to Mrs. Thornton explain about our mother to Mrs. Ginori, who had just begun her three years of service as our caretaker.

"Their mother ran off with this foreign millionaire, and left the poor little things. Imagine, a woman who'd desert her own babies! For a while, she lived openly with the man in New York. Nowadays people get away with things like that, but then it was a terrible scandal. It broke Professor Andrews' heart; he's never been the same."

Mrs. Ginori asked if our mother ever visited us.

"Not likely!" exclaimed Mrs. Thornton, triumph in her voice. "She doesn't dare set foot in this country—there's all kinds of criminal charges against her. She was born in Switzerland—the family was poor as dirt—and now she's what they call an undesirable alien. They say she's a very high-class singer, with concerts and operas all over Europe. But not in the U.S.A! The morals of an alley cat is what she has!"

I listened in pain and shame, knowing it was all true and wondering how I could face Mrs. Ginori after this. Maybe Mrs. Ginori didn't understand the story, since she spoke little English. That was my only hope.

The years had not softened my feelings. As I heard Pandora come down the stairs and go into the hall to ring for a taxi, I thought, "Let them be together. They deserve each other." I realized bitterly that she had come here today for only one purpose: to break this news to me. Earlier, she had attacked me because she knew her own guilt.

The front door slammed behind her a moment later and, rising, I stood utterly still in the silence of the house. Then I re-

Jessica North

membered the opals. I should have known from the beginning that they were a bribe, a salve for Pandora's conscience. I would have nothing to do with them!

I ran into the living room and snatched up the case that held the stones, but before I could reach the front door, I heard Pandora's taxi pulling away. Standing on the porch, I caught a glimpse of her—white hood obscured by the steamed rear window of the cab.

A knifelike wind whipped my skirt, chilling me, and the air swarmed with spiraling clouds of driven snow—veiling the campus, blotting out the street as the taxi vanished into the storm. Shivering, I went into the house, still holding the opals; not suspecting that they were Pandora's final gift to me and that I would never see her again.

Chapter Two

At the beginning of February I closed up the house and went to Arizona to enroll in a small, private college of arts and crafts.

Mrs. Thornton, although stony with disapproval at my leaving, agreed to come to the house once or twice a week to make sure all was in order, but warned me this was no guarantee against vandals or such hazards as fire and burst water pipes. "And if my sister in Florida takes a bad turn, I'll have to go to her, of course. What about forwarding mail?"

"Anything that looks like a bill or a business letter should go to Mr. Rowe at the bank. Other things can wait. And please don't give my address to anyone; I've told people I'll be traveling. I want a complete change."

She regarded me with a bleak eye, as though I were a criminal in flight. "I was thinking of mail from Italy," she said, her voice carefully expressionless.

"If there is any, it can wait until I come back," I told her, and for once Mrs. Thornton actually smiled.

I had received three picture postcards from Pandora. The

first, which came only two weeks after our quarrel, was a garishly colored photo of the Piazza San Marco and a scrawled message of no originality. "Venice is beautiful! Love, Pandora." The second, from a village in northern Italy, showed a view of a lake—a stretch of water that might have been anywhere in the world—and two equally universal rowboats. This time she informed me she had met "the most thrilling man," but did not name or describe this thriller.

A week before I left, the last card arrived, another Piazza San Marco, with the announcement that "we" were going on a long Adriatic cruise in the spring. Exactly who "we" might be was left unstated.

Although the cards, with the unvaried closing of "love," were clearly meant as an entreaty for peace, I did not answer them. The passing weeks had taken the edge off my anger, but I hadn't forgiven my sister, nor could I bring myself to send anything to Althea Hoffman's address.

Things could never again be the same between Pandora and me, I supposed. We had spoken to each other with the terrible kind of honesty that can never be wholly retracted. Yet, despite everything, we were sisters; we had grown up together as allies against the world, and our years together could not be erased. Eventually, her Italian adventure would turn sour; she would retreat homeward, tearful "little sister" needing comfort and protection again. When that happened, I would bow to the inevitable and welcome her as I always had—at least, I would try to. But until then, she would have no word from me.

Also, I had changed my mind about returning the opals. In a sense I had paid for them, paid bitterly, and if Pandora had them, the chance of their being sold by a pawnbroker seemed a very real threat. Family loyalty, I had learned, was not one of Pandora's virtues.

On the morning I left, when my bags were packed and the last dustcover had been put over the last chair, I heard the clink of the brass mail slot, went to the front door, and opened

the post box. Another card—this time a photo of a gondola—
and the longest message so far.

> Dear Catherine,
>   Met Gordon at the Danieli Restaurant. He's in Italy doing re-
> search, had some legal papers for me to sign. We talked about
> you for hours! Were your ears burning?
>   Love,
>   Pandora

The earlier cards I had simply glanced at, then put in a
drawer of my desk. But this one I read a second time, slowly
and deliberately tore it in two, then tore it again.

Arizona was a tonic—afternoon sunshine and crisp nights
of huge stars shining with unbelievable brilliance in the clear
air.

The school proved friendly and informal. I spent the mornings working in the jewelry studio and most afternoons painting—perhaps not very well, for I was a far better illustrator
than artist—but my enjoyment of the work was more important than the results.

Not far away towered mountains with magnificent slopes
for skiing, and I went to a ski lodge with other students on
weekends. After the snows melted, there were picnics and
cross-country horseback rides.

I knew this was a temporary world; a postponement of my
real life and future, whatever that future might be. But I was
content to go on day by day, week by week, until the weeks
had turned into almost three months without my realizing it.

On the morning in April when a telephone call shattered this
pleasant existence, I'd begun the day concerned with nothing
more than the fire opals—thinking not of their previous owner, but only of the stones themselves. By now I knew every
detail of the opals' shifting moods. They were dark, almost
black, but when light struck them they revealed an inner radi-

ance—a hidden fire in their darkness that could be cold and starlike or a blazing flame.

On my way to the jewelry studio, I stopped at the mailboxes and found a note Mrs. Thornton had sent from Florida. Her sister had indeed "taken a turn," but a mild one, and Mrs. Thornton would undoubtedly be home again by the time I received the note. She sounded annoyed that her sister, after summoning her so far, had been so inconsiderate as to recover at once.

I strolled into the studio, a long room crowded with workbenches, welding tanks and torches, and equipment for lost wax casting. The instructor, Mr. Burke, greeted me. "Good morning, Miss Andrews. Enjoy your vacation?"

"Very much, thanks."

There had been a holiday and, with two other students, I had taken a trip to the Mexican border. After prowling curio shops, I'd spent hours hand-buffing the new settings for the opals. Today would be the informal unveiling of my work.

At my own bench, I unwrapped the four gleaming pieces of the set and spread them out. Mounted in leafy silver, the stones glowed in the light from the window like the last moment of sunset.

"Oh, Catherine, how beautiful!" It was Pam, the friendly, plump girl who worked next to me. "Hey, everybody!" she called. "Catherine's finished resetting those opals. Come and see!"

"They don't look like the same stones," said a young man.

"The gold overpowered the opals, killed their light," said Mr. Burke.

I explained that the necklace was made of interlocking T-shaped settings, so that each stone could be separated from the others and the necklace shortened to a choker or even a bracelet.

"Put them on, Catherine," Pam insisted. "Model them!"

"With jeans, a shirt, and a smock? Really, Pam!"

But she was already placing the necklace around my throat and someone else handed me the earrings.

"Tremendous! And how great to be able to change the necklace to any length you want." Pam gazed at the final effect, then gave a twisted smile. "I hope they don't bring bad luck. Aren't opals supposed to be terribly unlucky?"

"Yes," said Mr. Burke dryly, "along with black cats, Friday the thirteenth, and clergymen on shipboard. He turned away with a sigh of despair for Pam's superstition. For a few minutes longer the opals were the center of attention, then the students drifted back to their own work.

Moving to the open window, I gazed down at the pendant, admiring the play of sunshine on its facets, the surface lights and inner lights. I didn't hear the telephone at the far end of the studio ring, but looked up when Mr. Burke called my name.

"Phone call, Miss Andrews," he said.

I went to answer it, apprehensive—only emergency calls were allowed to interrupt the work of the studios. Mrs. Thornton's list of calamities flashed through my mind: fire, flood, and burglary.

"Hello, this is Catherine Andrews."

"Thank goodness," said Mrs. Thornton. "I've been trying to reach you for three days."

"The school's been closed; a vacation. Are you still in Florida?"

"No. I got home last Friday." There was a long silence, then she said, "I'm calling about Dorrie."

"Yes? What about her?" So Pandora had come home, I thought, with a surge of relief. Everything was all right.

Mrs. Thornton spoke again, the words flat and terse. "She's dead. Died a little over two weeks ago."

"Dead? She can't be, it's impossible!" But the silence and Mrs. Thornton's heavy breathing on the line told me there was no mistake; the message was true. "Why didn't someone contact me? Why didn't someone call?"

"There was no way to reach you—no one knew how." Mrs. Thornton's voice rose angrily. "I told you I might have to go to Florida, that my sister's health came first. Well, when

I got back to the house on Friday, the first thing I saw was a cablegram and a letter from Italy. Then the phone started ringing. That was the first news I had.''

"Who called?" I asked faintly. "Was it . . . was it . . .''

"No, it wasn't *her*. They said she was still too weak and shocked to talk. *Her* shocked—I like that! I talked to some secretary or companion or something. I don't know.''

"How did she . . .'' The words seemed to choke me. "How did she die?''

"The woman wouldn't give me any details, treated me like a servant and insisted on having your phone number. Well, not likely! I'm not telling those people anything. All I could find out was that Dorrie drowned. Some kind of accident.''

Drowned? Vaguely I remembered her writing about a cruise in the spring. Had there been a sinking of a ship? I had read no newspapers. My mind was not functioning; everything was confused and I could comprehend only one thing: Pandora was dead.

"The funeral?" I asked. "Am I expected to—''

"The funeral's long over with. They couldn't reach you in time.'' She hesitated, then said eagerly, "Do you want me to open this letter and read it to you? I suppose it's got all the details.''

The blatant curiosity in her voice sounded ghoulish, obscene. What did her precious details matter? Nothing mattered except that Dorrie was gone. "Don't open it, and don't forward it. I'll be home soon, but I don't know when. I don't know what I'll do, I can't think right now.''

"It was a punishment on her for going to live with that woman. I told my sister only last week that—''

I hung up the phone, unable to bear her voice for another second.

Unsteady, I started for the door of the studio. Mr. Burke moved toward me. "Are you all right, Miss Andrews? Is there anything I can—''

"I'm all right," I said numbly.

Outside, I stumbled past the art gallery and the coffee shop, the sun blinding me. I wanted to weep, but no tears came; and Pandora's voice, her words spoken on Thanksgiving Day, echoed hollowly in my mind. *"I'm going to have a new life . . . a new life!"*

The iron bench I found was in a deserted corner of the campus. I sat there, dry-eyed but trembling, trying to accept her death—telling myself that grief was as futile as the remorse that now flooded over me. Why hadn't I answered her silly, pathetic postcards, her clumsy and childlike attempts to apologize? If I had been wiser, I would somehow have prevented her from going; and if I had failed in wisdom, at least I might have been kind. Now it was too late—the final words had been spoken, the last gesture made.

I realized I still wore the opals; how ironic that I should have put them on today. Their inner fires seemed banked and smoldering; a deep crimson, the color of blood. I gazed at them, remembering, and then the tears came.

A week later I sat alone with a single lamp burning in the big room that had once been Matthew's library. Half a dozen unanswered letters were spread out on the desk before me—representing decisions, various courses my life could follow—and I could not avoid answering them, for a decision not to reply was in itself an answer. I had reached a crisis; what I did now, or failed to do, would change my future completely, yet my will seemed paralyzed, my mind unable to concentrate.

Ever since arriving home this afternoon and reading the letter from a Miss Esther Sullivan, Althea Hoffman's secretary, I had felt dazed. I'd wandered from room to room, rereading what Miss Sullivan had written with increasing doubt and bewilderment. There had to be a mistake, some enormous error! But Miss Sullivan, to judge from her prose, was not a woman who made errors; her facts were as precise as her penmanship.

A southern wind warmed the night, and I had opened the windows. Next door, in Mrs. Sassman's rooming house, some students were spending a very intellectual evening—playing classical records and tapes, loudly debating the merits of Vivaldi versus Gluck. I remembered how Matthew had always hoped Mrs. Sassman wouldn't put music majors on this side of her house, especially in the spring or summer, then quickly put the idle thought from my mind. This was the sort of mental meandering I had been indulging in for hours, thinking about anything to avoid the problems I must eventually face.

I forced myself to pick up one of the letters, taking the easiest decision first. It was a note from Mrs. Foster, the real-estate dealer, saying she knew of an interested client if by any chance the house was for sale. My answer would be yes; I could not continue living here alone, every room filled with memories of Matthew and Pandora. Pandora's voice and my own, shrill and angry, seemed to me absorbed into the very paneling of the dining room.

I put the letter to one side, a problem solved, and considered next the note from Gordon Carr—a message of condolence written from Rome with no mention of his having seen Pandora earlier in the year. He added that his research on medieval pilgrimages was going well, and he "looked forward to seeing a great deal of you next fall."

No, I thought. No. He had once chosen Pandora, and for me that choice was final. I dropped the note in the wastebasket.

I did not touch the envelope I had brought back from Arizona; I had read its contents on the plane coming home. It was written confirmation of an offer made to me by the head of the school just before I left: a position as a teacher of commercial art and drafting while I worked toward an advanced degree, beginning in three weeks at the start of the summer term. I thought of those desert skies, translucent blue, and of the open, easy camaraderie of the students. I could be contented there; I could be free of the past. They expected me to accept what was a generous offer, and I had already halfway done so. But that had been before I arrived home and found the other letter.

The other letter. The pages were heavy as parchment and rich to the touch; it bore an embossed crest encircled by the name Villa Pellegrina.

Miss Sullivan began by explaining that she was companion and secretary to Althea Hoffman, who was too overcome by the "tragic death of her daughter" to write more than the brief note which was enclosed. There followed a rather stiff apology for their failure to reach me before the funeral—an apology that subtly, without actually saying so, managed to shift all the blame to me. Miss Sullivan, although better educated, seemed to have much in common with Mrs. Thornton. But it was the second page that I had reread so many times:

. . . As you know, Pandora was a keen sailor. She told us delightful stories about how she, with you and your late father, spent many happy summers sailing a yawl off Martha's Vineyard.

The villa here fronts a very large lake and we all enjoy sailing. But sudden winds coming from the nearby Alps raise enormous waves, making the sport rather risky, and so we have a household rule that no one ever goes out alone. Pandora, I am compelled to say, was a somewhat headstrong young woman. (I myself thought her independence was part of her great charm.)

Ten days ago she expressed a wish to sail to a village on the other side of the lake; this was on a gusty morning with an overcast sky. I, and others, warned her that a storm might break any moment, the lake was most hazardous, and no one should dream of sailing in such weather. She laughed at our caution, saying that a little weather was nothing to "an old Yankee salt." Still, I did not suspect she would ignore the warnings.

The boat was sighted at noon, apparently heeled over, and your sister's body was recovered by fishermen from the village several hours later. . .

Madame Hoffman, needless to say, has been crushed by this blow. Only last year she lost another loved one. This second loss is hard to bear . . .

. . . If you should care to come here, you are assured of a

cordial welcome, and if money is needed for transportation, I will make prompt arrangements.

Faithfully yours,
Esther Sullivan (Miss)

P.S. I do not know what to do with her possessions. There seems to be nothing of particular value. Are you her heir? Do I send you her trunk? Please advise.

I folded the pages and returned them to the heavy, cream-colored envelope. Miss Sullivan, of course, was unaware of the irony she had written; the letter that cordially invited me, the postscript that implied I would not come. But Althea Hoffman's note, a brief message on a slip of paper, said the same thing frankly.

Dear Catherine,
We share this sorrow, but my loss is greater. You were able to know and love Pandora for many years, while life gave me only a short time. Daughter, I cannot hope you will come to me even though I have asked. There is nothing to say but these words, written in love and grief.

Your mother

My mother. My eyelids burned as I stared at the paper. How could I believe what Althea Hoffman said, when I knew the pages Miss Sullivan had written were nothing but lies? Frightening lies, all the more sinister because they involved death—a strange and sudden death that could never have happened in the way it had been described to me.

Perhaps Miss Sullivan didn't realize that her story was false and totally impossible. She and Althea Hoffman must have been nearby when my sister died, and no doubt there were other witnesses to her last morning, but no matter what they may have heard or said or seen, *I knew Pandora*.

Music suddenly blared into the room, the record player next door pouring out the "Forging Song" from *Siegfried* at deafening volume, driving every thought from my mind. Angrily, I reached for the telephone, ready to complain to Mrs. Sassman, but the sound faded when I heard a girl say, ". . . Spare our eardrums, for heaven's sake!"

Forcing myself to concentrate again, I realized I knew only one thing for sure. Pandora's death was an unsolved and frightening puzzle, and I was the only one to suspect this. But what could I do? Write a letter to the Italian authorities telling all I knew and demanding they investigate? Hopeless, I thought, imagining their brusk dismissal of me as a troublemaker, a young woman long estranged from her mother, a person who had spiteful motives for lying. They would also say I had little to go on; no grounds for suspicion except one single fact. For me, this was quite enough, but I could never convince anyone else.

The easiest way was to turn my back, go to Arizona as I longed to do, forget my suspicions, forget Pandora. But could I ever forget? I had sent Pandora away in anger—the sister I had always been responsible for. I should go to Italy, I should see for myself; I owed that much to Pandora's memory.

But the thought of meeting Althea Hoffman paralyzed me. My mother . . .

I rested my head in my hands, pressing my temples, trying to decide. For Pandora, such a decision would have been easy. She had only to look at the sky and some miraculous sign would immediately tell her what to do. But I had no signs to guide me; I had only my own mind, my own warring emotions.

Suddenly an image of Althea Hoffman formed itself in my consciousness—not a picture of her as she must be today or as she would have appeared on the concert stage, but a childhood picture of my mother sitting beside my bed, holding my hand. I had dreamed this image, but it had never come to me as vividly as it did now.

Then I realized. It was the music, the record now being played rather softly next door. A contralto, not at all like Althea Hoffman's soaring voice, but it was the song she had sung so often, the words I knew so well.

When at night I fall asleep
Fourteen angels watch do keep
Two my head protecting,
Two my steps directing . . .

I lifted my head, all hesitation gone, knowing fully what I must do, realizing that underneath my hesitation I had known for several hours. Probably I had known when I first read Miss Sullivan's letter. From that moment, there had been no choice for me.

A week later I boarded a plane for Italy.

Chapter Three

The Locanda La Fiorita, a modest hotel in the village of San Tommaso, stood almost on the shore of the lake, but I hadn't realized this the night before, when the rattletrap bus from Verona had crawled through the opaque mist and deposited me at the entrance of the inn. Now, as I stepped onto the open terrace that served as a dining room, the lake took me by surprise.

"How beautiful!" I murmured.

An elderly waiter, standing nearby, heard me and smiled. "*Bellissima!*" he said.

The broad expanse of water gleamed with that cool sapphire blue one sees only in Alpine lakes, the fresh tint of a morning sky in spring. Far offshore, a crimson sail skimmed the surface like a great butterfly, and near me, just below the terrace, olive trees stood like a hedge, their leaves silver green and smokey.

"*Buon giorno, signorina,*" said the waiter. "*Una tavola?*"

"*Per favore. Vicino a la balaustra.*"

"You speak Italian, *signorina?*" he asked as he ushered me to a table.

"Not well, not enough." My sketchy and now-rusty Italian had come from three sources: Mrs. Ginori in my childhood, who spoke little English; a year in college when I had studied the language because I thought I had a headstart; and several weeks traveling in Italy on a tour for art students one summer. Ordinary conversations I could follow, but subtleties usually eluded me.

After ordering breakfast, I sat gazing at the lake and the high, rocky headlands on the far shore. I knew from studying a map that it was a long lake—more than thirty miles—but nowhere was its width more than a third of its length, and here it was narrow enough for me to see clearly the outlines of buildings on the far shore. A great turreted structure with a high tower dominated the view—an ancient castle, I supposed— and near it were other buildings, modern villas I could not see very clearly. The scene was so lovely and tranquil it was hard to believe that an act of violence had brought me here.

The week before, I had written to Miss Sullivan, asking her to convey my thanks to Althea Hoffman for the kind invitation and say that I had already planned a vacation in Europe and would no doubt visit the Villa Pellegrina. I gave no date of arrival, nor any indication of how long I expected to stay. Beyond spending a few days in this hotel and learning what I could about the household at Villa Pellegrina, I had no definite plan. When I felt ready, I would go there unannounced and see what happened.

The waiter brought a steaming pot of coffee and a basket of warm rolls. "Are you here for the opening of the museum, *signorina?*" he asked.

"Museum? What museum?"

"The Donato Museum." He seemed surprised I had not heard of it. "The great diva Althea Hoffman is building it in memory of Victor Donato. I am told she has gathered a magnificent collection."

"Of paintings?" I asked.

He shook his head. "No, no. Things having to do with music—mainly opera, but other things as well."

"Is the museum in the village?"

"No. Over there." He gestured toward the lake. "In the Castle Malaspina, the building with the tower. Hoffman herself lives in the villa you see to the left. She also has a house in Venice—a palace, they say."

So the long, two-story structure with the gleaming roof tiles was Villa Pellegrina, "Pilgrim House." I wondered why she had named it that.

"The museum is not yet ready for the public, but there is an advance viewing today for invited guests. We have some famous persons in the hotel; Fantonetti, the soprano from La Scala, and Trosske, the German tenor."

The names meant nothing to me, but the waiter seemed highly impressed. "Is there a celebration at the museum? Is that why they're here?"

The waiter lowered his voice. "The banquet has been canceled—Hoffman is still in seclusion. Her daughter was drowned not long ago and they say nothing consoles her."

"Really?" The bereft mother, I thought bitterly—what a wonderful chance for dramatics. "Did you know the daughter, did she ever come here?"

"Yes," he answered promptly. *Che bella!* A beautiful girl." Then, because he was an Italian male, he felt compelled to add, "Like yourself, *signorina,* if you will forgive me." He stared thoughtfully across the lake at the distant Villa Pellegrina. "She has lost two loved ones in hardly a year; one by water, the other by fire. Perhaps the devil extracts a price for money and fame."

He returned to the kitchen before I could question him about the other death. I looked at the castle and the villa with new interest, wondering what awaited me there. I would learn within a few days, as soon as enough time had passed so I did not seem to be arriving on the heels of the letter I had sent them.

I heard no one enter the terrace, but looked around when I

caught a sudden, strong aroma of perfume, a scent like lavender but sharper and sweeter. A tall man, silver haired and rapier thin, was passing my table. He would have been a figure to catch attention anywhere, but in a rustic inn his appearance was astonishing. His suit, perfectly tailored from some material that resembled raw silk, was trimmed at the cuffs, collar, and lapels with magenta velvet that matched the stripes of an elaborate ascot held in place by a stickpin whose glittering stones seemed impossibly large for diamonds.

But it was his face that startled me: an old man's face, hollow cheeks and hollow temples, yet strangely unlined, the pallid skin stretched without a wrinkle over the fine bones.

He passed my table, then turned back so quickly that I had no chance to avert my gaze and we were staring at each other. His hooded eyes held a sharp look of inquiry—not the appraising glance a woman becomes used to in Italy, but something else, something I could not define. The brilliant sunshine was merciless to the carefully applied rouge he wore just below his cheekbones, and it glinted on his eyelashes, which were heavy with mascara.

When his gray lips twisted into a smile and he murmured, *"Buon giorno,"* I felt a sense of physical revulsion. Tossing my head in the contemptuous manner of a Venetian or Florentine woman, I shifted in my chair, turning my back on him, and he moved toward the far end of the terrace. But as the waiter served the rest of my breakfast, I could feel the reptilian gaze on me, and was glad the restaurant was filling up with late risers. I had not enjoyed being alone on the terrace with the man.

Could his first look have been recognition? Had he seen me at the airport in Venice or on the Verona train? I doubted it, and, besides, my appearance had changed a great deal since yesterday. Not wanting to appear too conspicuously foreign, I had bound my hair with a bright scarf as I'd seen the Italian women do, and wore a pair of large harlequin sunglasses that were the current fashion in Venice.

When the waiter brought the bill, I asked in a low voice,

"Who is the man at the far table? The man with the silver hair."

"Silver hair?" A sly expression came over his face. "You mean the silver wig, *signorina*; he has as much real hair as a boccia ball. But he wears wigs of every color and today he is in a silver mood. It is the Prince Luigi."

"A prince?" I had never seen a prince before, but this was not my idea of what one should look like.

"*Si*. His family owned the Castle Malaspina for a thousand years."

At that moment the prince himself summoned the waiter, his voice a snarl of command. I couldn't catch the words that followed, but it was clearly an argument over the bill—the prince insisting he was being overcharged and cheated. Then he dismissed the waiter with a royal gesture, saying to his retreating back, "It does not matter. I will deduct the difference from your tip."

The waiter marched to the kitchen, then returned to my table carrying a small tray with change upon it. His face was stiff with barely concealed anger.

"The prince seems in a bad temper today," I said.

"He has the *toco malvagio*, the bad touch as we call it here. It is unlucky to know people like the Malaspina. *Eccome!*"

He moved off to another table and I rose to leave. The village was a small place, I thought; I was almost certain to cross Prince Luigi's path again—not a pleasant prospect.

The terrace had become so crowded that in order to leave I had to pass through a center aisle, near the prince's table, and I gave a quick, covert glance in his direction. I saw his hands, gray on the white cloth; slender, bejeweled fingers, with long nails enameled and filed like stilleto points. I realized he was still watching me; his eyes followed as I crossed to the double doors, measuring my steps, recording my features with a cobra's stare that cut the warm morning like an icy draft.

By noon more than a dozen chauffeur-driven limousines were parked near the hotel Locanda La Fiorita, rubbing elegant bumpers with sleek sports cars of every nationality, including a few humble Fiats. The cheaper cars displayed press cards.

Wandering down to the stone pier, I lingered at the edge of a crowd of about forty people who were waiting, I was told, for a launch to take them to the castle. They struck me as a peculiar collection; I had never seen such a weight of jewels worn in daylight—emeralds draped on huge bosoms, long drop earrings, and hawsers of pearls. Although some of them were quietly dressed, most appeared costumed for a coronation ball rather than a museum tour and an informal luncheon. A few eccentrics sought attention in the opposite way, flaunting threadbare clothing that must have been purchased in a flea market. But even these free souls were careful not to appear actually poor; a man in faded jeans and rope sandals wore a belt with heavy silver links.

The babble of languages was made even more confusing by the speakers' abruptly shifting from one idiom to another—from Italian or French to German, English, or other tongues I couldn't identify. A man and woman standing next to me were, for the moment, speaking English, although it seemed to be the native language of neither. "Of course, Althea was never a great artist," the woman was saying. "A good talent, but hardly major."

"With the Donato millions behind you, who needs talent?" The man remarked with a sour smile. "You can even afford to display Althea's temperament. We were at Spoleto together one season; Ponti was conducting, and she used to hurl scores at him with deadly aim."

A little man in a candy-striped polo shirt darted toward the couple and dropped to one knee, pointing a camera. The pair posed automatically, flashing smiles, the man rising almost on tiptoe to appear taller than his female companion. As I stepped out of range, a large open launch—gay with streamers and a checkered awning—arrived at the dock. A gangplank was made fast, and a man with a megaphone offered the crowd an official welcome—extremely prolonged and confusing because he translated each sentence from Italian into French and then English. The guests responded with rather bored applause and the chief guide's two assistants began to herd passengers aboard.

One of the guides approached me, touched his cap politely, and gestured toward the gangplank. "This way, please, *signorina*. We depart in five minutes."

Suddenly, impulsively, I found myself moving forward, joining the party—the idea had not crossed my mind until that second. This was my chance to see Althea Hoffman's domain, yet remain anonymous in the crowd, so why not take it? No one was checking tickets or invitations, and even if they did so later, I could hardly be thrown overboard. I would simply be a confused foreigner who thought this was a public tour.

As the launch pulled away from the dock, however, I suffered a moment of panic, remembering that a luncheon was to be served—there would be conversation, questions, and I was bound to be detected as an uninvited guest. But I reassured myself that the castle must be huge and the grounds spacious; I could slip off somewhere and wait until time for the launch to return. No one would notice—these people were far too self-concerned to pay attention to anyone else.

The launch sped swiftly toward the western shore, and the details of the rocky landscape became plainly visible. The lake divided two contrasting worlds: The world we had left was fertile, luxuriant with lemon groves, blossoming vines, and warmth-loving flowers. But the world we approached showed itself harsh and unwelcoming—stone crags and headlands rose from the narrow shore with a mountain crouched behind them, its peaks dusted with snow.

Now the Villa Pellegrina loomed ahead, larger than I had supposed. It was a pale pink building with carved ornamentation in a baroque style. Its wrought iron balconies were decorated with bright flower pots, and the white cornices carved like frosting struck a cheerful contrast to the stark background.

But the villa was overwhelmed by the huge bulk of masonry

that towered close to it: the grim fortress, Malaspina Castle.
The merlons that had once served as battlements and the slit
windows set high in the walls had been deliberately designed
centuries ago to strike awe in all who approached, and this intention still succeeded. Threatening, formidable, its presence
seemed to cast a pall over the company in the launch; chattering voices became hushed and puzzled, uneasy glances were
exchanged.

"The perfect setting for *Lucia*," a man remarked loudly.
"It only wants a little heather." He turned to the woman next
to him. "Marta, when we go inside, will you entertain us with
'The Mad Scene'?" There was scattered laughter.

The launch was quickly moored at a large pier, and our
guides led us up a steep flight of stone steps, halting at the top
for the one with the megaphone to deliver another address.

"Two things our distinguished guests should understand.
First, the museum is far from complete; there have been delays. Second, although I am certain you will find the collection
interesting, remember that the presentation is not designed
for tastes as sophisticated as yours. The appeal is to the public
in general, a popular museum."

A short, stout man with a heavy German accent broke in
with a question. "If it is to draw the public, why build it in so
isolated a place? A city would be better, *ja*?"

"This location was chosen because the late *Signor* Victor
Donato was born nearby. The western shore of the lake is an
area of poverty, and when Donato first thought of the museum, one of his motives was to create a tourist attraction that
would bring a little prosperity here. And it is not isolated; the
city of Verona is not far away and Brescia is even closer.
Thousands of visitors will come each year. This is Victor Donato's gift to his birthplace."

A woman behind me whispered, "And dear Althea's monument to her own vanity." Someone giggled.

As we mounted a second flight of stairs, our guide spoke
again. "The castle was built in the early tenth century on the

ruins of a Roman fort, a link in a chain of strongpoints to guard the mountain passes of the north.''

Approaching the heavy, iron-spiked doors, I saw a depression in the ground where an ancient moat had been filled in. On either side of the entrances, niches for sculpture had been cut into the walls, but they stood empty. We passed through a courtyard surrounded by gray masonry so high that the afternoon sun never warmed the flagstone paving. Then we were in the reconstructed rooms of the museum itself.

Before twenty minutes had passed, I thoroughly regretted my impulsiveness and felt I paid the penalty for insinuating myself into the party uninvited. The Donato museum, at least the part I saw that day, struck me as gruesome.

A score of rooms were set up as small stages, each showing a scene from a different opera with life-size figures of great singers of the past, lavishly costumed in clothing identical to that worn by the artist in the particular role. Everything was authentic, the guide assured us, down to the last rhinestone, ostrich plum, and bloodied dagger.

At the touch of a button, music appropriate for the scene was broadcast over a concealed sound system—Amelita Galli-Curci singing the "Bell Song" from *Lakmé*, Caruso intoning a bittersweet aria from *Rigoletto*. If a performance had been filmed, pressing another button changed the background of the stage set into a cinema screen, and film clips with sound were shown. The whole effect was opulent, astonishing, and, to me at least, funereal. All natural light, if there had ever been such a thing in the castle, was sealed out; shadowy areas separated the exhibits and sudden drafts chilled the bones.

Wax museums have always oppressed me, filled me with a repugnant sense of wandering through a public mortuary. Despite the elaborate trappings of light and sound, the museum seemed nothing more than a glorified, specialized version of Madame Tussaud's, complete with its own chamber of horrors—since opera is notoriously replete with murder, madness, and suicide.

Two women were standing close to me when lights came up in one room to reveal the "Sleepwalking Scene" from Verdi's *Macbeth*. One of them, who wore a droopy black hat, whispered to the other. "How revolting! Simply dreadful."

Her reaction surprised me. Although the figure of Lady Macbeth looked thoroughly tormented and the doctor and the gentlewoman were cowering in the background, this was mild compared to the ghastly dungeon scene from *Fidelio* we had been exposed to a moment before.

But she was not the only one in the crowd who found the display shocking. There were murmurs and whisperings all around me. I caught the words "killed" and "scandal." The visitors exchanged uneasy glances, and I longed to question someone directly, but this was impossible. When the woman in the droopy hat spoke again, I pressed closer, straining to hear more, but the music drowned her words. Obviously this scene reminded everyone around me of some scandal connected with Althea Hoffman. In time, I promised myself, I would learn what it was.

A few minutes later, while the others were fascinated by the appallingly realistic flames licking at the figure of Kirsten Flagstad as Brünnhilde, I slipped quietly away in search of an exit.

I wandered through a small but ornate theater, then into a corridor lined with shrouded figures which, I supposed, would in time take their places among the costumed exhibits. I passed them quickly, looking neither right nor left, trying to rid myself of a feeling that at any moment one of the swathed statues would raise an arm or step forward. My heels echoed on the stone floor. Then, turning a corner, I saw an open door and eagerly moved toward the sunlight.

I found myself in an open-air workshop where a dozen men were engaged in tasks to help complete the museum—two groups of craftsmen, carpenters working under an improvised roof and stonecutters working in the sun, stripped to the waist and acorn brown. They exchanged jokes, mock insults, and loud laughter while a small boy squatted cross-legged on the ground playing a squeaky concertina.

After the grimness, the deathlike atmosphere of the museum, this scene of lusty, good-humored life seemed so beautiful and vital that I longed for a sketch pad. I knew I'd never catch the force of the brawny carpenter swinging a maul to drive a spike, but perhaps I could at least record their faces—the faces of Lombardy peasants—strong boned and full cheeked, their moustaches ranging from blond to jet black.

The stonecutters were splitting marble to make facings, work I'd often watched in sculpture studios and had never seen performed with greater skill. As I walked past them, stepping around a stack of thin slabs, I heard the inevitable low whistles.

"Bella! Bella!"

I smiled to myself, for once enjoying the automatic flattery. This was healthy, natural, and there was no hint of the predatory leer of the cities. The air was warm but fresh, and a light breeze seemed to blow away the dankness of the castle; the remarks of the woman in the black hat, which I had found so strange and disturbing in the half-darkness of the museum, lost all plausibility in the brightness of the afternoon.

The path I followed led to a grove of laurel trees where I found a picnic table with plank benches—a good place to rest while I decided whether to wait for the launch to return or to find another means of getting to the far side of the lake. Higher up the slope I could see a road; if it were like most roads in Italy, sooner or later a bus would come rattling along and I could no doubt circle the lake.

The sudden trilling of a warbler in a nearby tree made me turn my head, and I saw I was not alone in the grove. A man, apparently unaware of my presence, sat on the ground, his back against the trunk of a laurel. A few feet away, resting on a thick trestle table, stood a block of Carrara marble so warmly beautiful that it was a shame to have it split for facings. The man was obviously another stonecutter; a chisel and heavy hammer lay on the ground beside him and when the sun struck his dark brown hair it sparkled on marble dust.

Now more than ever I wanted sketch paper. The stonecutter was the perfect summing up of what I had seen before: the Lombardy peasant, hard as a hatchet with ice-blue eyes and thick, tousled brown hair. When he slowly rose, I revised my mental sketch a bit—he was taller than I thought and not so heavy, but he still looked as though he could heft the marble block with one arm.

He took a couple of steps toward the stone, seeming uncertain, and then I smiled as I realized the marble puzzled him; he didn't know what to do next. Despite his age—probably about thirty—he must be an apprentice. Frowning, he scratched his head with the handle of the chisel, then moved to the table, where he ran his hand over the stone hesitantly, his deeply tanned face a study in perplexity. He seemed to force himself to a decision. He placed the chisel and lifted the hammer, apparently unaware that he was trying to split the stone against the grain—a mistake that could certainly cost him several days' wages.

"Signor!" I called. *"No!"*

He whirled toward me, so astonished that he dropped the chisel.

I went quickly to him, saying, *"Scusi.* You must not split it that way." But I realized my Italian was totally inadequate to explain the matter; I knew none of the technical terms used by local stonecutters. *"Permetta, signor."* Picking up the chisel, I tried to show him what I meant. He crossed his arms and leaned back, watching me closely. I ended by suggesting he ask the foreman of the stonecutters for advice. "It would be a shame to damage such expensive stone," I said.

"A desecration, my lady," he replied, crossing himself. "You have spared me a terrible error. How can a humble workman repay the kindness of such a lady?"

Humble workman? I suddenly felt uneasy. This was too much gratitude, too much humility. "You're welcome," I said.

"Permit me to ask," he went on smoothly, "do you devote all your time to rescuing the ignorant from their mistakes?"

His voice held no hint of irony; nothing in his expression prepared me for what came next. Suddenly the ice-blue eyes flashed with anger and he slammed the hammer on the wooden table with such force that I flinched. He shifted from Italian to fluent and furious English.

"Who the devil are you to give me lessons in carving? For two days I have studied this stone, planning, waiting for the right moment to begin. At last I am ready. Then what? A female, a busybody, pokes her long nose in, ruins everything!"

"I'm sorry," I stammered, so astonished by his cold rage that I seemed to have lost the power of speech. "I only thought—"

"Get out of here!" He took a menacing step toward me. "Go back to whatever mental hospital you escaped from. Go—leave—get out of my sight and don't came back!"

"I apologize for disturbing you," I said, my cheeks burning. "And thank you for this demonstration of Italian courtesy."

I retreated with what little dignity I could muster while he continued to shout at me in Italian—phrases I didn't understand, but recognized as words truck drivers yelled at each other when caught in traffic jams.

By pretending at first to listen to my advice, he had made an utter fool of me and it left me furious. Of course I shouldn't have interfered, but how could I have known the man was a sculptor—which apparently he was. They should post signs around him, I thought; public warnings that said, "Beware of the artist!"

In my anger and confusion, anxious only to escape the man, I'd paid no attention to the direction I'd taken. Now I halted abruptly, realizing I was much too close to the Villa Pellegrina, whose pink walls rose just ahead of me. To my left the headland, broken by terraces so that it resembled a gigantic stairway, fell steeply to the lake, while behind the house the mountain rose in magnificence. Althea Hoffman had chosen a spectacular site. And this meeting place of mountain and lake would be natural for her; she had been born in Geneva.

A stone walkway led from the house to the castle. I decided to follow it, seeing that it would bring me back to the museum entrance, yet give a wide berth to the grove where the terrible-tempered sculptor worked. I had gone only a few steps when I saw a woman coming toward me, her eyes downcast as if she were wary of the unevenness of the flagstones, but moving with smooth confidence and strength. At first I thought she might be from the group visiting the museum, then I realized this was impossible—I would have noticed the severe black dress unrelieved by any touch of color, and the iron gray hair combed tightly back and caught in a bun.

Yet her plainness of dress did not make her drab, but striking, and her hair emphasized her handsome features. She was only a few steps from me when she looked up. I saw wide-set eyes and a firm mouth. The woman looked at me, hesitated only an instant, then smiled—a brilliant smile that conveyed warmth and pleasure.

"Good afternoon, Miss Andrews," she said. "I'm delighted to welcome you. In fact, I've just been to the museum to see if you were with our visitors. I'm Esther Sullivan."

I stared at her, astounded and unbelieving. How could she possibly have recognized me? It was uncanny. I managed to summon enough composure to say, "How do you do, Miss Sullivan?"

"How good of you to have come to Italy so quickly! It was more than we dared hope for. Shall we go into the house?" She put her hand lightly on my arm. Her touch was cool, yet gracious. "I'm sure you'll want lunch. We had very little notice, of course. But I think everything is prepared for your arrival. Yes, I think so."

"I'm puzzled, Miss Sullivan," I said. "You seemed to recognize me instantly."

"Of course. Prince Luigi called me an hour ago. He saw you board the launch in San Tommaso; he even described how you were dressed."

But how could the prince have known me? Her explanation merely added to my bewilderment. I started to protest, but suddenly Esther Sullivan's hand tightened on my arm. She halted, standing as though frozen.

Then I, too, heard the wailing. It came from the road behind the wall, a sound of women's voices raised in shrill, keening lament—faint, but growing louder, closer. Miss Sullivan's face had turned pale.

"There's a graveyard farther up the mountain," she said softly. "It's near the ruins of the old monastery. The peasants still use it sometimes, but it's not consecrated. Suicides are buried there. Suicides and those the villagers say have died without God. It's a cruel thing to be kept apart from one's own family in death."

I heard the sound of a horsedrawn wagon passing, and one woman's voice rose above the others in broken sobs, grief-stricken and wordless.

Miss Sullivan sighed, shaking her head. "Of course, your mother has heard this and it's bound to affect her. Her condition is far from good. Any emotional disturbance is difficult for her."

I had no doubt about Miss Sullivan's concern for Althea after seeing her expression as the funeral passed the wall. Anyone so devoted to Althea Hoffman was the last person I could trust, and despite her cordiality, I inwardly marked her as an enemy.

"Forgive me for mentioning a tragic matter," she said quietly. "But I must tell you I remember my pleasure in welcoming your sister here. She was so lovely! May I say I feel the same pleasure now! I hope you will be very happy here. Shall we go inside? As I said, everything is ready."

Chapter Four

I followed Miss Sullivan up the broad stone steps to a terrace at the front entrance of the villa, my thoughts in confusion since my plan to observe the scene anonymously had been shattered by Prince Luigi's uncanny recognition of me. How *could* he have known? There was no possible way.

Now that my attempt at a secret arrival was exposed, the whole idea seemed childish and embarrassing, I had no way of accounting for my sudden, unannounced appearance here, but I was thankful that Esther Sullivan gave no sign that she found the situation extraordinary.

"Please come in." She opened a heavy door of carved oak. Your arriving so soon is a wonderful surprise for Althea."

I could detect no irony in Miss Sullivan's voice; the serene smile remained warm and welcoming.

"What did Althea say when you told her I was here?" I asked.

"Oh, but I haven't told her. I went to her room after Prince Luigi called, but she was sleeping and I hadn't the heart to disturb her. She was ill last night and hardly slept at all."

"She's ill? Then I'm intruding. I can return when—"

Miss Sullivan glanced at me with apparent surprise. "The arrival of her own daughter after so many years could hardly be an intrusion." She seemed to believe what she said, as though Althea, who had ignored me all my life, had miraculously changed.

We crossed a tiled entrance hall, mounted several more steps, and I found myself in the enormous living room of the Villa Pellegrina—a hushed and somber place with velour draperies, tightly closed, that masked the windows and shut out the sun. A vaulted ceiling arched upward to a lantern dome where panes of stained glass filtered the brilliance of the afternoon, admitting only a glow that tinted the white walls with mauve and sea green.

There were no obvious signs of a household in mourning, but somehow I felt the cavernous room was shrouded in black crepe. A spray of white roses in a marble urn seemed a funerary offering, and their fragrance, blending with the perfume of pale flowers growing in jardinieres, made the air oppressive and dolorous. Moving through the gloom beside the dark figure of Miss Sullivan, I struggled against the same sense of entrapment that had assailed me in the museum—a longing for escape, a desperate need for sunlight and the open air.

How could anyone live here? But I knew the answer—no one did. This hall, with its gigantic candelabra, massive couches, its jungle of drooping ferns, was not a place for living, but a temple where Althea Hoffman's worshipers could gather to pay homage. Now the goddess was in seclusion, the worshipers had been turned away, leaving the shrine deserted.

Miss Sullivan seemed to sense my thoughts. "This part of the villa hasn't been used since Pandora's death. It's hard to believe how cheerful and lovely this room is when it's flooded with sunshine."

At the fireplace I paused to look at a portrait above the mantle. "Althea?" I asked, although there could be no doubt.

"Yes. Painted by Ives Gros almost twenty years ago."

She touched a switch and a concealed spotlight illuminated the picture, making the bold tones glow with life. Althea Hoffman stood swathed in magenta satin, the folds and swirls of the gown shimmering against a background of mist. Intelligent eyes, so large and piercingly blue that they dominated her face, gazed out upon a world she had conquered. Her hair shone like a crown of spun gold, and she had a radiant beauty—even though the cheekbones were too strong, the chin too firm. The painter had seen only planes and angles in her face; there were no softened edges, no tempering of her strength with gentleness.

"I always supposed Pandora resembled her," I said. "But she didn't. Not at all."

"No. You are much more like your mother than Pandora was."

"I don't agree!" I resented the opinion and I certainly did not believe it.

Esther Sullivan, staring at the portrait, seemed not to hear me. "Althea was not in the least pretty, but she was beautiful. No one ever forgot her, ever failed to be impressed. I suppose she was born with a talent for fascination. That's a gift that can work great good or cause terrible damage. I'm afraid it never brought Althea happiness." As she studied the portrait, I thought the gray eyes concealed some unspoken pain. Esther Sullivan, I realized, was a woman who had suffered deeply, and the suffering had left its scars—hollowing her temples, etching faint lines around her lips. Had she taken on Althea Hoffman's burdens? I felt that she had.

She turned from the painting to me, her glance resting for an instant on my face as though making a judgment. It was a brief look, yet so penetrating that I found myself drawing back. In that single second I seemed to have been weighed, measured, and evaluated. Then she smiled, as though I had passed some test. "Yes, you are very like your mother." Her hand moved to the electric switch, extinguishing the spotlight, and the portrait again blended into the shadows.

But the vivid impression of Althea Hoffman did not fade from my mind. Soon I would meet this woman—this imperious stranger who was my mother—and I felt bewildered, unprepared. I had planned this trip to Italy with quiet resolution, sure of myself and my purpose. But I should never have come here, I thought suddenly. No matter what I suspected about Pandora's death, I should not have come.

"Let me show you to the terrace room," said Miss Sullivan. "It's more cheerful there. Then I'll break the good news of your arrival to Althea. You'll want lunch, and I must see that your room is ready."

"Please don't go to any trouble. My luggage is at the hotel. I can spend the night there and return tomorrow."

"I'll send for your things. Althea wouldn't dream of your staying anywhere but here."

Reluctantly I agreed, knowing it was useless to put matters off until tomorrow. We continued toward another short flight of steps, to a second level of the room. Then, with a gasp, I halted, paralyzed by what I saw.

Moving slowly toward us was some kind of animal—a cat, but gigantic and far more ferocious looking than any feline I'd ever expected to encounter outside a zoo. It was a tawny, black-spotted creature with terrifying yellow eyes, and it stood examining me with what seemed a ravenous expression, its long tail flicking menacingly.

"A leopard?" I whispered, hardly able to breathe and fearful that the least sound might cause the beast to spring.

"Oh, I'm so sorry," exclaimed Miss Sullivan. "Please don't be frightened. I should have warned you about Rajah, but I'm so used to him I didn't think."

Stepping quickly forward, she grasped the animal by a jeweled collar buckled around his neck. "He's a pet, friendly and completely harmless."

"He doesn't *look* harmless," I replied, still far from calm. "What sort of cat is he?"

"An ocelot, born in Paraguay."

I profoundly wished they had left him there. The other side

of the world was hardly far enough away. Miss Sullivan
scratched the giant feline behind the ears, and he yawned, dis-
playing an arsenal of gleaming fangs.

"Althea bought Rajah years ago for publicity. The newspapers loved it, of course. *Prima Donna tames savage five-foot-
long cat!* That sort of thing. Actually Rajah's only four feet
long and was always gentle. Althea used to lead him on stage
for curtain calls, and he was a sensation—a trademark for her!
Haven't you read any of the magazine stories about Rajah?"

"No, I'm afraid not." I might have added that avoiding stories about Althea was an ingrained habit with me. But there
really wasn't much to avoid; she hadn't sung in America since
the beginning of her career and the press there paid her little
attention. Her fame was in Europe.

"Reporters used to go on and on about Rajah's diamond
collar," said Miss Sullivan. "A gift from Victor Donato and
worth over a million dollars. Nonsense, of course. The jewels
were rhinestones or paste. But the public dotes on fabulous
stories." She clapped her hands sharply. "Rajah, go away!"

Obediently the big cat padded off, vanishing among the
ferns and the tall, potted philodendrons like a tiger retreating
into a jungle.

"He just wanders loose in the house?" I asked, still apprehensive. I had never been timid with animals, but Rajah,
whether five feet long or merely four, remained disconcerting.

"In the house or on the grounds, wherever he likes. We're
very fond of Rajah. You'll get used to him," she assured me.

I nodded, saying nothing. I would not be at the Villa Pellegrina long enough to become accustomed to Rajah or any other inmate of this oppressive house. Two or three days, I
thought. I could endure it that long, and surely by then I'd
know more about Pandora's death. And that, I reminded myself, was my purpose here: to learn the truth about what had
happened. And if I couldn't discover the truth, at least I could
put the lie to the story of the tragedy Miss Sullivan had written me, a tale that I alone knew was impossible. Beyond the
living room the character of the house changed. We passed

through an inviting library, with shelves of books bound in warm leather and a clutter of comfortable furniture from a dozen countries and periods. The terrace room, as Esther Sullivan called it, jutted from the house and, with windows on three sides, commanded a breathtaking panorama of the mountains, the lake, and the far shore. From here, on the southern side of the villa, one could not see the dismal castle that housed the equally dismal museum.

"If you'll excuse me, I'll go to Althea." But Miss Sullivan hesitated. "I hope you won't think it ungracious if she doesn't welcome you in person immediately. As I told you, she had an uncomfortable night and felt quite weak this morning."

"I understand, and I'm sorry she's been ill," I said.

"Her strength comes and goes. She hadn't been herself since Pandora's death. She's suffered terrible grief."

"Naturally." Was it grief or remorse she suffered? Althea could not possibly have loved Pandora, a daughter she had abandoned and later known only for a few months. Althea seemed to have withdrawn from the world, yes. But guilt could explain this as easily as sorrow.

"This has been a difficult time for all of us," Miss Sullivan added. "Losing two loved ones within a single year—and in such dreadful ways—has been hard to bear."

"Of course," I agreed. Again, two? She must mean the death of Victor Donato, I thought. But surely I had read newspaper obituaries for the millionaire almost two years ago, not one.

After Miss Sullivan left, I put the sketch pad I'd been carrying on a coffee table and went to the eastern windows to gaze across the lake, trying for a few minutes to close my mind to memories of Pandora.

The far shore, several miles away, appeared deceptively close. I could easily identify the hotel and, near it, the spire of the village church. Smaller buildings, shops and houses, seemed pastel cubes framed by whitewashed fences. But one peculiar structure loomed above the others, its grotesque oddity marring the landscape—a tower of some sort, but like no other tower in Italy. It rose stiff and ugly against the horizon, a glare of angry orange paint at war with the gentle colors of the village. Nothing could have ruined the magnificence of the view, but the orange tower tried its best.

The lake lay glassy; no craft moved across its shimmering surface, but a few hundred yards offshore a wooden skiff with an outboard motor swung gently at anchor. In it, a woman in a huge straw hat sat motionless, a bamboo fishing pole clasped in her hands. The scene was a picture of tranquility, yet against my will, I could not help imagining it transformed; the surface of the lake lashed by storm-driven waves, dark water writhing as it must have writhed and foamed on the morning Pandora died.

The sheer drop of the cliffs concealed the villa's landing dock and boathouse from me, but anyone standing at the windows of the villa could hardly have failed to see the helpless sailboat trapped and foundering. Yet Miss Sullivan's letter made no mention of any alarm being raised.

Lost in thought, I did not hear anyone enter the room, but whirled abruptly, startled, when just behind me a man's voice said, "*Buon giorno.*"

He stood a step or two away—a slender, aristocratic man of about thirty, with fair hair swept back from a deeply tanned forehead. There was an air of easy authority about him, a careless self-assurance.

"*Buon giorno*," I said, recovering from my surprise.

He replied with a hint of a bow and a courteous but definitely questioning smile that asked who I was and what the devil I was doing here. "You are, perhaps, one of the museum tour guests? You have lost your way?" He spoke a cultivated English with a trace of a foreign accent that seemed not to be Italian.

"No. I'm Catherine Andrews," I explained. "Althea Hoffman's daughter. I've just arrived from America."

For a second his poise deserted him; he looked thunderstruck. Obviously he recognized my name and apparently I was the last person in the world he expected to find here. "*La figilia! Però che—*" Then he managed to summon back his debonair manner; the smile returned. "Forgive my confusion. No one told me you were arriving."

"My plans changed." And *that*, I thought, was certainly the truth! "I came earlier than I expected and without warning, I'm afraid."

"How fortunate for us. We have an ancient saying here: The unexpected guest is doubly welcome."

I suspected this ancient saying was about one second old, but he spoke it gracefully, gesturing for me to sit in one of the rattan chairs flanking the coffee table.

"I am Konrad Donato," he told me. "Son of the late Victor Donato."

It was my turn to be surprised. The thought that Victor Donato might have had a family of his own before he met Althea had never crossed my mind. So their affair, I thought bitterly, had destroyed not just one marriage, but two.

Victor Donato's son would be a man of great wealth, and Konrad filled the role perfectly. The white silk sport shirt had sleeves so full and dramatic that only a man completely sure of his bearing would have worn it. A scarf, emerald green, knotted loosely at his throat gave a touch of careless elegance. He was clearly a member of a class usually encountered only in magazines; the people photographers await in airports, the ultrarich and ultrafashionable few whom reporters interview in Monaco or Palm Springs even though they seem to have little to say.

"Do you live here, *signore*?" I asked.

"Please, not *signore*. I am Konrad and I will call you Catherine. After all, I am your stepbrother in an informal way, am I not? That is what your sister used to say. It was one of her jokes to call me *fratello*, her brother."

I glanced at him quickly. Could Konrad Donato be the "thrilling man" Pandora had mentioned in the postcard? Had they been lovers? Certainly he seemed a type of man she might pursue—rich, attractive, and sophisticated.

"I have troubled you and I am sorry," he said, misreading

my expression. "I should not have reminded you of your sister. Forgive me."

"There's nothing to forgive," I answered. "I'm over my shock at her death, and I hope you'll talk about Pandora. Her memory shouldn't be hidden away as if it were something terrible."

He nodded slowly, studying me. "Good. You are most sensible. In fact, that is how Pandora described you."

"Oh?" Somehow being called "sensible" did not strike me as entirely a compliment. I wondered what else Pandora had said.

He took the chair opposite me. "You asked if I lived here. Yes, here and elsewhere. I am a wanderer, but I always return home to the lake and my two mothers."

"Two mothers?"

"Yes. Did not Pandora describe our curious situation?"

I chose not to admit that Pandora had never written me a letter or that her few postcards were hardly more than a scrawled sentence. "She was rather vague," I said.

A flicker of amusement came into his hazel eyes. "You see, I am lucky enough to have two mothers, and unlucky enough that both are very difficult ladies." His light tone somehow managed to suggest that being difficult was a highly charming quality. "There is Althea, who came into my life when I was ten years old. I feel that I am her son and she regards me as such. Then there is my real mother, Ilse, the *Signora* Donato, who is my father's widow. To her, also, I am devoted."

"And they both live in this house?" I asked, astonished.

"No, no!" Konrad chuckled. "What a battle that would be! A pair of tigresses in the same cage! No, years ago my mother built a house on the opposite shore of the lake. You must have noticed it. It is painted bright orange and is quite the most hideous building in all Italy—perhaps in all Europe."

"Yes, I noticed it. The color makes it conspicuous."

"Conspicuous indeed! That is what my mother wishes to be. She moved here hoping her presence would be a constant reproach to my father. Now she stays on to shame Althea."

"I think that would be difficult."

His eyebrows lifted a fraction. "Perhaps difficult to shame her, but easy to provoke her rage. My mother manages that with great skill."

He moved to the window where I had stood earlier and gestured for me to join him. "Look," he said. "Do you see the woman fishing?"

"Yes." The scene was unchanged; the woman still sat hunched in the skiff.

"That is Ilse Donato, my mother."

For a second I thought he was joking. The woman was wearing one of those broad, straw hats that both men and women wear when toiling in Italian rice fields. Even at this distance, I could see that the dark dress she wore was a shapeless sack. I had supposed her a peasant woman fishing to supplement a poor family's diet.

"A pity she has come to this." Konrad spoke softly, both sadness and resignation in his voice. "She is from Vienna, a city where the women love sparkle and style. But hatred of Althea has destroyed much that was charming in my mother. Tragic, is it not, to waste one's life brooding about the past? Perhaps it is also an extreme selfishness."

I wasn't sure what he meant by selfishness in this case, but his remark disturbed me and, unwillingly, I suddenly thought of my father, whose bitterness toward Althea had deepened, not lessened, with the passing years. But that, of course, was ridiculous. There was no true parallel between Matthew Andrews and the woman in the boat who had built the ludicrous spite tower across the lake.

Konrad turned from the window and moved toward a bell cord in the corner of the room. "Forgive me, Catherine, I am thoughtless. We must arrange a room for you. And have you had lunch?"

"Miss Sullivan is taking care of everything, thank you."

"Ah, yes. Sullie always does. I should have known."

"Sullie? Is that what you call her?" I could hardly believe the redoubtable Miss Sullivan would tolerate a nickname.

"Yes. Sullie is like a member of the family. She was my father's personal secretary before Althea snatched her away from him—against Sullie's wishes, I think. But Althea had her way." He shrugged, gesturing the inevitable. "She has always had her way, except now and then with Mario and Lillian."

"Who are Mario and Lillian?"

He seemed puzzled. "Did not Pandora write you about them? Althea's adopted son and daughter?"

"No! I had no idea she had adopted children." I was standing beside one of the wicker chairs, and I felt my hand tightening on the woven back, gripping it, as I realized that Althea not only had abandoned Pandora and me but had long ago replaced us. Other children, adopted children! During the years when I was growing up I had struggled to banish all pictures of Althea from my mind, but sometimes, against my will, I'd imagined her and her unknown life in Europe. I'd envisioned her emerging from a limousine, swathed in ermine, aglitter with diamonds; or I'd thought of ballrooms in Vienna or Paris where Althea, elegant and treacherous, moved beneath the great chandeliers. But this picture had never entered my mind—Althea with children, children she looked upon as her own, children who called her "Mother."

What did it matter since Althea meant nothing to me? But it *did* matter, and I could not understand my own feelings, this sudden welling of new resentment. "Do they—the adopted son and daughter—live here, too?" I asked.

"Mario lives wherever his work takes him. Now he is staying here, completing reliefs and statues for the museum. He is a sculptor and quite famous for a young artist. You have not heard of him? Mario Donato?"

"No," I said, suddenly remembering my encounter with the dark-haired stonecarver outside the museum. Could that terrible-tempered artisan be the adopted son? I hoped not. "You mentioned a daughter?"

"Yes. Lillian." Konrad hesitated, seeming to search for words, and when at last he spoke his voice was curiously flat and guarded. "Lillian died a year ago. She was very young, even younger than Pandora."

I knew then what Miss Sullivan and the waiter had meant when they had spoken of losing "two loved ones in a single year." Not Pandora and Victor Donato, as I had assumed, but Pandora and an adopted daughter named Lillian.

"How tragic for Althea," I said. "Two daughters dying so young. Tell me, was Lillian's death also an accident?"

"Yes. Another accident and a very cruel one." He frowned, shaking his head as though to dismiss a painful memory. "We will not talk of this now, or of any other sad subject. The day of your arrival here is no time for gloom. Ah, I see your lunch has arrived at last."

A uniformed maid appeared carrying a tray laden with pungent dishes of pasta and shellfish, but I was too disturbed by what I'd just learned to be concerned about the meal, however delicious. Two accidents! Pandora's death now seemed even more sinister, and I was determined to learn more about Lillian.

But Konrad abruptly and deliberately shifted the subject, talking glibly about the cuisine of northern Italy, giving me no chance to learn more unless I interrupted him with the bluntest questions; and blunt questions, I felt sure, would gain me nothing. Despite his outward affability, Konrad made it plain he would permit no inquiries about Lillian. At least not now.

I had finished lunch and was sipping strong, aromatic coffee when Miss Sullivan returned. Althea, she announced, was delighted by my unexpected arrival and would see me in an hour. Meanwhile, if I had finished my lunch, would I care to inspect the room she had arranged for me?

"How is Althea today?" Konrad asked her.

"Much as usual." A look of sympathy and understanding passed between them, and Miss Sullivan's voice was gentle when she added, "Not at her best, even with Catherine's arrival. But we shouldn't expect miracles."

Just as I was rising from the table, there came a shout from somewhere in the house. "Sullie! Konrad! Where the devil are you?"

Konrad moved past me toward the door. "In the terrace room," he called, then turned to me with a smile. "That is Mario. He sounds excited just now, but for being entirely Italian he is usually a quiet man."

I had recognized the voice instantly; I knew it was the explosive sculptor and I sat waiting, determined not to be caught off guard again. When he strode into the room a moment later, he seemed to bring a thunderstorm with him. Konrad stood between me and the doorway, and Mario Donato did not realize I was in the room when the first angry words tumbled out.

"I just heard the launch is on its way to the village to bring Althea's daughter here! You know this is impossible! There must be some way to stop her, to—"

Then he saw me, and recognition dawned even before Konrad said, "Catherine, may I present my brother, Mario Donato?"

For a moment we faced each other in silence, neither of us attempting to conceal the mutual enmity we felt. After what he had said upon entering, any polite words between us would have been useless. We were opponents—we both knew it.

Then, ignoring me, he spoke to Konrad. "Has she seen Althea yet? Talked to her?"

"Not yet." Konrad's manner was smooth as oil. "But she looks forward to that pleasure soon."

Mario shifted from English into Italian, assuming I wouldn't understand. "*Bene.* You should have told me the moment she arrived. She will not speak with my mother today, tomorrow, or ever. We will get her out of the villa and on her way—the faster the better."

He spoke rapidly, but I managed to follow his words and my anger blazed.

"Ridiculous!" I exclaimed, my tone sharp enough to make him face me. "I have no intention of leaving or of listening to this madman. Miss Sullivan, please show me to my room. Remember, I have an appointment with my mother."

Mario Donato glared at me, the dark face filled with suppressed rage. "Why have you come here?" he demanded. "After all these years, why do you now appear? Is it money you are after? How much? Go away and perhaps I can persuade Althea to grant you an allowance."

Although my cheeks were still burning, his taunts turned my anger into an icy calm. "I am here to visit my mother at her own invitation, and it is none of your business. Excuse me." As I moved toward the door, chin high, I almost expected a heavy hand to seize my shoulder and stop me by force. Instead, it was the quiet intensity of Mario Donato's voice that caused me to hesitate, and then to turn back.

"Why must you hurt her more than you already have?" he asked, his features taut. "For years you have ignored her, neglected her. Now she is ill and has suffered. Since she has never meant anything to you, *signorina*, why will you not leave her in peace?"

His accusations, I told myself, were stupid and untrue. Althea, not I, had been guilty of neglect! Yet the words, which he so obviously believed, stung like blows. And his question—why had I come?—was one I dared not answer. I looked from Mario to Konrad, who watched quietly, his aristocratic face unreadable; yet I felt his deferential expression was a mask concealing feelings as violent as Mario's.

Then Esther Sullivan moved swiftly to my side and clasped my hand, her touch warm and firm.

"You must forgive Mario," she said. "There can be no excuse for this, but you should understand that he is trying—however mistakenly—to protect Althea."

"To protect her from me? That hardly seems necessary," I replied.

"Let us hope not." Mario shrugged his shoulders, seeming to concede this skirmish, if not the whole battle, to me. He glanced at Miss Sullivan. "I do not need you to apologize for me, Sullie, nor do I thank you for explaining my feelings. This woman has been warned to leave. What happens now is her own fault.''

Miss Sullivan took my arm, a gesture more reassuring than any words could have been. "Let me show you to your room. I'm sorry this misunderstanding has marred your welcome."

I left with her, grateful that in Miss Sullivan I had found at least one friend at the Villa Pelligrina. But as we mounted the stairway, moving silently through shadowy coolness, I could not erase Mario Donato's words from my mind. "What happens now is her own fault," he had said.

And I thought of Pandora.

Chapter Five

Somewhere, far away in the still house, the chime of a clock sounded the hour. I was late for my meeting with Althea, deliberately late, and knew I could delay no longer, that I must control the dread and confusion I felt.

The room Miss Sullivan had led me to was next to Althea's suite and had been part of it until Pandora's arrival. Althea, Miss Sullivan said, had wanted her daughter near her; the connecting door had been locked and draped on both sides to muffle sound, so Althea and Pandora could feel close but private.

It was a spacious, pleasant room, I kept telling myself. The colors were cheerful shades of yellow and rust; French doors opened onto a small balcony overlooking broad lawns and a grove of cypress trees.

"I put away all of Pandora's things," Miss Sullivan had said in a hushed tone. "When you want to go over them, tell me."

She had done her work thoroughly; no trace of my sister was left, not the least reminder. But nevertheless, I had the impression Pandora stood near me, just beyond my range of vision. When I glanced into the gilt-framed mirror, I almost expected my eyes to meet hers.

"Stop this!" I said aloud, and, permitting myself no more time to brood, I went quickly into the hallway to Althea's door. Then I hesitated again.

I knew my mother only as the dimmest memory; a figure sitting on the edge of my bed, the melody of a song, and, perhaps, although I was not sure, a vague impression of a tall woman brushing her lips across my forehead, turning off a lamp, then tiptoeing from my room. Perhaps my memories should be left that way, and I realized that now was my last chance to turn back.

Then, squaring my shoulders, I knocked firmly on the panel.

"Come in, Catherine." The voice was soft, but richly vibrant.

Opening the door, I stepped once more into dimness. Althea Hoffman sat erect in a leather chair at the far end of the room, her back to a tall window that admitted diffuse illumination through a web of net curtains. On her right hand a tiny spark flashed—a ring—and I could see a crown of pale hair against the leather chair; but her face remained shadowed by the high winged collar of the brocaded robe she wore. Perfectly straight and unmoving, she seemed as rigid as a mosaic of a Byzantine empress.

I could think of no greeting; eternity seemed to pass before she chose to speak. I do not know what I'd expected her to say, but whatever I might have imagined, it was certainly not the words she finally uttered. "So you have come here at last, Catherine. I did not think you would."

"Why not? I believe you invited me." My voice sounded uncertain, tense. I forced myself to be calmer.

Althea rose slowly and moved to one side of the window—only a few steps, but her least movement showed natural grace, even majesty. When she touched a switch near the window, an electric motor hummed and one layer of the curtains swept back, admitting more light.

Then she turned to me, and I caught my breath. Her face was that of the portrait downstairs, in some ways remarkably untouched by age. The bones were as fine and firm as they had appeared twenty years ago, the eyes a brighter gentian blue with only the lightest trace of wrinkles around them. Yet hollows darkened her temples and her cheeks were waxen. It was a face, I thought, more ravaged by illness than by time.

The astonishing thing was not her appearance, but the swift, sudden realization that I remembered her. I was hardly more than three years old when she abandoned us—how could I possibly know her now? I was surely tricked by having seen the portrait today—I had to be. But at the same time I knew this was no illusion: I remembered her as my mother. The figure at my bedside was no longer obscure; the tall woman turning out the light was Althea. A feeling akin to panic swept through me and unexplainable tears threatened to form in my eyes. Confused, I took refuge in defiance.

"Was I mistaken in thinking you meant the invitation?" I asked, lifting my head.

Her smile seemed wintery, forced. "No, the invitation was sincere. Foolish, I grant you, but sincere. You see, I was badly shaken by Pandora's death." She hesitated, then forced herself to continue. "I made a number of futile, emotional gestures at the time. I suppose asking you to come here was one of them. Certainly I knew it was a mistake when I received your uncharitable reply."

"Uncharitable?" I exclaimed. "I wrote no such reply."

"That depends upon your point of view." She gestured toward a small settee. "Do sit down, Catherine. I am going to order tea. Will you join me?"

"Thank you, no."

"Perhaps a drink?"

"No, nothing."

She crossed the room to a huge bed with a fantastic headboard carved to resemble a swan spreading gilded wings. Near it hung draperies which I supposed covered a narrow window, but she opened them to reveal the sliding doors of a small cabinet set in the wall at table height.

"It's a kitchen lift," she said. "What Americans call a dumb waiter. A repulsive term, dumb waiter! I had this little elevator installed so I could practice without any interruption." She pressed a button. "Three short rings means tea. I used to work for days on end without seeing a soul."

She took a chair facing me, and I realized that perhaps Althea felt as ill at ease as I did, although she was better able to conceal her emotions. For a moment we sat in silence, regarding each other politely but cooly.

"You mentioned a letter I wrote," I said at last. "You called it uncharitable. I don't understand."

"Really?" She did not look directly into my eyes. "Lack of kindness isn't always a question of the words you use—it can be the timing of the words. I wrote you during my grief over Pandora's loss; I was searching for any help or comfort." For an instant her eyes rested on my face, then moved away. "I did what I had sworn never to do in my life. I appealed to you. I asked you to come to me."

"And I answered that I would. How can you call that uncharitable?"

Althea's features remained calm, her voice controlled, but the whiteness of her knuckles as she gripped the arms of the chair betrayed her emotions. "I called out to you in grief, and you replied with a polite message saying that since you expected to be in Europe anyway, you would doubtless pay me a visit. Until then, I had not understood the cruelty of mere politeness. Thank you for the lesson, Catherine."

She spoke with terrible simplicity, a candor that made the words devastating. "I'm sorry, I certainly meant no cruelty," I said. "I don't remember exactly what I wrote."

"Of course not! It meant so little to you. But I shouldn't blame you for hurting me when I place myself in a position to be hurt. After all, I know your nature. Why should I have de-

luded myself that Pandora's death would change your coldness toward me, your lack of sympathy?''

I stared at her, unbelieving. How could she, who had never
displayed one whit of love or concern for her own children, sit
there and quietly accuse me of coldness? The years of hurt
and loneliness, the pain of her desertion, welled up in a flood.

"What could you expect?" I demanded. "Nothing I could
possibly do could hurt you the way you hurt me—you and the
way you hurt Dorrie and Matthew. You say you cried out to
me in grief! Where were you when I was a child who needed
comforting? What you did to us was . . . was . . ." I could
think of no term strong enough, but she supplied one.

"Wicked," she said. "Wicked is the word you are searching for. It is the sort of word Esther Sullivan uses when, like
you, she delivers high moral judgments." Althea made a gesture of impatience, and the jewels on her fingers flashed in the
light. "Let us not waste time abusing each other. I am aware
of your opinion of me. Pandora told me exactly how you
feel."

"I don't believe you," I said. "Dorrie wouldn't discuss me
with you."

"Come now, Catherine! You know that's exactly what your
sister *would* have done. She was my child and I loved her, but
I was not blind to her character. Spare me any noble nonsense
about Pandora!"

A bell sounded softly. Althea rose, went to the cabinet elevator, and returned with the tea tray. Her hands were not
quite steady as she poured, and there was an unnatural stiff-
ness in the way she held herself erect.

"No, I shall not argue with you, Catherine," she said, lifting her cup. "After all, I would surely lose to a girl who was
president of the Eastfield School Debating Society for two
years."

She had succeeded in startling me. "How did you know
that?" I asked. "Of course. Pandora told you."

She shook her head. "No. Pandora talked of your opinions,
not your talents. She did not, for instance, mention your win-

ning the school prize for drawing, or that you designed the
scenery for a production of *Blossom Time*."

"Who told you that?" These were certainly not things Pandora would mention. I doubted she had even remembered
them.

Althea sipped her tea thoughtfully, ignoring my question.
"I would have preferred you to have sung the soprano role in
the operetta, but designing scenery also requires talent. I
especially liked the scrim you painted as a background for the
'Ave Maria.' Clouds, as usual, but the suggestion of thunder-
heads struck me as original."

"You couldn't have seen it!" I exclaimed.

"No, I couldn't have. That was not permitted me!" Suddenly she was on her feet and pacing; her vibrant voice, although quiet, seemed to fill the room.

"Years ago you passed a terrible judgment upon me, Catherine," she said. "But what have you ever known of me or
my life? Nothing! Only the lies you learned from Matthew
Andrews."

"Don't say that about Matthew. I won't listen—"

My protest went unfinished. She whirled upon me, eyes
flashing in anger. "You will listen to me, Catherine! There is
no other way you can understand your own life."

She began speaking then, telling her story, and within a few
minutes I found myself drawn into the events and listening in
fascinated silence. Althea Hoffman had gained fame as a singer, not an actress, yet with one gesture she could set a scene,
create an atmosphere. She lived her story, and I soon found
myself living it with her.

She was born, as I knew, in Geneva, and her childhood had
been unremarkable until her father died when she was ten
years old. There were no close relatives, and her mother, a
seamstress, decided their only hope of prosperity lay in emi-
grating to the United States.

"But for us, America was an unkept promise. Our hard-
ships in Boston were as great as in Geneva. My mother was ill

much of the time and her death, a few years later, was a blessed end to suffering.

"No one who knows me now could imagine what I was like at sixteen!" Bitterness tinged Althea's voice. "Shy, ignorant, frightened! Even then I sang, but I was afraid to let anyone hear me, afraid of their laughter. I worked as a maid, I took care of children; finally I became a waitress."

The first time she sang in public was in a restaurant in Cambridge, an imitation rathskeller frequented by Harvard students. Once, when the dining room was deserted and the small band was practicing German folk songs, Althea, not thinking anyone would pay attention, began singing. The manager, hearing her, urged her to perform that evening.

"I was terrified when the time came; my knees were trembling, I didn't know what to do with my hands. The band began to play *Musse Den*, and suddenly I was singing. There was no more fear, there was only the music! Then everyone was cheering and applauding. Oh, it was magic to me, pure magic! No other performance was ever so exciting; not my debut at La Scala, not the first time I sang *Lucia* in Rome—even though the audience covered the stage with roses that night.

"A few months later, Matthew Andrews came to the rathskeller. I remember it was summer and he had returned to Harvard to finish his doctorate. I hardly knew him when he asked me to marry.

"It was very tempting to me. Matthew was attractive and kind, ten years older than I—which seemed proper in my European way of thinking. More than anything else, he offered security and safety.

"But I foresaw troubles. He was educated and so were his family and his friends. I felt ignorant when he discussed books I had not read, plays I had not seen. When I told him this, he laughed at me; he said he wanted a wife, not a literary scholar. Then he kissed me on the forehead, as one kisses a child, and told me I was his dear girl and must never change."

Althea moved slowly across the room and paused at the

window. She seemed to have forgotten my presence and for the moment was reliving her life for herself alone.

"How little we understood one another!" she said. "Like a fool, I did not believe Matthew Andrews. When he told me he loved me just as I was, I thought he was merely being kind, reassuring me. It seemed impossible that anyone could really value ignorance above education. How could he find charm in my lack of cultivation and learning? But I discovered he had meant every word he said.

"After we were married, my education began. I devoted every free hour to improving myself—not just studying piano and voice, but attending classes in history and literature. I did this mostly because I had a thirst for knowledge, but partly because I wanted my husband to be proud of me. After all, he was a college professor, and what had I been? A waitress who sang! Not that I was ashamed of this—there is no disgrace in humble work. But I had noticed Matthew was careful never to mention my background to his friends.

"But our first quarrels were about having children. I wanted them; he didn't. He found a dozen excuses, but I think his real reason was jealousy. He would have been jealous of a child. God knows, he was jealous enough of everyone else! Physically, he loved me desperately. Apart from that, I hardly existed.

"He was tolerant when I was chosen as soprano soloist in a community production of *The Messiah,* but not so happy when I was invited to repeat my performance in another town."

During the next year it became obvious that Althea was a musician of extraordinary talent. Only her marriage to Matthew Andrews, who was astonished and intransigent, stood between her and a brilliantly promising career.

"I could have had both," said Althea angrily. "I would have made compromises, yielded much. But who can compromise with blind jealousy?" Suddenly her hands clenched, and color surged to her cheeks. "And then Matthew, in the disguise of love, did an unspeakable thing.

"Always he had been adamant about not having children. Now he changed his mind. And I was overjoyed, not suspecting that he was using motherhood as a weapon—or should I say a padlock and chain? But when you were born, I had no such suspicion. I knew only happiness, fulfillment.

"Pandora came soon after—too soon, I felt. But it was only when Matthew began to accuse me of neglecting my children for my music that I saw the plan he had designed for me. There would be another child and then probably another. Not because he wanted a family, but to keep me in my proper place as wife and brood mother. He had chosen the wrong woman! I rebelled!"

Pacing the floor, Althea tossed her head—a lioness, defiant and proud. "I did not neglect you! But I could not have stopped singing anymore than a bird can stop. I appeared only in New England and twice in New York. I was never away from home longer than one night or, at most, two. Because of you and Pandora, I refused a dozen important engagements, but nothing satisfied Matthew, for it was not really my absence he resented, but my accomplishment, my independence.

"Backstage, after my first New York recital, I met Victor Donato. We fell in love—and, yes, we had an affair. Our plan was to marry as soon as I could arrange a divorce. But Matthew struck first."

She shrugged her shoulders, a gesture of weariness. "I assume you know the ugly story. Matthew filed not for divorce but for legal separation, charging me with adultery and gross immorality. The judge who heard the case, a village prude, granted Matthew's petition and deprived me of my own children.

"I was called an evil woman! An immoral foreigner who had betrayed a respectable American husband with another foreigner. I was frantic—I appealed the decision but it was futile. Then, in desperation, I was driven to attempt a foolish thing. I hired men to kidnap you and Dorrie."

"To kidnap—?" I drew my breath sharply as the half-remembered nightmare came back to me. The walk to school, the car, and the strange men shouting. So it was not just a dream; it had really happened, and now I knew why.

"I thought if I could somehow get you to Europe, Victor's power and money would protect us. But Matthew learned of my plan, or guessed it. The attempt failed and brought disastrous consequences.

"I had never applied for American citizenship—I simply never thought about it. I was not sent to prison for the kidnapping plot, but I found myself declared an undesirable alien in the United States. Not only were my daughters taken from me, but I was exiled from them. Year after year, Victor's lawyers battled to have that decision reversed. Always failure! I wrote Matthew, begging him to let you and Dorrie visit me in Europe or Canada or anywhere. My letters were returned unopened. So were the gifts I sent you on your birthdays and every Christmas."

She sat beside me on the settee, but did not look into my face; her eyes were turned away. "How did I know about the prize for drawing and the stage design? Because your school published a weekly paper and I arranged to have it sent to me. I never missed an issue—but often your names were not in it, and no papers came in the summer.

"Victor used to tell me that I was morbid, that I had made a cult of my loss. When we learned we could have no children of our own, we adopted Mario and later Lillian. I loved them deeply, but it did not change things.

"I had faith that as soon as you and Dorrie were old enough to understand, you would write me. But your fourteenth birthday passed, and when the fifteenth came, I sent no present, but I still waited. I am not sure when I faced the truth that your minds were poisoned against me, your hearts hardened."

Althea straightened her shoulders and lifted her chin slightly. "I, too, have my pride. How long could I beg for a crumb of affection?"

She hesitated, then rose quickly. "Come with me, Catherine. I want to show you something."

I followed her into an adjacent room, where she slid back the doors of a tall cupboard. Two shelves were lined with objects wrapped in transparent plastic. I saw a great, golden-haired doll, a cuckoo clock, an autograph album with a silver clasp.

"Gifts that were never received," Althea said quietly. "I thought someday you might enjoy seeing them; then you would know you had not been forgotten, and I would be proud to show you. But now I find no joy in it. None." She unwrapped an elaborate music box decorated with a carved scene of two children in a forest. "This was for you," she said, handing it to me. "Long ago. So very long ago."

When I raised the lid, the familiar lullaby from *Hansel and Gretel* chimed gently.

> *When at night I fall asleep,*
> *Fourteen angels watch do keep . . .*

"At last it is yours," she told me. I nodded silently, fighting back tears.

When we returned to the bedroom, I saw how much the telling of the story had cost her. She no longer appeared fierce and dominating, but looked vulnerable, drained of strength. She sank into a chair near the tea table.

"A year ago Lillian, my adopted daughter, died. Her death was tragic and . . ." Althea paused, her eyes closed, then shook her head. ". . . horrible. Forgive me, but I still cannot bear to speak of it. Victor had died, then Lillian was taken from me. It is impossible to imagine my loneliness. Then, like a miracle, Pandora's first letter came. Oh, what a wonderful letter! She told me how loyalty to her father had kept her from writing before; that since his death she had been so busy with her career as a television actress that time had slipped by. But now she was eager to visit me, and would come as soon as she could fulfill her contracts as an actress."

I nodded, not permitting my expression to give away my true feelings. How like Pandora! Even in the first letter she had ever written her mother, she could not resist boasting, could not be honest.

"So Pandora came to me, but after such a little time she, too, was taken." Althea rose to her feet, unsteady now, and clutched the back of the chair for support. "Is it any wonder that I feel some evil force destroys those I love, my own children? Is it any wonder that I feel . . . haunted?"

"What can I do?" I asked. "Tell me, and I will try."

She looked at me, both hope and apprehension in her eyes. "Will you stay here a while, Catherine? Let us become acquainted. Who knows? We might even learn to like each other. We might be friends."

"Yes," I said. "We might."

The Catherine Andrews who left that room a few minutes later was not the same young woman who had entered it an hour before. Except in legends of miraculous conversions, no one is utterly changed in a single interview—yet I knew something deep and important had happened to me. Whatever the full truth of the past might be, I no longer hated Althea. I had dropped a terrible weight, a burden of resentment I'd carried for years without even knowing it was heavy. What had this long-nurtured hatred done to me? How had it changed my life? I could not tell. I only knew I felt light—uplifted.

The lengthening shadows in the corridor did not bother me, and when I opened the door of my room, it seemed only natural that Esther Sullivan had decorated the dressing table with a bouquet of fresh daffodils and had welcomed me with a bowl of Spanish oranges and grapes. There was even a selection of books and magazines in English. Of course I was being welcomed! At that moment I felt myself the beloved daughter of the house returning after a long absence.

My suitcase and flight bag had been upacked, at Miss Sullivan's orders, I supposed. Dresses hung in the wardrobe on heavily padded hangers; the drawers of the bureau were neatly arranged.

I placed the music box Althea had given me on the bedside

table. A birthday present, belated by fifteen years, but all the more precious for that.

No sense of Pandora's presence remained in the room, and now I felt chagrined to have imagined such a ghost. Even my suspicions about Pandora's death now seemed improbable. There must be a simple explanation for the one fact that made the accident of her drowning so unlikely. I stretched out on the bed, intending to rest for a moment; then my eyes closed without my realizing it, and when I awoke to a tapping on my door, the room was almost in darkness.

I switched on a lamp, calling, "Yes, come in."

Esther Sullivan entered, carrying two unlighted candles and a box of matches in a brass holder. "Protection against our erratic electrical system," she said. "The power fails at the most inconvenient times."

I noticed again what a striking figure she presented: tall, severe in the unrelieved black dress, slender but strong.

"Supper is at eight-thirty, and a very light meal unless there are guests," she told me. "When there are guests, it's a heavy meal at some dreadfully late Italian hour. There are no guests tonight."

"A light meal is what I'll want, thank you."

"Good." She hesitated. "Tonight everyone is having supper out except Althea, who has a tray in her room, and Mario Donato. It would be just the two of you in the dining room." She gave me a delicate, inquiring look.

"Thank you for the warning." I smiled at her. "A tray will suit me very well."

Her relief was apparent. "I'm sorry about this awkwardness. Mario will soon recover his good sense and apologize."

"Oh, I can endure his wrath, and I don't especially need his apology." Mario Donato's insults and even his final threat had dwindled to unimportance. Now I felt I could dismiss him as an unusually dramatic Italian male with no manners. He could not lessen my new sense of well-being.

"I've just been with Althea," Miss Sullivan said. "Perhaps

it's not my place to comment, but whatever happened between you this afternoon was like a miracle for her. I actually heard her laugh! For the first time in months. And before I left she said a strange thing."

"What was that?"

"She asked me to remember you in my prayers. Althea knows that I *do* believe in prayer—it's my only real strength. But she never mentions my faith except lightly." Then she added quickly, "I don't mean she scoffs; it's that she feels I'm very old-fashioned, and I suppose that's true. But tonight she was quite serious when she mentioned you."

"How kind of you to tell me."

"Not at all. I—I—" She averted her eyes, seemed to study her folded hands. "I have no gift for words—it's hard for me to express my emotions. But you must know how grateful I am that you've come here, and I will, indeed, pray that you stay."

I was again touched by Miss Sullivan's concern. I sensed that she was a lonely woman and had probably never had a real life except as a satellite to Althea. No doubt the collapse of Althea's world had meant the destruction of her own.

"Miss Sullivan, if I am to stay, there is something I need to know," I said. "Tell me about Lillian Donato. How did she die?"

Her pale cheeks turned ashen, and for a moment I thought she would make no answer at all. Then she said, "I have no right to speak of that. You must ask your mother."

"Was she drowned?" I asked sharply. "Tell me!"

"Drowned? No, that was Pandora." Esther Sullivan seemed bewildered, unable to think. Then she murmured, "Lillian died by fire. I saw her die. I will carry that memory to my grave."

But immediately her iron control seemed to reassert itself. She drew herself up, clasped her hands to conceal their trembling. "After Pandora's death, Althea was hysterical for several days. She seemed to blame herself for both accidents.

But, of course, that was part of the hysteria. She could not have prevented Pandora's drowning; no one could."

I couldn't quite catch the implication of Miss Sullivan's words. Was she saying that while Pandora's death had been inevitable, Althea was somehow responsible for Lillian's perishing by fire? Surely that was not her meaning!

"The fire you spoke of, Miss Sullivan. How did it happen?"

"You must ask Althea. I can tell you nothing—it is not my place to talk of it." She turned from me, ending the conversation. Then, as she started to leave, something caught her eye and she stepped toward the bedside table. She was looking at the music box.

"Isn't it charming?" I said. "Althea gave it to me this afternoon."

Miss Sullivan looked astonished. "Really?" She touched the carved lid gently, almost reverently. "This surprises me very much. You should be flattered. I thought nothing in the world would induce Althea to part with this."

"Is it so valuable?" I was puzzled by Esther Sullivan's manner. Why should Althea *not* part with it, since it had been bought for me in the first place?

"It has deep sentimental value," she said. "This music box was one of Lillian's most treasured possessions."

"Lillian's?" I exclaimed.

"Yes. Althea gave it to Lillian on her twelfth birthday."

"Are you sure?" I asked, unbelieving. "Perhaps it was another music box."

"No. I remember that for once we were all together at the villa. So often we were separated on birthdays, but that time we were together. The cook brought in a cake with twelve glowing candles, and Lillian lifted the lid from this box. I remember how she clapped her hands and said, 'Oh, it's the "Children's Prayer"!' Then Althea and Lillian sang together along with the music from the box. It was a beautiful moment, one of my most loved memories. It was that day, when they were singing, that we realized God had given Lillian a great talent. She would surpass Althea; her voice would one day be the most beautiful of her generation."

I started to protest, to say there was a mistake. Althea must have bought two identical gifts—one for me, one for Lillian.

"Look," she said. "See how this corner is dented? You would never notice if you didn't know about it. Do you see?"

She held the box toward me, and I drew back as from something unclean, afraid she would try to place it in my hands.

"Lillian kept it on her bedside table and one night here at the villa she had a frightening dream. I slept near her and heard her cry out in her sleep. As I was coming to wake her, she must have knocked the music box from the table. I remember it was on the floor, playing, and Lillian was in tears. I took her in my arms; I comforted her."

Miss Sullivan's voice became a whisper. "After Lillian's death, I found the box in her room. I took it to Althea and I suppose she put it away with the other keepsakes of Lillian. With her doll, the cuckoo clock, the calico rabbit . . ."

I did not hear what else she said. Instead I heard in my mind the sincerity of Althea's voice when she had given me this gift. *"It was for you . . . so long ago."*

Miss Sullivan was bidding me goodnight, taking her leave. I nodded and spoke; I believe I even managed to smile.

After she had gone I stood staring at the music box. I did not lift the lid; I knew the chimes would not sound the same to me now. There would be a different tone . . . hollow . . . false . . .

Chapter Six

In the morning I was awakened by another chiming: the tinkle of sheep bells on the nearby mountain slope. Rising quickly, I put on my robe, opened the draperies, and stepped onto the balcony.

The world was washed in the cool, yellow morning light of Italian spring. Two children, wearing broad, fringed hats that must have once belonged to their fathers, herded a small flock of sheep toward patches of new grass higher on the shoulder of the mountain. Turning, they waved to me, and I waved back. From some hidden place—perhaps the cypress grove—came the single trilled note of a songbird. Since songbirds are so rare in Italy, I took the greeting to be a favorable omen. At least I hoped so.

The turmoil Esther Sullivan had raised in my mind the night before had not evaporated in the morning light. Before going to sleep, I'd twisted and turned on my pillow, wakeful with doubts, uncertain of what I should do—and at last decided to return the music box to Althea, tell her frankly that keeping it seemed like robbing the dead, and then see what she would reply.

Now, with my emotions somewhat less stormy, such a course seemed unwise and useless. I had no doubt Althea would be quick to offer an explanation. Surely she must have realized that everyone in the household knew the box had been Lillian's. Of course she'd have an answer! But could I believe what she might tell me? Could I believe anyone at the villa? Mario? Konrad? I knew I shouldn't even trust Esther Sullivan, although she was the only one I had no reason to doubt.

No, I would not confront Althea. I would wait and watch; I'd pretend ignorance until the truth became known. Soon, I thought, there would come a chance to mention the box casually without arousing any suspicions.

In the shower I was pelted by drops as cold as hailstones, and made a mental note to ask the schedule of the water heater; continuous hot water is regarded in Italy as one of the more sinful extravagances. I dressed and went into the hallway, where a maid was swishing a long rag dustmop across spotless, dustless tiles, and asked where breakfast was served.

The dining room was on the lower floor, and its windows framed views of both the lake and the mountain. Copper warming dishes were placed on a sideboard with a bowl of fruit and a basket of hot crisp rolls. Near it, an angular man of middle age was drawing himself a cup of espresso from a hissing machine that stood on a metal stand. His well-worn tweeds with their elbow patches had an out-of-date, professorial look; the slightly stooped shoulders suggested hours spent in libraries. He resembled many of the academic gentlemen who had been my neighbors all my life.

"Good morning," he called cheerfully. "You must be Althea's daughter, Catherine. Althea has asked me to show you about the place this morning, but help yourself to breakfast first. That egg dish with olives and cheese is a marvel. By the way, I'm Richard Halpin. I'm director of the museum."

Over breakfast I learned that Halpin was also a composer, particularly of opera. "A ridiculous profession these days, my dear," he said, with a morose shake of his head. "Like designing hoopskirts or making spinning wheels. The small demand that exists can be met by antiques. I'm given encouragement from time to time, of course. A one-act of mine was performed at Spoletto a few seasons back, and next year my old college in England will stage my *Macbeth*."

"*Macbeth*?" I asked. "Isn't there already a version? Didn't Verdi compose it?"

Richard Halpin shuddered, his moustache seeming to droop even more than it did already. "One of the worst misconceptions in the history of opera! Masses of witches and enough syrupy singers to fill a sweetshop. But Lady Macbeth is a show-off role and ten years ago Althea showed off very well in it. So she commissioned me to write a version in English that would be more faithful to Shakespeare."

"Has it been performed?"

My question so obviously surprised him that for a moment I thought I had just revealed an ignorance that was insulting. Perhaps his *Macbeth* was a work of major international fame.

"You mean you don't—" He stopped, fumbled for words, then said, "No, it really hasn't been performed. Last year we did a scaled-down, concert version of it here at the museum. We used some costumes and scenery. Althea sang, of course, and she brought in a good baritone. Her daughter Lillian doubled in a couple of small roles."

"Miss Sullivan told me Lillian was a singer of great talent," I ventured.

Halpin looked uncomfortable. "Well, let's say she had a certain potential. But a true diva is a great singer who can also act. Lillian was more an actress who sang rather well. I never heard her in actual performance. Our production was left unfinished." He rose from his chair. "Shall we start with a quick look at the grounds?"

He proved to be a fascinating guide who knew the name of every plant and flower, and his admiration for the lake, the villa, and the ancient castle showed in every comment he made. Such enthusiasm was contagious, of course, but I was already a convert to the beauty of northern Italy's lake country.

As we rounded a long arbor heavily hung with unripe table grapes, I heard a faint rustle in the vines and suddenly Rajah emerged as from ambush, leaping toward us in what I hoped was a playful caper.

"Absolutely harmless, of course," said Halpin, regarding the huge cat uneasily. "I must say the old fellow seems frisky this morning."

When the ocelot rubbed against my leg, I gathered my courage and reached out to scratch him as I had seen Esther Sullivan do.

"I wouldn't, if I were you." Halpin sounded grim. "You might make a friend for life and a constant companion."

"Better a friend than an enemy," I replied. Rajah's coat felt velvety, and he enjoyed my hesitant attention for a moment, then ambled off on some ocelot errand.

Halpin led me to gates where the driveways of the villa and the museum met to join the mountain road. "There's a piece of carving I want you to see," he told me. "A Santa Cecilia."

I expected something traditional—a nun at a keyboard with some entranced cherubs watching her. But when I looked up at the arch above the gates, my eyes widened. The saint herself was not shown; there was only a suggestion of lovely, tapering hands and an indication of some instrument—a lute or even a lyre—clasped by the curving fingers. Bursting from this center, the flowing lines of music caught in stone rippled, then pulsed to arcs and swirls. It seemed a living, moving thing.

"Glorious." I had dropped my voice as though we were standing in a museum. "It's one of the most beautiful works I've ever seen."

"Yes, it's remarkable," agreed Halpin. "I think it's Mario's masterpiece—even better than the memorial monument he did in Rome two years ago."

I had suspected that Mario Donato was the sculptor, but it was difficult to believe. When I recalled his face and voice, I had an impression of force and strength, even of violence. The Santa Cecilia conveyed that power, yet it expressed far more than that. There were delicacy and an almost fragile gentleness in the fine tracery of line—a sensitivity I'd never have suspected in Mario Donato.

Leaving the gates, we crossed the lawn to a small but perfectly designed rose garden, not yet in bloom. Then someone called my name and I saw Konrad Donato approaching, dressed in tennis clothes and carrying a racquet.

"Good morning!" he called. "You are taking a stroll?" The sunshine made his fair hair even lighter. Yesterday he had seemed like an advertisement for the best men's shop in Rome; this morning he resembled a Hollywood ideal of a tennis player—unrumpled, gleaming white, perfect. I thought of his mother, Ilse Donato, huddled in her fishing skiff, and it seemed impossible she was connected with this young man.

Konrad joined us, smiling. "You are in good hands, Catherine," he said. "Richard is an expert on the Villa Pellegrina. He knows all the horrible details of its history."

"He's a wonderful guide," I said, and then exclaimed, "Look! Over in those trees. I think I saw a deer, but it's gone now."

"I'm sure you did," said Konrad. "There are at least a dozen behind the fence in that grove. My father first saw them in England. English red deer. I think they are called fallow deer, also. He thought they were the most beautiful animals on earth, and he brought them to Italy and made a park for them."

A deer park, I thought. Yet another royal gesture by Victor Donato. "Can we get close to them?" I asked.

"Oh, yes," Konrad assured me. "They are not tame, but they approach the fence. I will show you."

Richard Halpin glanced at his watch. "Konrad is a better guide to the deer than I am, Catherine, and I have work awaiting me at the museum. If you'll drop by this afternoon, I'll show you our exhibits. They're not yet complete, but you'll find them most interesting, I think."

I was not eager to return to the castle, but there was no way to refuse and I thanked him. After Halpin left us, Konrad and I strolled along a flagstone walk lined by irises and ferns.

"I am truly sorry about the unpleasantness yesterday," he said. "Mario behaved like a savage, as I later told him."

"It hardly matters," I said, and surprisingly this was true. Much of the hurt and outrage I had felt yesterday came because many things Mario had said were dangerously on target. I had indeed arrived bearing a grudge against Althea. Now that I knew more of her story, my resentment was gone. I still couldn't trust her—learning about the music box proved that—but she had certainly awakened my sympathy.

"I suspect Mario may have been angry with you simply because you are Pandora's sister," said Konrad.

"He didn't like Pandora?"

Konrad shrugged. "Let us say that at first things were very good between them, perhaps too good to last. And later things were bad."

"Are you saying that Pandora and Mario had a love affair and then quarreled?" I asked.

Konrad's smile was mocking. "My dear Catherine, what would I know of love affairs? Especially Mario's love affairs. I said only that they were friends and then were not friends." And he would say no more.

The deer park, to my surprise, was the same grove of cypress and firs visible from my balcony. The wire fence was interwoven among the trees and camouflaged by low, bushy pines.

"Pasquale!" shouted Konrad, and an ancient man with a magnificent white moustache emerged from what appeared to be a toolshed. He seemed to know what was wanted, and hobbled toward us carrying a reed market basket heaped with coarsely chopped carrots and other vegetables. He bowed to me, gave a toothless grin, then, cupping his hand to his mouth, made a strange yodeling call like the cry of some giant bird.

There was a rustling in the thickets and suddenly the deer appeared as if by magic. Two great stags with many-tined antlers, several lovely hinds, and a fawn so charming I wanted to adopt it cautiously approached the fence. Still untamed, they would not venture too close to the wire barrier, but they eagerly accepted our tossed offerings of food. The older stag even showed off for us, rearing on his hind legs and shaking his antlers.

"Hello, Catherine, hello, Konrad," said a voice behind us. It was Miss Sullivan. She nodded with grave courtesy to the old man, murmuring, "*Buon giorno, Don Pasquale.*"

"*Buon giorno, excellencia!*" He swept off his battered hat, and his bow to her, although hampered by rheumatism, was deep.

"I see you've met Don Pasquale," she said to me. "He's our genius with plants and animals—a landscape designer, born veterinarian, and herb doctor." Reaching into the basket, she tossed a carrot to the fawn. "Althea seems very well today, Catherine, but a little tired from the excitement of your arrival. She'll spend the day resting. Mr. Halpin and I are having lunch at the museum. Will you join us?"

"Yes, thank you," I said.

"Good. About one o'clock. That will give you time to have a brief look at what we're doing." She glanced behind her. "I wonder where Rajah is. He was following me a moment ago."

Her question was answered almost before it was spoken. No one saw where he came from, but suddenly Rajah charged across a stretch of lawn toward the fence.

"He can't leap it!" Konrad exclaimed. "It's too high."

Bur Rajah had no need to leap from the ground. In a flash he scaled a tree trunk near the wire and, from the lower branches, jumped easily to earth inside the pen. The next moment was utter confusion—all of us shouting; deer scattering, crashing through thickets; and the fawn, maddened with fear, hurling himself against the wire of the fence, then falling as his thin legs collapsed beneath him. After wild kicking, he righted himself and staggered away, dragging one leg painfully.

Meanwhile, the creator of the uproar had grown tired of the game. Rajah leaped easily into the tree and curled up in the thick lower branches, his tail twitching happily.

"*La pistola!*" Don Pasquale shouted. "I need the pistol."

"It's in a cabinet in the office," said Miss Sullivan. "I'll get it." She hurried away toward the museum.

"Not a pistol!" I protested. "What for?"

Without realizing it, I had seized Konrad's arm and was clinging to it. He smiled at me and I let go.

"We are not shooting the fawn," he assured me, "or shooting Rajah, although I admit my temptation."

"Then why send for a pistol?"

"This is not a pistol that shoots bullets. It shoots a little needle thing—how do you say it in English? Like a dart. This has a drug that will make the fawn quiet so Pasquale can examine him."

"It won't hurt the fawn?"

"Not at all. It is a drug used now in zoos and all places where wild animals must be handled. Without it, we could not even catch the fawn except at the risk of hurting it still more."

A moment later Esther Sullivan returned with the special gun—not at all like a pistol, but much longer to accommodate the "bullets": little hypodermic needles slightly larger than kitchen matches.

"They look sinister," I said.

"The fawn will be paralyzed only for a few hours. Have no worry, Catherine."

Konrad and Don Pasquale shouted and waved their arms to shoo Rajah from his perch. When he leaped down, Miss Sullivan took a firm hold on his jeweled collar.

"I'm ashamed of you," she scolded. "You've never done such a thing before!" Rajah rubbed against her leg contentedly.

"Don't wait for us," said Konrad as he and Don Pasquale started toward a gate in the fence. "The park is only a few acres but it may take hours to get close to the fawn."

When we were alone, Miss Sullivan said, "By the way, I've had Pandora's trunk sent to your room. I thought you would want to sort through her things as soon as possible. A saddening task, I'm afraid. Would you like me to help you?"

"No, thank you," I told her. "I think I'd rather do it alone."

Her expression of sympathy made me feel guilty. She assumed I wanted to be alone because I might be overcome with grief, which was not the case. My mourning had ended, and besides, the few possessions Pandora had left behind held no meaning for me: they were not my sister, they were simply . . . things. But they might reveal a message, some answer to the question of her death. And that message was for me alone.

The trunk, which long ago Pandora and I had shared when we went to summer camp, stood on a rack in my room. Opening it, I saw clothing I recognized—things originally expensive but now well-worn because Pandora had found them as bargains in resale shops. Suddenly I hesitated, my eye caught by a glitter of sequins.

The dress I lifted and held to the light was certainly no hand-me-down. It was new and I recognized the label of an extravagantly expensive fashion boutique of a New York department store—a shop that offers flamboyant styles for stage and television celebrities. I could only guess at the price of this silk sheath, with its hand-embroidered collar of sequins and seed pearls, but I was sure that never before had Pandora owned a dress so costly.

Nor was this all. I found two more party dresses with the same label, as well as a lounging outfit as thin as gossamer. How had Pandora been able to afford such a wardrobe for her trip to Italy? Had Althea sent her the money? I doubted it. Air

fare and probably a little more, yes. But Pandora's means of
paying for these extravagances remained a mystery.

Putting aside the clothing, I smiled ruefully at plastic-
protected snapshots of Matthew and myself. Another envelope contained assorted photos of people of the villa. Mario
Donato stood on a pier wearing a turtleneck and an Italian
fisherman's cap with a round tassel. He was smiling broadly.
Then Mario leaning against a stone wall, Mario playing a flute,
Mario on the Rialto Bridge in Venice. The identity of Pandora's "exciting man" seemed apparent now.

But then a surprise: a flash picture—probably taken by a
street photographer— of Pandora and Konrad seated at a table in a sidewalk cafe, laughing, with a bottle of champagne
before them. His arm circled her possessively, like a
lover's.

Near the bottom of the trunk, its glass carefully protected
by cardboard, I found a large drawing, in pencil dressed with
charcoal and India ink. Even without the signature, the work
would have been unmistakable. This was the design—the
original, I supposed—for the Santa Cecilia I had seen earlier
today. At the lower right the mat board was signed, "Merry
Christmas from Mario."

This was not a work any artist would have given away lightly, and I wondered if Pandora could have understood its value. Mario had known Pandora only two or three weeks when
he had given her this. What had Konrad said? "At first things
were very good between them, and later things were bad."
How bad? That was a question I would have to answer.

Next I came across a letter postmarked in Venice and addressed in a handwriting once dear and familiar to me. I had
known Gordon Carr was in Italy doing historical research. He
had written me, and Pandora had written me about him, but in
the rush of events I had forgotten. Not long ago I would have
found reading a letter from Gordon to Pandora almost painful.
Now I felt nothing, not even that I was an intruder in their
lives, when I slipped it from the envelope.

There was no salutation, no date, and the handwriting was jerky with an emotion I soon realized was rage.

As I told you on the phone, you won't get away with this. I'll be at the villa two weeks from today and expect to settle accounts with you once and for all. This is final.

Gordon

I stared at the note, unbelieving. What could Pandora have done to arouse such anger in Gordon, who was almost unfailingly gentle and patient? Their divorce had been settled before Pandora left the United States; everything was supposed to be finished between them. Although the postmark was slightly smudged, the date was clear enough to read—but for a moment I didn't see its significance. Then I realized that Gordon would have arrived at the villa to "settle accounts" with Pandora on the day before her death.

Gordon must have returned to the United States by now; there was no way to question him directly about the quarrel. But I could certainly send him a note asking about Pandora's welfare when he last saw her. I resolved to do this tonight.

The trunk was almost empty now. There remained a few toilet articles, Pandora's camera, and some rather pathetic souvenirs. I picked up a wrinkled program for an off-Broadway play. *I Saw You* was a mystery drama in which Pandora had played a fairly important role. Such hopes she had pinned to that part! And the play closed after three performances, an utter failure.

Slowly I repacked the trunk, trying to fit together what I had learned. But now there seemed more questions than ever, and I had not found the most important object of all: Pandora's diary. She *must* have kept one! She had always recorded her life in some sort of journal, ever since childhood. She didn't write every day, and often a week would go by with no entries. But then she would fill several pages. As I put away the expensive clothes, I searched every pocket, the two purses and evening bags, even the lining of the trunk itself. But no diary was to be found; I felt sure someone had taken it.

An hour later I entered the courtyard of Castle Malaspina and passed between the great open doors of the museum into the lobby, where a workman directed me to the offices and working studios on the second floor. When I reached the top of the marble staircase, I suddenly heard an angry uproar of quarreling voices, and three men wearing billed caps and paint-stained coveralls emerged from the doorway nearest me. Looking back, one of them made a gesture of contempt known to anyone who has ever watched a street argument in Italy.

"An end to these questions!" the first man exclaimed. "Our honesty is insulted! We will not be called thieves!"

They stormed past me just as Richard Halpin appeared at the door calling out an apology in correct but bookish Italian. The painters, ignoring him, stomped down the stairs.

"I seem to have arrived at an unfortunate moment," I said. Halpin's rather sallow complexion had turned noticeably red.

"No, no. This is really nothing," he said, ushering me into a large office where Miss Sullivan was seated at a desk. She was wearing, I noticed, a brown smock over her dark dress.

"A show of temperament," Halpin went on. "If there is anyone who can surpass a dramatic soprano in outrage, it's an Italian workman."

Esther Sullivan greeted me, then explained that the painters had been questioned about a theft. "They were not being accused. We only wanted information. The diamond necklace for the Countess in our *Figaro* exhibit is missing."

"A diamond necklace!" I exclaimed.

"Oh, not real diamonds," she assured me. "Paste. But even stage jewelry is expensive. The necklace cost a good deal more than any of those workmen earns in a week. We've had too many such losses."

"I simply can't understand how it happens," said Halpin,

frowning. "The thefts all take place at night, yet our security seems perfect. There's never been a sign of a break-in."

"So the thief must be the Malaspina family ghost," said Miss Sullivan, with a faint smile.

"A ghost? I've always been fascinated by ghost stories." This was true, but I wasn't sure I would enjoy listening to tales of hauntings in the gloomier parts of this building.

"You couldn't possibly have an Italian castle without a whole crowd of ghosts," Halpin said. "But here we have an especially larcenous specter. In fact, the shade of a robber nobleman. I'll tell you about him at lunch. First, if you'll excuse me for a few minutes, there are some invoices I must check."

Miss Sullivan rose. "That gives me an opportunity to show Catherine our studios." She led me into the corridor. "I'm sure you'll be interested. Pandora told us you were interested in arts and crafts. I believe she said you design jewelry."

"I'm still a beginner, but it's fascinating work."

"We don't make costumes and properties for the museum exhibits here," Miss Sullivan explained, showing me into a large, sunny studio. "Most things come from Rome or Paris. But we have equipment for repairs and changes, and there's also a scene shop that will be used when the theater is opened."

Money, a large amount of it, had been spent on the various working areas of the spacious room. There were a complete center for sewing, a section set aside for plaster molding, and a modern bench for delicate welding, soldering, and lost wax casting.

On a worktable I noticed a huge belt buckle studded with beads of amber glass, and exclaimed, "What a handsome piece!"

"Isn't it? It belonged to the great Chaliapin, who wore it when he sang *Boris Godunov*. The clasp is broken and I'm going to repair it."

"You'll repair it?" I asked, surprised.

"As soon as I find time." She permitted herself a smile. "I

love to work with my hands; I suppose it comes from my father. He was a watch and clock repairman. But in our little town in Canada there were never enough clocks that needed mending, so he made things to sell. Ship models, lamps and carriage lanterns, fancy weather vanes. All the family helped. We learned skills—we had to.''

From a little town in Canada, and from a poor family, I thought. Miss Sullivan had made a long journey.

She seemed to sense the questions in my mind. "I went to London to study to become a singer, although my parents didn't approve of the opera—it was too much like the theater, they said. But I had great ambitions in those days." Her smile had become rueful. "Young singers have so many false hopes! I worked in a typing pool and at night I was a volunteer with a small opera company. Oh, not as a singer. I served as mistress of properties. I ironed costumes, pasted together tinsel crowns. Eventually I was promoted to stage manager. Victor Donato helped support the company for a time, as he aided many other musical groups. After a while he decided our troupe was not promising, but he'd been impressed with my efficiency, and I am quite well-organized, of course. So—" She glanced around the room, made a gesture of dismissal with her tapering hands as though to say, "So I am here. That is the entire story of my life."

An offstage existence, I thought: She was always a background figure for others. Had those youthful ambitions and hopes faded quietly? Or had she yielded them up one day in bitter anger?

"You seem to accomplish so much," I told her in honest admiration. "Althea, the villa, the museum work."

But her denial was quick. "Not really. Since Althea retired from public life, my duties have been few. I have to be active, occupied. Otherwise the days would seem endless."

I did not understand what she meant, but I had the sense Esther Sullivan spent these days—that might have seemed endless—awaiting something. The opening of the museum?

Perhaps Althea's recovery of strength and eventual return to her career? Miss Sullivan's face was now closed, unrevealing.

"Ready for lunch?" called Richard Halpin, appearing in the studio. "This way please."

He escorted us through a maze of passageways leading to a small dining room furnished and decorated in the Italian baroque manner—a fantasy of gilt and glitter.

"This will be used to entertain distinguished visitors," Halpin said, indicating a long refectory table surrounded by a dozen red plush chairs. "Of course, the kitchen isn't in service yet. We'll have trays that were sent over from the villa."

As I took the chair Halpin offered, I noticed the large painting on the wall opposite me. It appeared to be very old, and I supposed it the work of some early Renaissance artist. Whatever its merits as a picture, it was a work few people would care to contemplate while dining. The composition was based on the famous *Judith* by Botticelli; it showed a young woman holding a dripping sword in one hand and, gruesomely, the decapitated head of an evil-looking man in the other. But there the similarity to *Judith* ended. This woman wore a white robe adorned with a scarlet cross. Tiny figures wearing the same cross were painted as angels hovering in the clouds above.

Richard Halpin was smiling at me. "I see you are admiring our pilgrim."

"Is that what she is?" Then I remembered that a red cross was the insignia of religious pilgrims in the Middle Ages. "It's a bit gory for my taste, especially at lunch."

My remark did not trouble him in the least. "Indeed? I never thought of it in that connection. It needs a place of honor. But we do have some milder recallings of the legend of the thirteenth pilgrim in tapestries. One in the museum, another in the villa."

"A local legend?" I asked.

"Oh, my dear," said Halpin, "it is *the* local legend—the most famous tale about the castle. The villa takes its name from this lady." He gestured toward the painting. "La Pellegrina. The pilgrim. I've almost finished an opera based on the tale."

Then, while a maid served us lunch, he told me the story; a brief recounting, for the details were lost in the remote past.

Castle Malaspina was built in the Middle Ages by an evil count who placed his stronghold athwart a route used by pilgrims traveling from Germany to Rome; the faithful who, in some cases, were attempting to reach the Holy Land. For his supposed services in protecting the road, the count extracted tolls from all comers.

The count himself was actually the worst brigand in the land, but he preyed only on the helpless. If he encountered a party rich enough and without defense, he would invite them to spend the night in his castle. His hospitality always proved fatal, yet for years these crimes remained undiscovered.

"How was it possible to hide such things?" I asked. "I should think the secret would have become known."

"That is the diabolical part of the tale. Come and look out this window."

I followed him to the window, where he pointed to ancient ruins of stone walls far away on the mountainside above the villa.

"Centuries ago that was a monastery. The monks could look down on the road that circled the lake to the south, and always they saw the pilgrims, at a distance, leave safely. What they really saw, of course, was the count and his henchmen disguised in the clothing of the victims and riding their horses.

"Once around a bend in the road and out of sight of the monastery, the brigands returned to the castle through a secret tunnel in the mountain.

"In this manner the count did away with eleven helpless maidens, all pilgrims who ended their journeys not in holy shrines, but in graves in the cellars of the castle. But during the twelfth attempt a young page escaped and made his way back to Germany with the horrible tale. When the victim's sister learned what had happened, she swore a vow of revenge.

Dressed as a pilgrim, she came to the castle—the thirteenth maiden to enter its gates—and beneath her pilgrim's cloak she carried a sword."

Halpin gestured toward the painting. "And that is the legend. She extracted a terrible vengeance for the murder of her sister. Afterwards, some say, she herself was then imprisoned and starved. Others say she escaped."

"The story doesn't lend much charm to the castle, does it?" I commented. "I wonder if there's any truth in it."

"Undoubtedly some," said Halpin relighting his pipe.

"Very little, I would say," Miss Sullivan remarked. "When Victor Donato purchased the castle and the villa, one of my tasks was to check the buildings and the antique plans with an architect from Rome. There are no traces of dungeons or even cellars, except a small one for wine. And, of course, there is no tunnel."

"That's very strange," Halpin said, shaking his head. "Usually the lords of castles like this one made some secret provision for escape in case of prolonged siege. In any case, I'm trying to assemble ancient maps and plans. Two thousand years ago the Romans had tin mines in these mountains. Something like that might account for a tunnel."

"Then history is another of your interests?" I asked him.

"Not really, except the history of music. But, as I told you, I've almost completed an opera based on the legend. What good luck for me if I could prove the story! Think of the publicity!"

"If the production of your opera depends upon proving that legend, it may wait a long time," said Miss Sullivan, raising a disbelieving eyebrow.

"Nevertheless, I believe the story really happened," Halpin insisted.

"Why?" I asked.

He stared at the painting of the thirteenth pilgrim and a shadow seemed to cross his features. "Because I sense it in the corridors of the castle. I can feel it here—a presence, an atmosphere."

"Sheer imagination," said Miss Sullivan, but I saw her glance uneasily at the painting of the young woman with the bloodied sword.

That afternoon I descended the steps to the stone jetty and stood for a moment gazing at the locked doors of the boathouse where a yawl had once been kept. Then, turning toward the lake, I tried once more to picture what Pandora might have done that last morning.

The cliff above concealed me from the villa; no one there could have seen this spot. But might there have been a witness on the lake itself? A fisherman, perhaps? No, everyone agreed the day had been too stormy.

Today there were several small craft almost within hailing distance, and standing a little farther offshore—today as yesterday—was the anchored skiff with Ilse Donato. I was unable to distinguish her features—she was too far away—but I felt certain her eyes were watching me. On impulse, I lifted my hand and waved a greeting, but there was no response from the silent, huddled figure.

Slowly, I climbed the stairs from the boathouse to the villa; not the broad stone steps I had used coming from the museum a moment before, but a narrow wooden stairway roofed against the rain with sides protected by vine-tangled lattice work.

If the story they told at the villa were true, this was the way Pandora must have come down to the boathouse—and here, too, she would have been unseen. For no reason except perhaps the uneasy rustling of the vines, Richard Halpin's story of the thirteenth pilgrim returned to my mind, bringing with it a strange chill. A sister slain; another sister drawn to the Castle Malaspina by her death. In memory, the painting of the avenger seemed to take on added terror.

I hurried on, not liking the concealed, deserted stairway. When I reached the top I heard a rhythmic, thudding noise— the sound, I thought, of wood being chopped. Walking toward it, I found myself again at the deer park, and the woodcutter

proved to be a young gardener who was cutting down the tree
Rajah had used to clear the fence.

Don Pasquale, supervising the work, smiled when he saw
me, touching his battered felt hat. "*Buon giorno, signorina.*"

"*Buon giorno, Don Pasquale.*" Since I could not remember
the Italian word for "fawn," I asked, "Is the little one all
right?"

"Ah yes! He had injured a hoof on the wire of the fence,
but the leg was not broken. Come, I will show you." He mo-
tioned to the gardener to continue his work with the axe.

At the shed, Don Pasquale undid a padlock and opened the
door. The fawn lay stretched out on the floor, a strip of canvas wrapped tightly around one hoof. He was so still, so unnaturally still, that for a moment I feared him dead, then saw a
slight lift of his chest and knew he was breathing. When Don
Pasquale knelt beside his head, I thought I detected a flicker
of terror in the open eyes.

"He cannot move yet," said the old man tenderly, "but before sunset he will stir, then sleep, and tonight I will take him
back into the park."

"Poor little one," I murmured, wondering what inexpres-
sible fear must be behind those liquid eyes—a wild creature,
used to freedom and flight, lying helpless and paralyzed, surrounded by those who might be his deadly enemies. Don Pasquale patted the fawn's head, making cooing sounds, and although I knew he meant only kindness, I wished he would
again close the door, to leave the fawn alone in comforting
darkness. To me, the silent terror of the animal seemed almost palpable.

"I am pleased you like my beautiful deer," the old man
said. "Your late sister, may she rest in happiness, also enjoyed watching them. Many afternoons she came to the park;
she would sit on a bench, very quietly. Sometimes she would
write in a book, and then she would smile. Ah, what a beautiful smile. *Bellissima!*"

"A book?" I asked. "She wrote in a book?"

"*Si.*"

A diary, of course! I had not been mistaken. Pandora in Italy, a new adventure, meeting new acquaintances. Naturally she kept some sort of journal. And it had been taken away, hidden after her death. What could she have seen, have written, that no one else could be allowed to read?

The warm sunlight seemed suddenly chill. I looked down at the fawn, and again saw in his eyes the terror and helplessness; a mute, anguished plea. I pressed my hands against my ears, trying to think, trying to shut out the beating sound of axe strokes as the blade hacked and tore the woody flesh of the tree.

Chapter Seven

It was the following day that I met Lisa, the strange, ragamuffin child from the mountain village.

I remember that I rose so late I found breakfast being cleared from the sideboard when I came downstairs. Taking a roll, a piece of fruit, and my sketch pad, I was heading for the rose garden when I met Miss Sullivan.

"Good morning," she said. "Seeing you saves my writing a note. Althea is feeling much better and would like to see you later on. Noon perhaps? At two she's having lunch with her attorney."

"Noon will be fine," I told her. Then, as Miss Sullivan was about to leave, I decided to ask about Pandora's diary. "It wasn't in the trunk," I said. "But she always kept one—it must have been misplaced."

"Yes," she said quietly. "I noticed it was missing."

"You did?" I exclaimed.

"I remembered it for two reasons, I suppose. Once she read a few lines from it aloud. A description of a sunset over the lake, very brief but quite beautiful. And then . . ." Es-

ther Sullivan hesitated, looked away. "My last memory of
Pandora involves that little book. She was very impatient that
morning; fretful about the storm, restless. I saw her jot something down, then she snapped the book shut and put it in the
pocket of her raincoat."

"She was wearing a raincoat? Indoors?"

"Not exactly wearing it. The day was chilly and she'd put it
around her shoulders like a cape."

I could picture it so clearly. Pandora loved capes and
cloaks, anything that trailed or floated or swished dramatically.

"I don't remember a raincoat in the trunk," I said.

"No," replied Miss Sullivan quietly. "The coat was never
found. We supposed that when the sailboat . . . that
is . . ."

"Please, I understand."

Miss Sullivan left, apparently relieved at not having to spell
out the details for me, and as I went toward the rose garden I
decided her explanation of the loss of the diary was probably
true. I had magnified a small mystery, and I resolved not to do
this in the future.

I chose a place in the garden where four paths intersected.
Several benches of lacy wrought iron stood beside the walkways and, sitting down, I enjoyed my brioche and the pear I
had brought from the house. Then I began to draw—not the
roses, which demanded color, but the curvilinear patterns of
the ironwork, trying to catch in charcoal the flowing scrolls
and sudden flourishes that lend gaiety to Italian iron of every
century. It was pleasant to lose myself completely in my
work, to forget for a while all problems.

Some time later I glanced up to see a small girl standing
near me, shyly watching. She was perhaps eight years old,
and wore a boy's shirt, much mended, and a dark skirt that
had become colorful from frequent patching. On a chain
around her neck were not only the expected miraculous med-
al, but also a tiny cloth bag, the kind I had been told contained magic charms.

"*Ciao, signorina,*" she said with a bashful smile.

After I had returned her greeting, she spoke very slowly in English. "My name is Lisa. How are you?"

"Fine, thank you, Lisa."

She seemed to understand me, but this was the limit of her English vocabulary except for a few scattered words such as "tree," "sky," and "path." I was about to ask where she had learned these when she said quite distinctly, "Pandora."

"Did you know Pandora?" I asked, concealing my surprise.

Lisa nodded. "It was cold then. She brought me a warm coat from Venice. A beautiful coat."

I had supposed Lisa was the daughter of one of the servants, but this was not the case. Sitting beside me, losing her shyness, she explained she lived far up the mountain near a small village. Her father was dead, her mother "sold things" for a living.

"What things?" I asked. But Lisa was vague—unable or unwilling to explain her mother's occupation—and I might never have learned the truth had not one of the workmen, on some errand, chosen to take a shortcut through the rose garden. Approaching us, he slowed his walk to a snail's pace to give me the appraising look I'd come to expect from Italian males, but then his eye fell on Lisa. Recognition flashed across his face and he automatically folded his middle fingers under his thumb—making the goat's horns gesture as a ritual to ward off the evil eye—then continued on, carelessly crossing himself.

"Why did he do that?" I asked.

Lisa shrugged. "Because he is foolish." She looked away from me, much too innocent, and after some questioning I learned that her mother sold potions, charms, and curses. Lisa was the daughter of a village witch, a *strega*.

"Last year, when I was just a little girl," she said with great seriousness, "I came here to steal apples and pears from the trees. Also I would hide and listen to the lady sing." She pointed toward the villa. "Sometimes the lady would stand on the balcony, and when she sang it was the most beautiful sound in the world. Her daughter sang, too, but not so well. Then I heard the daughter was dead, and the lady never sang again.''

"And Pandora?'' I asked.

"She was also the lady's daughter. But now she is gone; I don't know what happened to her.'' Then Lisa explained proudly that she no longer stole things from the garden. She knew everyone at the villa and, if she was hungry, she was given food in the kitchen.

"I would like to draw,'' she said. "Will you teach me?''

So we began a drawing lesson, starting out with oval-bodied cats. We were progressing to striped cats when Lisa looked down the path, dropped her charcoal, and with a squeal of delight ran to greet Mario Donato, who was coming toward us. A few steps away from him, Lisa hurled herself into the air and Mario caught her by the waist—lifting her high, whirling her while she shrieked in pretended fright.

When he returned her to earth, they spoke such a slurred and excited dialect that I could catch nothing beyond Mario's refusal to marry Lisa, claiming he was both too old and too ugly.

She led him toward me, pointing. "I am learning to draw. The *signorina* is teaching me.''

Mario lifted a dark eyebrow. "Then let us see how well she herself draws.'' Without warning he picked up my sketchbook and began leafing through it.

"That happens to be private!'' I exclaimed. He ignored me and there was nothing I could do except, perhaps, try to snatch it back—which seemed ridiculous.

Closing the book, he dropped it on the bench, then patted Lisa on the head, smiling. "*Si.* You should learn from this lady. She does not draw badly at all.''

"Thank you,'' I said, hoping my tone dripped acid. "You are much too kind!''

"Not kind at all. I meant it,'' he said pleasantly. "You have no reason to conceal your work. Most of the sketches are very promising.''

I slowly realized that the man believed he was paying me a compliment.

"Little one," he said to Lisa, "I was on an errand, and now you will do it for me, please. Go to the kitchen and tell the cook I want a basket with bread and cheese and wine. And, yes, some sausage. Take the food to the main stairway in the museum. I am working there."

Lisa's small face darkened. "The cook does not trust me; I am not allowed to take food away, only to eat it there. How will she know it is really for you?"

He took a heavy silver ring from his finger and dropped to one knee, putting an arm around her. "Show her my ring. She will recognize it and know it is a sign."

Lisa, enthralled at such a fairy-tale mission, glowed. Clutching the ring in both hands, she ran toward the villa.

Mario sat beside me, examining my sketch of the wrought iron patterns critically. There was no trace of self-consciousness in his manner; he behaved as though our first two meetings had never taken place.

"This is better than much of your work, a freer line than the sketches you made a few days ago."

"May I ask how you know my drawings?" I inquired cooly. "You seem given to instant judgments."

"Oh, but I have studied your sketches closely." His smile was sardonic. "After our unfortunate meeting in the terrace room, you rushed away leaving your sketchbook behind. Naturally I examined the drawings."

"Then you pried into something private."

"Of course I would try to learn more about a possible enemy." His gesture showed surprise that I had not grasped this simple fact at once. "An artist's work reveals much about its creator. But you, I discovered, are as secret in your art as you were secret in . . . in your arrival here, perhaps?" There was light mockery in the tone and the smile, but suddenly I

was more curious than irritated. I felt he was trying to convey
that it was time to call a truce.

"I'm sorry you considered me an enemy," I said, testing
the possible offer of peace. "I think you should have waited
to know me better."

His smile broadened. "Yes. But sometimes that is hard to
do, very hard. At times we all make judgments without evidence, no?"

"I think you are telling me something, and I wish you'd say
what you mean," I said.

"How Americans love bluntness!" He sighed. "Very well.
Because of things Pandora had said, I believed you came here
without love or sympathy for your mother—who happens also
to be my mother. Why would I welcome such a visitor?"

"I understand how you felt," I answered, looking away
from him. The gaze of those clear eyes, surprisingly blue in
his dark face, was too knowing.

"Also, you are Pandora's sister. I admit I did not look forward to having a second Pandora here," he continued.

"Why? I thought Pandora and Althea were devoted to each
other."

Mario Donato shrugged. "Pandora was devoted to Pandora. Who knows what Althea felt?" He shook his head, then
smiled. "Now I have spoken enough evil of the dead. Let us
forget this subject. And with your permission, I will call you
Catherine. It is a stupidity to say *Signorina* Andrews when
you are my mother's daughter."

"I agree . . . Mario." But saying his name did not come
easily to me. I still found him formidable. There was a quality
in Mario Donato that left me unsure, and I believed it was a
sense of suppressed violence.

"I think we will have much to thank you for, Catherine. For
instance, I am told there will be a dinner on Monday night."
Reaching out, he picked a dark red rose from a nearby bush
and carefully began to remove the thorns from the stem. "A
small celebration, but the first since Pandora's death. Mother

is even talking about opening the house in Venice. So I think your being here is good for her.''

"Thank you. I hope so." I hesitated, then said what had come into my mind. "Forgive me, but it seems odd to hear you call Althea Mother.''

He straightened slightly and his voice was cool. "On the contrary, it seems odd to me that you should call your mother Althea. I suppose it is an Americanism.''

"Please don't be offended," I said quickly. "I only meant that for years I never thought of her as having other children.''

"I understand. But, you see, she *is* my mother. *Mama, Mutter, Mère.* In childhood our language changed as we wandered from country to country. But Althea was always the same and almost always was with us. We were gypsies camping in the most expensive hotels. For a long time there was no single place we could call home, so home was where Althea was.''

"She adopted you when you were very young?" I asked.

Absently he tucked the rose into the bandana he had tied around his forehead. "No. Only Lillian came to us as a baby. I was nine years old, but had no memories except of an orphanage." He leaned back on the bench, crossing his arms. "The orphanage is near here and that is why I look like every other Lombard peasant, except a little darker than most. My dark hair and the location of the orphanage once caused gossip that I was Don Victor's illegitimate son. *Che cosa!* One glance at Konrad should end such talk—we are nothing alike.''

"So Althea found you at the orphanage?"

"No. Only once in her life did Mother go to an orphanage. She longed to take every single child with her, and I am told there were sixty. It so saddened her that she never visited another such place. Miss Sullivan did the searching. Sullie heard me singing in a boys' choir and brought Althea to the next concert. I am fortunate that Mother's love did not depend upon my voice! After it changed, no one ever urged me to sing again. Meanwhile, I had learned to play the flute. Every one in the family had to know music. Perhaps it was music that *made* us a family."

"Your sister, Lillian, was a singer, wasn't she?" I inquired.

His face seemed to close, the smile faded. "Yes. But not, I think, a very good one." Abruptly he rose. "I must return to work. It has been pleasant talking with you, Catherine."

"I've enjoyed it. I—"

"*Ciao.*" He turned away, striding toward the museum, the rose in the headband giving him a rakish look. And the story of Lillian, the daughter no one would talk about, remained a mystery.

But Mario hesitated on the path, for a moment seeming undecided, then called to me. "If you would like to see what I am working on, come along."

His invitation was awkward, almost gruff, and I suspected he seldom asked anyone to see work in progress. When I joined him, he said, "This piece is the last of my commissions for the museum, except for finishing a few details. I will be pleased to be done with it. Let others worry about completing the museum—if it is ever completed."

"I was told it would be open for the public soon."

He gave a short, dry laugh. "Illusions! The work is at least three months behind schedule. Every possible accident has delayed the work. Poor Konrad!"

"Why poor Konrad?"

"Because delays and accidents cost money. The money comes from Konrad's share of the Donato estate," said Mario. "The museum must be paid for before Konrad inherits the rest of his fortune."

"Who decides when it is finished? Does a committee pronounce it complete?"

He shook his head. "Not a committee. Althea has control. The Donato museum is finished when she says it is."

The interior of the castle, even in the bright midmorning,

retained its disconcerting chill. Halfway up the great staircase, where it divided at a landing, stood a marble wall panel lashed to scaffolding. Yesterday it had been covered with canvas, which was now removed.

"I do not work in a studio if I can avoid it," said Mario. "I want to see constantly the place where the work will one day be shown. It must be part of an entire atmosphere."

The high-relief sculpture was far from complete, but I could see it followed classic lines and the figure of Pan was already identifiable.

"You do not like it," he said abruptly. "I can see your disappointment."

"How can I tell?" I countered. "You've just begun. But I think it's very different from your other work."

"Exactly!" His eyes snapped. "This will be a classic bore, a photograph in stone. I am doing this for Althea's sake, because this is the way she wants it." Mario glared at the work. "Perhaps I can find some spark to give it life, but I doubt it. Yet you must admit it suits the atmosphere." His broad gesture encompassed the whole museum. "Dead! Dead voices singing through lifeless tapes. You touch a button and entire orchestras play for you, although not one of the musicians still lives. All these statues remind me of mummies or corpses. What a terrible place, what a terrible idea! No wonder everything about it has proved unlucky. Since my father bought the castle and the villa, we have had nothing but troubles. His own death, then Lillian and Pandora. My mother's strength is gone. And I do not think the troubles are yet ended. No, there will be more."

"Why do you say that?" I asked, suddenly feeling uneasy.

But he smiled in self-mockery, and lifting his hand made the sign against evil. "Because I am a superstitious Italian, *signorina*. Is that not reason enough?"

Althea greeted me wearing a dressing gown as rich and scarlet as a cardinal's cape. Miss Sullivan had said she was better and stronger, but I was unprepared for the change I saw. Color had come into her cheeks, her eyes had brightened, and there was a new lightness in her steps and gestures.

"It's having you here," she told me, laughing and kissing me on the cheek. "You're a tonic for me, Catherine. But I must admit that having two nights of sound sleep helped."

She led me to the balcony, which was separated from that of my own room only by a few feet. "We'll sit out here. It's too beautiful a day to be indoors."

She ordered espresso for us, sending a note to the kitchen on the tiny elevator, since there seemed to be no special signal on the service bell for that particular request.

From the balcony I could see across the lawns and over the wall of the villa. A farm cart moved lazily along the road, and high on the shoulder of the mountain the ruins of the ancient monastery lay bathed in sunlight. While Althea was bringing the espresso, I watched the road—imagining palfreys and horses with jeweled harnesses, pilgrims dressed in cowls and wimples as in the legend Richard Halpin had told.

"A lovely view, isn't it?" said Althea, returning.

"Yes. But I'm surprised you didn't choose rooms to the front, where you could see the lake."

"Oh, I did at first. Victor and I had adjoining suites across the hall from this room. But I changed because I couldn't bear being spied upon. I found myself living behind closed draperies night and day." Althea took a tiny sip from her cup. "There is this madwoman who happens to be Konrad's mother. Victor married Ilse when he was quite young. I suppose he married her for her money, although he never insulted her by admitting it."

She ignored my look of surprise. "He was a poor young man with great ambitions. He left Italy to find work in Vienna, and Ilse's father hired him. So they met and Ilse's small fortune proved irresistible. I must say he put her money to good use. He had a Midas touch, but it did not, alas, turn Ilse into a golden maiden."

"Were they divorced?" I inquired.

"My dear Catherine! They were living in Italy; no divorce was possible then." Althea shook her head sadly. "I wonder why she hates me so. They had been separated five years when Victor met me. I did not take him away—she lost him long before. But she is still consumed with vicious jealousy."

"Konrad said it was an obsession with her."

"Yes, that is the word! Some days she stares openly at the villa through binoculars! Madness, of course. She writes vile, anonymous letters to me, bribes servants to learn about our lives here. Ilse has even entered the villa at night. But what can I do? She is Victor's widow and Konrad's mother. I am helpless." With an impatient hand, she waved the subject away. "Let us talk of other things."

I hesitated, knowing I must mention the music box, yet afraid. Althea and I had the beginning of something precious, I felt. But this was still a time of discovery; our relationship remained fragile, tentative. I dreaded the thought of losing what I had just found. But I could not allow the question of the music box to remain between us like a stone wall.

"Miss Sullivan was admiring the music box you gave me," I said, hoping to sound casual. "She told me Lillian had one very much like it."

"Did she?" Althea gave me a cynical smile and lifted an eyebrow. "I don't think you are quoting Sullie correctly, Catherine. I am sure she accused me of giving away Lillian's music box and was furious with me."

"Not furious, only surprised," I said, and told myself never again to try to deceive Althea with a tactful lie. I had underestimated her shrewdness.

"I am happy that Sullie was not too upset." Althea seemed not to regard the matter as important. "She believes the box was Lillian's, and in a way it was. It happened about ten years ago. I'd been on a concert tour too tightly scheduled, and I came home exhausted. I was astounded the first evening when Sullie appeared from the kitchen with a birthday cake and a present for Lillian. I felt dreadful, I'd never forgotten a birthday before! But I carried it off well. I rushed out of the room and brought back the music box. Matthew had sent it back to me a year or two before. I fooled Lillian, and I must have fooled Sullie, too, although at the time I believed she suspected something.''

I felt a surge of relief at hearing Althea's explanation, and at the same time guilt for having doubted her. I suddenly wondered if my suspicions about Pandora's death might be as easily answered.

Althea smiled, but her smile was tinged with sadness. "This is remarkable, Catherine. I have been talking about Lillian without realizing it, without pain. I think that is another step forward for me.''

She put her hand on mine, and it came to me that in finding Althea I had at last found someone I could confide in, someone I could trust.

"Would it be painful if we talked about Pandora for a moment?" I asked. "There are things I wonder about, things I don't understand.''

"Then I think we must talk," she said.

"I went through Pandora's trunk. I found a letter from Gordon Carr, who was married to Pandora.''

"I have met him." Althea sounded cautious. "He came here twice. I liked the young man, even though the circumstances of his being here were not very favorable.''

"What do you mean? Why did he come here?''

Althea considered a moment, then she said, "He came to collect money. I daresay everyone in the villa overheard the scenes about it.''

"But their divorce was final, everything financial was settled," I objected. "I don't see how—''

"Pandora still had a charge-a-plate for an account at some New York shop—I don't remember the name of it. The account should have been closed, but somehow it was overlooked. Before leaving America, Pandora made several expensive purchases.''

"The dresses," I said. "This explains the dresses I found.''

"Pandora behaved foolishly. She expected to pay the bill with money due her from television commercials. The money did not arrive and naturally her former husband was furious. The amount was several thousand American dollars."

"Television commercials!" I thought bitterly. Yes, there was just enough possibility of the commercials being repeated to give Pandora hope. She had never been able to distinguish the real from the make-believe, and was always sure that any delightful possibility, however remote, could not fail to prove true.

"Pandora tried to borrow the money from Konrad," said Althea, frowning. "He refused her. Very rich men—and Konrad is extraordinarily rich—are sensitive about requests for money, especially requests from beautiful women. Konrad felt he was being used, taken for a fool. It was most unpleasant.

"Mr. Carr, who was desperate by this time, came to me. I paid the account, and afterwards told Pandora what I thought of her irresponsible behavior. I was harsh with her, much harsher than I intended."

Althea rose and stepped to the railing. She stood with her back to me, her hands resting on the black iron. "That was my last conversation with her, the last words I spoke to Pandora. So often we are angry with those we love—we quarrel, we say hateful words. And we never think that those words might be the last ones; that we can never call them back, never amend them or say we are sorry. This has happened twice with me. First with Lillian, then with Pandora."

I went quickly to her side, but whatever emotion she felt was under tight control. When she spoke, her voice was steady, even. "And that is the story. Mr. Carr remained at the villa that night and left sometime the next morning, but I did not see him that day. I understand he returned to America recently."

For a moment we were silent, then I said, "Thank you for telling me this, it was important to me. And thank you for helping Pandora."

Her head lifted almost defiantly. "But of course I helped her! After all, I was her mother!"

That afternoon, trying to put my thoughts in order, I left the villa and went down to the quay, crossed a strip of sand that served as a beach, and then followed a path where the mountain seemed to rise almost straight from the waters of the lake.

I climbed slowly, following the tortuous path that soon turned into a goat trail and finally ended at a narrow mountain meadow ablaze with wildflowers. I was not far from Castle Malaspina; the meadow lay well above it and I could look down on the stone turrets, the triangular merlons to shield defending archers, and the ruined watchtower. From this vantage point I could picture the entire landscape as it must have been centuries ago—the castle's portcullis rising to admit a company of travelers, a drawbridge being lowered to span a moat no longer there.

My gaze moved on to the villa, so tiny compared to the castle, and I thought of the people I had come to know in my brief time there. Today I felt especially close to Althea. I had resolved to be wary about accepting anything she told me about the music box, but found myself unable to doubt her story. And Althea had solved the small mysteries of the trunk, putting Gordon Carr's letter into perspective as an angry but justified demand for payment—not the dire threat I'd supposed it to be.

When I thought of Pandora's going to Konrad for money, the feeling of humiliation I had known so many times returned. Why had I always taken upon myself shame for Pandora's conduct? I must learn to resist such feelings.

The sun had grown too warm; I regretted not wearing a hat or at least a bandana, and I started toward the castle, thankful to be moving downhill now instead of climbing. I approached from the side opposite the public entrance to the museum. The door of an arched postern stood open, and I passed into the main courtyard. This part of Castle Malaspina had not been restored and much of it lay in ruins. But one building, which seemed in better condition than its neighbors, caught my attention.

The structure was not large, but its proportions were perfect; a simple stone basilica that must have been built as a nobleman's chapel very early in the Middle Ages, perhaps even two or three centuries before the castle itself. At one time there had been double doors, but they were missing, and I stepped across the threshold onto a floor made of Byzantine tiles that reminded me how near we were to Venice and how close Venice was to the eastern world.

Sunlight poured through great gaps where parts of the roof above the nave had collapsed, and on the walls of the clerestory only traces of red and blue frescoes remained. There was no altar, but against the rear wall, behind the place where an altar would have been, there remained a tall altar screen of nine panels which seemed affixed to the building.

The paneled screen, which I remembered was called a reredos or a retablo, covered the full width of the nave and rose at least twenty feet against the wall. It was wood, carved and painted, and had a strange, almost barbaric splendor, at once repellent and fascinating. Each panel was as large as an ordinary door and all of them were heavily framed with carving and gold leaf, although only traces of the gold remained. At the top, above all the panels, stood a statue of a woman—a young woman, I thought—and she carried a staff with a pilgrim's cross.

I moved toward it, down the center aisle, passing several wooden posts that had been installed to help support the crumbling roof and arches. The posts looked rather new, but already they were falling prey to termites, and coarse woody powder lay in small heaps on the tiles. Now I could distinguish the details of the panels; low-relief figures portraying the final agonies of martyrs, deaths by sword, rack, and arrows. Although ravaged by time, it retained its fearful effect.

I was almost close enough to touch the carvings when a whispered voice said, "Stop! Don't move!"

The command conveyed such desperation that for an in-

stant I stood frozen, then turned back very slowly. Esther
Sullivan stood in the doorway of the chapel, her dark figure
silhouetted against the sunlight, but even in shadow I could
see the pallor of her face. She whispered again, so softly that
it was hard to hear, but I could not miss the intensity of her
tone. "Catherine, come back. Walk slowly, lightly. Stay near
the pillars, but don't touch them. Don't speak. It's dangerous . . . the roof . . . the least sound . . ."

At first I didn't understand the desperation of her warning,
then a bit of powderlike sawdust fell on my shoulder and I
looked up. Overhead, a wooden crossbeam resting on two
posts braced the ceiling. I could see the beam was worm-eat-
en, its surface almost papery. Miss Sullivan's meaning
dawned on me fully. The least movement, even an echoing
noise, might bring the ceiling or even the whole structure
down.

I moved toward her cautiously while she nodded encouragement, but I could see she was holding her breath in fear. I
felt curiously calm, even when a faint breeze caused the brac-
ing of the clerestory to creak loudly. Then, as I saw more of
the ominous wood dust fall, the extent of the danger struck
me, and the next twenty steps seemed to take an eternity.
Panic came afterwards—when I had reached the safety of the
entrance and found myself in Miss Sullivan's strong, comforting embrace.

Together we drew back from the front wall of the chapel,
and then her alarm changed to anger.

"Everyone knows that building could be a death trap!" she
stormed. "Where are the boards that block the doorway? And
the danger sign is gone! Who could have done such a stupid,
criminal thing?"

I stared in astonishment at an Esther Sullivan I had not
known existed. I had seen her under strain before, but never
imagined her raising her voice in rage. This was an outward
anger I might have expected from Althea, but not from Miss
Sullivan. Partly, I supposed, this was her release from the ten-

sion of watching my perilous retreat from the chapel. I realized how frightened for my safety she'd been.

Calmer now, she said, "The engineers from Milan warned us that the chapel should be pulled down, that it might collapse at any time. But Althea felt it was a shame to destroy such a beautiful ancient building. Someday it can be restored, so we put boards across the entrance and a danger sign. Now they're gone!" She brushed her hand across her brow, shook her head. "Oh, my dear, when I saw you going into that place, I thought my heart was stopping. Maybe nothing would have happened, you might have been fortunate, but there are tons of stone and tile and plaster in the roof and upper walls." She shuddered, closing her eyes. "Enough to entomb you."

"Please don't be upset," I said, touched by her concern. "I'm quite all right and nothing has happened."

"But I feel responsible! What if something harmed you? I could never forgive myself if you—" She broke off in midsentence, not wanting to speak the thought that was in her mind. But I had already caught her meaning.

"Forgive me for being overly alarmed," she said. "Now I must find a workman to replace the boards and the danger sign for the doorway."

She left me then, and I pitied the miscreant who'd removed the barrier if he fell into Esther Sullivan's hands.

I started toward the villa, my nerves none too steady. Miss Sullivan had probably exaggerated the danger in the chapel. But it was easy to understand how, after Pandora's death, she might feel overly protective toward me. Not only Pandora, I reminded myself, for Lillian had also died in some violent way.

I felt sure Esther Sullivan had intended to say, "I could never forgive myself if you died as Pandora died." But why should she think of such a thing? Was it only because of my brush with danger in the chapel? I did not believe it. Those words she had left unspoken must have been in her mind for a long time, perhaps ever since I'd arrived.

I hurried toward the villa, moving quickly along the stone walk as though my rapid steps could somehow outdistance thoughts I did not want to consider, but could not banish from my mind.

Chapter Eight

"This is not a party tonight," Althea told me on Monday morning. "Just a family dinner plus Richard Halpin. And I've asked Prince Luigi, who is eager to meet you, and his niece." Her smile was gay and her eyes twinkled like bubbles of glass. "Not a party, but we shall dress for one. We shall be flamboyant! My hairdresser is coming later in the morning, and he's a marvel. Shall I send him to you?"

"No, thank you. I'll manage."

The brilliance of the morning sun had driven us from Althea's balcony and we sat just inside the open doors. Outside I saw Lisa skipping down the path toward the rose garden, a few minutes early for a promised drawing lesson. She carried a drawing pad and a new box of crayons.

"I have a surprise," Althea said. "I've told Sullie to call Venice and make arrangements to have the house there opened for us next week. I am venturing into the world again, and expect to have a wonderful time!"

Althea's high spirits were contagious—perhaps that was

one of the qualities that made her a great public personality—
and I found myself humming a tune as I went to meet Lisa.

The last three days had been uneventful. Spring was blossoming into summer and the rose garden blazed with crimson,
yellow, and pink. The lime tree below my balcony put out pet-
als so fragile that the least breeze caused a flowery snowfall.
Afternoons, the Villa Pellegrina lazed in golden sun.

Every day peasant women came to the gate; women in
fringed black shawls carrying baskets of fresh lettuce, to-
matoes, and new peas. The shawls and black dresses seemed
incongruous in this land of instant smiles and quick laughter,
and it seemed wrong that these women, who sang at any excuse and slapped their hips at peasant jokes, were garbed in
perpetual mourning.

By now I had learned the routine of the household. I knew
one never saw Miss Sullivan in the morning except in passing.
Her days, filled with duties—many of them self-imposed—
seemed to begin at dawn. She often reminded me of a nun, an
efficient and silent nun charged with the operation of some
large convent; she glided quietly through the rooms, automatically checking the work of the maids. If she merely glanced at
a neglected flower bed, a man appeared immediately to weed
it, and Richard Halpin constantly praised her help at the museum.

Konrad seemed always occupied with various errands of
pleasure, and Mario I hardly glimpsed. "He is suffering one of
his sculpting seizures," Konrad explained to me. "He is like
Althea used to be, a compulsive worker." Konrad, who was
anything but a compulsive worker, had leaned back in his
deck chair, frowning. "Life is too precious to waste it practicing scales or chiseling rocks."

I had learned nothing more about Pandora. When I questioned the servants, they piously crossed themselves and murmured praise of the dead. But today I had a new plan. I had
decided to have lunch at the inn across the lake and learn what
I could from the talkative waiter who had seemed to know a

good deal about Prince Luigi. If I were to meet the prince to-night, it would be wise to gain some information in advance.

The drawing lesson with Lisa was brief, even though we had graduated from cat drawings to ocelot pictures. Rajah, asleep on his back with his paws in the air, snored softly under the lemon tree, giving us a splendid model.

A little after noon I went down to the jetty where the villa's boats were moored. There were two of them—sturdy, easily handled speedboats: the *Thais,* slightly lumbering but roofed for all weather, and the smaller, open *Tosca,* which I chose for today. The beautiful weather had brought out on the lake a whole fleet of pleasure craft. I felt a part of the gaiety as I cruised slowly among the polka-dot and candy-striped sails, past a yawl with a huge painted dragon's eye, then turned sharply but easily as a little inboard, decorated to resemble a speckled fish, cut across my bow.

Enjoying myself, I did not notice Ilse Donato's skiff until I was within twenty yards of it. But she must have sighted me well before that, because when I first realized who she was she had already balled her thick, blunt hand into a fist.

"Go! Go away!" she shouted in broken English. "The fish you are scaring! Go!"

Both her fist and the bamboo fishing pole were being waved at me threateningly, although her accusation was preposterous. With a dozen boats in the vicinity, the *Tosca* could hardly frighten away any fish that had not already made for deep water. I let the motor idle and the *Tosca* drifted a little closer to her.

"Hello, *Signora* Donato," I called cheerfully. "I wish you a good catch."

She shook the pole at me again. "To me you dare speak? I know who you are, what you are!" She shifted to German then, uttering a string of what must have been the most unspeakable curses and imprecations.

"Good day, *signora,*" I replied, and waved good-bye as I pulled slowly away from her.

Ilse Donato, it now struck me, had no resemblance at all to Konrad. Her face was jowly, the nose broad and flat. She could not possibly be poor, yet her faded brown dress was shabby and shapeless. Her skiff had not been painted in years and the little outboard motor looked too small to propel it. No matter how much she hated me for being Althea's daughter, I felt sorry for her, the poor, pathetic madwoman. I wondered what was in the leather case that hung from a strap around her neck, then realized it was made to hold binoculars. Part of her spying equipment!

Did she raise such a howl every time a boat from the villa approached? I supposed so, and marveled again at her strange and enduring preoccupation.

At the village quay a trio of urchins moored the *Tosca* for me. After rewarding them with a few lire, I strolled along the lakeside avenue to the inn and entered its dining room just as the doors were being opened for lunch.

The waiter, Giovanni, recognized me at once and, beaming hospitality, ushered me to a table on a shady corner of the terrace.

"Benvenuto, signorina! Forgive me, but is it *Signorina* Hoffman? Everyone in the village already knows who you are, but no one is certain of your name."

"Catherine Andrews," I answered. "But I don't understand how I can be so well-known so quickly."

"But you are of the Villa Pellegrina!" And that, he seemed to feel, explained everything. It did explain things, when I thought about the servants and the workmen from the village coming daily to the villa. Everyone would know the smallest detail about Althea Hoffman's household.

Giovanni lowered his voice, "Also, I hope the *signorina* will excuse any indiscreet remarks I may have made when I did not know who the *signorina* was. I do not remember exactly what was said, but be assured I have only the highest esteem for that noble friend of your family, Prince Luigi."

"Oh, stop this!" I burst out laughing. "You find him just as detestable as I do, Giovanni. I can't imagine why anyone puts up with him."

The old man chuckled and smoothed his white moustache. "Exactly, *signorina.*"

"Giovanni, since it's too early for other diners, please join me for a glass of wine. Is that permitted?"

"Permitted!" He squared his shoulders with dramatic hauteur. "Would Giovanni Tedeschi accept a position in an establishment where he could not join a beautiful lady for a glass of wine? I am enchanted, *signorina.*" Any fear I'd had about being unable to draw him out proved completely groundless. To Giovanni it seemed only natural to gossip about his customers, and and he did not find it odd when I asked for every detail of Pandora's visits to the restaurant.

"She came here several times, *signorina.* At first it was with the dark son, the artist Mario. It was a pleasure to watch them because one does not often see two people so beautiful together. The *signor* always ordered a simple pasta and our own red wine, which is pleasing in a man who can afford so much fancier food and drink. They laughed, they seemed happy.

"Then one evening there was great talk because the *signorina* was escorted by *Signor* Konrad Donato."

"Why did that cause talk?"

"Ah, *signorina!* Everyone in town knew that Don Konrad was practically betrothed to Donna Giulia, whose uncle is Prince Luigi. Naturally everyone wondered about it. Don Konrad did not behave like a man whose marriage is settled."

Giovanni gave me a knowing look, then he shook his head and sighed. "The last time we saw her she came in the evening and was with Prince Luigi himself. In the kitchen there was a joke that he had brought the lady here to poison her and this way he would clear the aisle to the altar for his niece. The cook became angry and said this was not a thing to laugh about. The prince's ancestors had done that very thing a hundred times and we should keep an eye on the wine decanter.

"But they were friendly until almost the end of their supper. Then some terrible quarrel started. The prince seemed to have been insulted beyond rage. I could not hear what he said to the lady, but his look would have frozen the blood. He stared at her, and when he lifted his glass the wine spilled, he was shaking so.

"You may believe I rushed to the table with a napkin, hoping to hear anything, but neither one spoke. The lady was not at all angry. She smiled at him, a very contented smile, as though she had just won a fortune from him at cards."

Giovanni stared balefully at his glass. "Three days later the poor lady was dead, drowned. I am not a superstitious man, but I saw Prince Luigi's eyes that night, and I will swear in church there was a curse in them."

He could tell me no more about Pandora, but before he left to serve the arriving diners, I asked him if he knew anything about Lillian Donato's death.

"I only know what the village knows, and that is very little. There was a fire in the castle, in a hall that they have made into a theatre. Afterwards the police came, high ranking officials. Naturally there were unpleasant rumors, all lies."

"What were the rumors?" I persisted.

"*Signorina*, I would not listen to such gossip!" he said piously, and since no amount of questioning would make him reveal what he'd heard, I realized the rumors must be about Althea, and thus could not be repeated to her daughter.

An hour later, as the *Tosca* started back across the lake, I considered the slowly building picture of Pandora's months at the Villa Pellegrina. It was not an appealing picture and not one I wanted to accept, but I had to admit that all I had learned was typical of Pandora. I'd confirmed again that the "most thrilling man" she had mentioned was Mario. She had taken this affair with at least some seriousness, because she had written of plans to travel with him. She had expected the attraction to last, but it had not. Whatever lasted with Pandora?

Apparently she had turned to Konrad, until that friendship—or whatever it was—exploded when she asked him to loan her money. She had quarreled with Konrad, then aroused Althea's anger; and something she had said to Prince Luigi had enraged him. Was there no one at the villa she had not hurt or offended? Only Miss Sullivan seemed to have escaped without trouble. And so the last months of Pandora's life had been exactly like the years that preceded them—Pandora sowing mischief, bringing to the villa her special gift for trouble and discord. She had spoken only the truth those months ago when she said to me, "Everywhere I go I cause trouble."

Yet I'd loved her, even if my love did not always reach as far as forgiveness.

That night, to judge from the flurry in the Villa Pellegrina, we might have been preparing to entertain at least a hundred people instead of "just the family and two guests," as Althea had put it.

The confusion was great enough for a banquet. Would supper be served in the dining room or on the terrace? Althea changed her mind hourly. Twice, Japanese lanterns were hung to light an outdoor dinner, then removed. Music was to be played in the living room before supper, then Althea decided the living room was too baronial for so small a group and shifted the arrangements to a downstairs parlor—only to have it discovered that the parlor piano was out of tune, so back to the living room once more.

Miss Sullivan executed the orders and counterorders with cool dispatch, and when I expressed amazement at Althea's concern over preparations, Miss Sullivan said quietly, "This is the first time she had had a meal out of her room in months. To her this is not a small occasion."

I dressed early, choosing a gown that was not quite white and not quite egg shell—a color perfect for the fire opals I would wear. I had just taken the opals from their case when

Althea tapped on my door, then opened it only a crack before I could answer.

"I won't interrupt," she called. "But do not go downstairs until I come for you. We will enter together. And very late!"

The door closed quickly and I smiled at my own reflection in the mirror. Althea and I could not merely go downstairs, could not simply join the others. We would, naturally, "enter"! I wondered if Althea, like the great soprano Mary Garden, always made noise in the wings to attract attention before she swept on stage.

It was quite dark now, and I moved a chair to the balcony, where I could enjoy the breeze that usually stirred after sunset. The lawns, the arbors, and the rose garden were fragrant in the evening coolness. Along the drive amber lights and lanterns had been turned on, and soon I saw Richard Halpin, impeccable in black tie, strolling toward the villa. He lived, I had been told, in a cottage beyond the deer park, but seldom had meals there—he was always expected at the villa.

Now, before turning the corner that would remove him from my view and lead him to the front entrance, he carefully checked his watch, inspected his cuff links, and looked down to observe the shine of his shoes, critically lifting one foot, then the other. Satisfied that all was in proper British order, he went his way, giving the tips of his moustache a final tweaking.

The other two guests arrived much later, whirling up in a silvery sports car, and I had only a glimpse of them; an impression of a slender young couple, the man in a startling mauve dinner jacket. Not Prince Luigi, I thought, but a much younger man.

Leaving the balcony, I finished dressing by putting on the opals, shortening the necklace by removing two links, then, not quite pleased with the result, replacing one. I had just finished when Althea burst into the room, a fantasy of chiffon and dazzle, swirling in a gown that appeared a froth of gold miraculously pinned together by sapphires.

"Do you like it?" She posed, then pirouetted like a school-girl. "La Challes designed it for my South American concert tour, and I've never worn it since. It's a bit 'Dance of the Seven Veils,' but why should I not be Salome tonight? I am—"

She broke off, staring at me, eyes wide, and for an instant I saw an expression of anger. Then it vanished. "The fire opals," she whispered. "The settings are changed, but there cannot be other opals like them."

"They were my grandmother's," I said, suddenly self-conscious. "But of course you know that."

"And they were mine! A wedding gift from Matthew Andrews. Take them off, Catherine," she commanded. "Take them off at once."

Instinctively my hands went to the opals. "No, I will not," I told her. "These are a gift from Pandora, and I intend to wear them tonight."

She gave me a glance of incredulity. "You do not, I hope, believe I want them back! Opals are unlucky— disastrous. I am not surprised Pandora gave them away. Catherine, you must listen to me! Lili Rossi wore opals when she sang Lucia in Paris, and she tripped on stage and broke her hip. I saw it! And there's a story about Alma Gluck and—"

I laughed then. "Althea, don't be silly. You sound like some peasant woman from a mountain village. You can't believe such superstition. Now let's go downstairs before everyone has supper without us and goes home. You look beautiful."

"Very well, since I can hardly snatch them from you. But this is not my last word on the subject. Meanwhile, we can only hope for the best."

Rajah, glittering in a rhinestone harness and gold chain, was waiting outside the door like a faithful spaniel, and the three of us descended the main stairway of the villa—Althea an arriving goddess, I her acolyte and attendant even though she linked her arm with mine.

When the stairway turned and we became visible to those in

the living room, I almost expected her to burst into some mighty aria. Brünnhilde's "Battle Cry"? No, she had never sung Wagner. But the "Queen of the Night" would do.

Instead, she called out in a ringing tone that had almost the same effect. "Good evening! Welcome! *Ciao!*"

Her gesture was so regal that I was almost persuaded a vast multitude was present as she proclaimed, "I want you to meet my daughter Catherine, recently arrived from America!"

Of the six people composing the audience, there were only two I did not know and only one I did not recognize. The guest in the mauve, brocaded dinner jacket was, after all, the aged Prince Luigi. I had been deceived by a wig of close-cropped yellow curls, which was meant, I suppose, to suggest the Golden Age of Greece, but reminded me more of the Decline of Rome. His other cosmetic disguises were more subtle by electric light than they had appeared during the day.

"*Enchanté!*" He breathed, bowing low and taking my hand. "Please permit me to introduce my niece, La Contessa Bartolo," he said smoothly. "She is better known to the film and television audience of Italy as Giulia Lombardi."

Looking at her, I thought instantly of Pandora. Giulia was equally lovely, gifted with that fair Lombard beauty that often seems more French than Italian. Her gown of royal blue might have been copied from a Pompeian fresco, but was so sheer that no Roman matron would have dreamed of appearing in it.

"*Ciao*, darling," she said in a husky, languid tone acquired through years of practice. Her tilted eyes appraised my dress, dismissed it, then lingered a second on the opals. Her resemblance to Pandora, I realized, was not in features but in mannerisms; the small gestures designed to show the tapering of her fingers, the calculated little toss of her head.

"Prince Luigi," I said, "please solve a mystery for me. How did you recognize me in the hotel across the lake?"

"I should pretend clairvoyance," he replied, "But my talent is only an excellent memory. Your late sister showed me a photo of you. I never forget the face of a lovely woman. Especially when that woman reminds me of the young Althea

Hoffman." He drew his carmine-tinted lips into a poor imitation of an admiring smile.

A waiter in a white jacket with great golden frogs embroidered on it passed drinks. After a few minutes, Althea clapped her hands to command our attention. Then she spoke as though announcing a full symphony orchestra. "Tonight we are honored to hear the overture to a new opera, *The Thirteenth Pilgrim*. It will be played by the composer."

Richard Halpin took his place at the piano, and from the first chords it was apparent he was an excellent musician. The overture, appropriately grim and medieval, evoked corridors lighted by flickering torches, swords hidden by cloaks, and, in its happier moments, the tinkling of harness bells. I thought it completely appropriate to the legend.

At the end, the small audience applauded warmly. Halpin rose, bowed, and said, "Now a long interval while the composer and the audience enjoy some champagne."

I thought of what I'd learned today at the inn across the lake, and when I looked at the faces around me, they seemed like masks—each hiding a special knowledge of Pandora's death. I crossed the room to the couch where Mario Donato sat alone, drinking champagne and staring gloomily at Althea's portrait above the mantle.

"I have a question I hope you'll answer," I said, thinking I had little to lose by a direct approach.

"Then sit down," he replied. "But I warn you I have had more wine than I usually take."

"I heard today that Pandora and Konrad were lovers," I said, and then added recklessly, "I also heard they had planned to be married. Is that true?"

He beckoned to the waiter to refill his glass, and considered his reply. "I do not know what understandings were between them. I am sure Pandora had hopes, but she played her cards badly; she asked him for money. My brother fears that his greatest attraction is his wealth, not his person or his soul. I think that is why he did not marry long ago."

"Pandora never cared about money," I insisted. "You're

misjudging her. Pandora's first husband was a penniless actor, and she knew Gordon Carr would never be rich."

"*Scusi! Scusi, Madonna!*" He lifted his hands in mock apology. "I cannot always understand the virtues of fine ladies like your sister."

Then the mockery turned to bitterness. His voice became quiet and cold. "I was stupid about Pandora, stupid enough to imagine I had fallen in love with her and to believe she cared for me. I suppose at first she did not know about my father's will, did not realize I had inherited very little of the Donato fortune. Konrad, not I, was the son by blood. But my father treated me fairly and generously. I never envied Konrad his wealth, even when I learned it could buy Pandora."

"I don't believe that," I told him.

"Catherine, do not be like a child! I know nothing of this actor Pandora married, but I am certain that in those days she imagined she would be a great actress, a film star. It must have been the same when she met this *Signor* Carr who came here to demand money from her. But she had learned that fame and wealth do not fall upon us like showers of rain."

Looking away from me, he shrugged his shoulders. "If Pandora wished to be a film star, then Konrad could buy her a studio in Hollywood. Perhaps a play in London or New York?" Mario snapped his fingers. "Simple! Konrad can produce it. All very practical, no?"

"You sound as though you hated her," I told him, the words coming out almost in a whisper.

"*Si!* You cannot imagine how much." He gazed across the room, where a laughing Konrad was toasting Giulia. "But when it ended, I think my brother hated her even more."

Rising, he made a slight bow. "If you will excuse me, we have had enough questions. Also, I find the subject unpleasant."

The second part of our musical entertainment began. Now Miss Sullivan was at the piano and Halpin showed his versatility by playing the cello, and playing it very well. I didn't recognize the music, but thought it was probably Bach.

Prince Luigi sat with his hooded eyes closed, an expression of serene elevation frozen on his countenance, and the eyes popped open only once to impale Giulia with a murderous glare when she applauded during a pause between movements.

In my mind I kept repeating Pandora and Mario, Pandora and Konrad. She had hurt both of them. She was not deliberately cruel, I told myself, but thoughtless and impulsive. Yet in this room were three men who had hated her.

The music ended, supper was announced, and we moved to the long table in the dining room. There were no place cards and Konrad took the chair to my right. "I think you have been avoiding me," he said. "But you cannot escape me at the dinner table."

Prince Luigi, on my left, overheard Konrad, and I received a stare of royal disapproval. Then the stare changed to a flattering smile. "We must become friends, my dear. Your sister and I were very close. Such a talented child!"

Down the table Althea announced abruptly, "I am opening the house in Venice. I need color and crowds for a little while. We all do."

"It's very difficult," Esther Sullivan remarked. "There are so many final decisions about the museum you should make."

"Decisions!" Althea was irritated. "Let someone else decide things. After all, I am paying enough money!"

"It is more accurate to say that *I* am paying," said Konrad. Then, seeing Althea's expression, he added, "At any rate, the estate is paying."

"That is one of the main purposes of the estate." Althea, when nettled, did not disguise her annoyance. "If I wish to go anywhere, however, the museum's problems will not detain me."

"Giulia and I leave for Venice tomorrow," said Prince Luigi. "Shall I tell your housekeeper to expect you soon?"

"I have arranged it," said Miss Sullivan.

The prince turned to me. "I have a small but quite exquisite apartment in Venice; a tiny corner of the grand mansion Althea now owns, the Palazzo Malaspina."

"Malaspina?" I asked. "It belonged to your family?"

"*Si*. For four centuries. Or was it five? I am a poor historian," he said in a tone of dismissal. "When Victor Donato acquired it from my creditors, he gave me a tenancy on a small apartment. A kind gesture, no?"

No one could have accused him of ungrateful sarcasm, yet he was conveying how abused he had been by Don Victor.

"Life and fortunes change," the prince continued. "To think that Victor Donato's father and grandfather were woodcutters on the Malaspina estates! Nevertheless, I am content with my small house here at the lake and my tiny apartment in Venice." He leaned forward, speaking to Richard Halpin across the table. "Who knows? Perhaps your new opera, *Signor* Halpin, will restore my family's fame."

"Yes, quite," said Halpin, seeming surprised that anyone would want his family immortalized by the story of murder and theft.

"But I hope you will change the ending you described to me," said the prince. "As the legend is told in my family, after the girl killed my wicked ancestor, his brothers seized her and imprisoned her in a dungeon, where she starved in the finest Italian tradition of vengeance."

"But Castle Malaspina has no dungeons," Halpin remarked.

"Of course not," agreed the prince, smiling. "They must have used the tower as a prison."

Althea was deeply engaged in conversation with Konrad, and Giulia, noting this, lowered her voice and spoke to Mario in Italian. "Bart Hutchinson has returned from America. He is staying at their house in Venice and still has that terrible film."

Mario frowned, glanced toward Althea, but said nothing.

"Who is Bart Hutchinson?" I inquired.

"He was Lillian's lover," she answered, still in a low tone. Althea did not hear, but Esther Sullivan did, and her face blanched. Glaring at Giulia, she changed the subject abruptly. "Konrad is buying a new motor launch for the villa."

"Another?" Prince Luigi turned to me with a knowing smile. "What a pity you do not enjoy boating, Catherine. It is the greatest pleasure of living at the lake."

"What leads you to believe I don't enjoy it?" I asked.

His smile became a grin. "One night, a night like this one, we were having supper here and Pandora amused us with stories of childhood. She told us how she and your father sailed a yawl on a bay called Nar . . . Nargasett?"

"Narragansett," I said.

"*Si.* You were furious because water and boats terrified you. A phobia!" He steepled his thin fingers, enjoying the tale. "She even told of the time you cut the sail to pieces so you would not be left alone on shore."

Althea protested. "Luigi, Catherine was only a child!"

"Naturally. And what child who feared water would not resent a sister who took to it like a gull?" His manner was indulgent as he spoke to the table at large. "I confess that on the day of Catherine's arrival here, I was surprised to see her enter even so large a craft as the launch the museum had rented that day."

"I say, thank God!" Althea's voice hushed the table. "It is more than enough to lose one child because of senseless daring."

The moment of decision had come, the inevitable time when I must speak or be silent, and I did not know which was the wiser course. But after hesitating, I spoke into the silence at the table. "Not a word of this is true. Not any of it. That's the strange and perhaps dreadful thing."

At first no one seemed to comprehend what I had said. Then Prince Luigi bridled. "On the contrary, I have told the story exactly as Pandora did."

"Yes, I'm sure you did, but you misunderstand me. None of you really knew Pandora." Everyone at the table was leaning forward, their eyes fixed on me.

"Pandora often told lies, and this was one of them," I said.

The stillness around me was tense, unnatural. "She couldn't help herself; she was frightened and unsure. Making up things was a way to be important, to get attention and be admired."

I felt strangely detached as I spoke, although I had known ever since reading Esther Sullivan's letter about Pandora that one day I would have to tell these things.

"The childhood story about slashing the sail was true, except she shifted the characters. It was Pandora who feared the water, who couldn't swim, who wouldn't sail. Once at summer camp she had hysterics when some girls forced her into a canoe and pushed it a few feet from shore. It was a deathly fear."

I paused, and Esther Sullivan, her face pallid, said, "She must have changed later on. No one afraid of water would have insisted on sailing the day she had the accident. I warned her at least twice that the lake was dangerous."

"Yes, so did I. I told her." It was a chorus around the table.

"Can't any of you *see*?" I rode over their voices, suddenly impatient. "Of course she chose an impossible day! She knew you would insist the weather was too risky! If it had been a fine day, everyone would have told her to go ahead and enjoy sailing. What would she have done then?"

"I do not understand this," said Konrad, frowning. "Why would she invent tales that were easily detected? She spoke of sailing several times, she told stories—and we live on a lake. In time the truth would have been learned."

"She couldn't help herself!" I insisted, trying to make them understand. "People like Pandora believe their own fantasies when they tell them."

"They do!" Richard Halpin spoke with conviction. "Some singers in opera, quite famous ones, will claim roles they've never sung. Yet all the facts are on record and it's easy to discover their lies. And I've known several people who believed their own daydreams."

I said, "When Miss Sullivan wrote that Pandora had died in a sailing accident, I knew it was impossible."

The atmosphere at the table seemed charged. I could feel shock, doubt, and hostility.

"So Pandora talked about sailing, did she?" I went on. "Well, which of you ever saw her in a boat?"

No one could meet the challenge. I saw Miss Sullivan lower her eyes, shaken. Althea's face was bewildered.

Then Mario spoke. "I saw her in a boat," he said. "We spent a weekend together. She was in a boat with me twice, there is no doubt at all."

I was so startled, so taken aback that I gasped. I did not believe him for an instant, but there was nothing to be gained by flatly contradicting him.

"The circumstances must have been unusual," I said quietly. "But it is still difficult for me to believe she climbed into a boat alone on a stormy day."

Again, silence. Then Giulia, perplexed, said, "All this talking in English! It is not clear to me. If Pandora did not go sailing, then what happened to her?"

The question, which had been hovering in the air for some minutes, was almost drowned by the loud scrape of Althea's chair on the marble floor as she arose abruptly.

"Shall we return to the living room?" Her voice was unsteady at first, but then she controlled it. "There is an excellent cognac. I believe we would all feel better for a drink."

The next half-hour was a time of confusion. Everyone seemed to speak at once, then sudden stillness would descend. I was astonished at how quickly explanations were rushed forward.

Konrad speculated that Pandora had climbed into the yawl and waited at the doors of the boathouse for someone to discover her and forbid the outing. The boat had been tugged by a sudden wave and drifted out before Pandora could escape.

Miss Sullivan wondered if the drowning and the sinking of the yawl might be unconnected. "If the boat broke loose from its moorings, she might have run along the pier trying to catch a line to stop it. She could have fallen into the water."

Althea came and sat beside me. I said, "I hope I haven't brought you more distress. I didn't want to do that."

"No, you have not," she told me. "Nor shall I worry about how the accident took place. Somehow Pandora found her way to that boat, but learning an explanation will not bring her back to us."

She rose, moving toward the door to bid Prince Luigi good night, and her shoulders seemed firm, her back held proudly. She inclined her head to the prince and Giulia, the regal but gracious hostess. I had no clue to her real thoughts or feelings.

Later, on the way to my room, Mario Donato intercepted me on the staircase, his face grim. "Was it necessary for you to do that?" he asked quietly. "There was nothing to gain. Why could you not leave the past undisturbed?"

"No, it *was* necessary," I replied. "And tell me, why did you lie about seeing Pandora in a boat?"

"But I did see her," he said, and then looked at me gravely, shaking his head. "They say that an avalanche starts with one rolling pebble. Now you have started your avalanche, Catherine, and I do not think you can stop it. Someone may be crushed in this." Before turning away from me, he added, "Who knows? The one crushed may be you yourself."

Forcing myself to ignore his words, I went to my room, feeling that the ordeal of the evening was done. I would rest easier, I told myself, now that the secret I'd kept for so long was in the open. But the tension of downstairs did not leave me as I propped open the balcony doors to admit any breeze that arose in the night. I undressed and prepared for bed, haunted by uneasiness, and although I was exhausted, I did not quickly fall asleep.

When at last sleep came, it brought dreams—dreams I struggled against, fighting to sink into deeper unconsciousness, refusing to allow imagined sounds and images to awaken me. For a long time I kept the realization that I was dreaming, that what I thought I heard and saw was only in my restless mind. Then the sensation of dreaming faded; I became lost in the nightmare.

Someone, some presence, had entered the room from the deserted corridor unhindered by the locked door, and now stood beside my bed, its visage shrouded and featureless. But I thought that great dark hollows of eyes gazed down upon me, intent and remorseless. I tried to sit up, to cry out, but I had lost all power of movement. In the distortion of the dream, I felt I'd been transformed. Like the fawn in the shed near the deer park, I could not stir or speak. I lay helpless, paralyzed before an unknown enemy.

"Who are you?" I could not cry the words, but I thought them desperately. "Who are you? Is it Pandora? Who is it?"

There was only silence as the figure leaned toward me. Then a name was spoken faintly, not near my bed but echoing in the distance. "Lillian . . . Lillian . . ."

The presence vanished. I felt I was no longer in my bed, but had entered the museum and was standing before the *Macbeth* exhibit, as I had done that first day. But this time I was alone; the crowd of whispering visitors had departed. The "Sleepwalking Scene" unfolded before me, but although the waxen figures of the singers performed only a few steps away, their voices were muted, almost inaudible.

Lady Macbeth moved toward me. I tried to retreat, but found myself rooted to the spot. Her face, now changed to the dark countenance that had stood beside my bed, thrust itself nearer; lips formed, parted, and I heard a faint scream. Then the scream rose in a horrible ear-splitting crescendo, and its shrillness somehow released me from the grip of the nightmare.

I was sitting bolt upright in bed, awake and shuddering.

Someone—a real person, not a figure in a dream—had screamed, a cry filled with agony, loud enough and close enough to have awakened me. Rising, I snatched my robe from the back of a chair and ran to the balcony, parting the net of the mosquito curtains. The grounds below, the shad-

owy deer park and the stone walkways, lay hushed and deserted in cloudy moonlight. Nothing moved. Nor was there
the least sound as I gazed across an untenanted world frozen
in the paleness of the moon.

Then a light came on—a light in Althea's room, the next
window to my right. Listening, I heard shuffling footsteps,
stumbling and uncertain, then a louder sound as though someone had fallen against a piece of furniture.

Was Althea weeping? I thought so, but was not sure; nor
was I certain that the word she had said was, "Lillian."

I stood in confusion—wanting to go to her, feeling I should,
yet afraid that my knocking on her door, trying to talk with
her, would be not a comfort, but a terrible and unwelcome intrusion into the privacy of some grief whose history I had
been forbidden.

Then, as I hesitated, the light was switched off, the villa left
in darkness. But on the lawn below I caught sight of a figure
running toward the villa from the direction of the castle.
Drawing back behind the net curtains, I watched Mario Donato approach. He was barefoot and shirtless, wearing only a
pair of dark jeans, and in his right hand he carried a heavy,
short-handled hammer—a mallet or a maul.

He halted beneath Althea's window, stood gazing upward,
then moved a step back, as though uncertain of what to do.
Then for a moment the clouds parted, and in the cold moonlight I saw his face, clear and hard-edged. There was anguish
in his look, but far more than that, an expression of rage I
would never forget.

Chapter Nine

Midmorning when I went downstairs for a late breakfast, I noticed a handkerchief looped over the knob of Althea's door. This, I had been told, was a signal—her equivalent of a "Do Not Disturb" sign. It meant she felt exhausted or ill and no one was permitted to knock except in the gravest emergency.

Exhausted or not, I thought, Althea would have to see me later today and no handkerchief would keep me out. After last night I knew what Miss Sullivan really meant when she said, "Althea spent a difficult night" or when she calmly observed that Althea "had been troubled."

Troubled was hardly the word! I knew Althea suffered no less than torment, and was astonished the household seemed not to realize it. Of course, no servants slept at the villa, Konrad and Miss Sullivan had bedrooms downstairs, and Richard Halpin's cottage stood too far away for him to hear anything. But Mario had heard; it must have been Althea's scream that brought him running across the lawns.

When I reached the dining room, I found Mario there alone, looking as though he had slept little.

"*Buon giorno.*" He glanced at me, then stared silently at his coffee cup.

"This is a surprise," I said, helping myself to rolls and fruit from the sideboard. "I haven't seen you here for breakfast before."

"Usually I am too early for breakfast. I take something from the kitchen and go to work."

I joined him at the table. "Konrad said your work was your whole life. I begin to believe him."

"You make me sound inhuman," he answered with a faint smile. "*Si*, when I work it is important, sometimes desperate. But when the work is finished, you see the other Mario Donato. I am lazy then and care for nothing except enjoying myself."

"Which Mario are you today?"

He frowned. "Not quite either one. I am not working; I do not know when I will begin again." He hesitated, glanced toward the door, then spoke. "I have been waiting here for you, Catherine. I wish to talk about the things you said at dinner last night."

"Good. I'd like to talk about them, too. But it would be easier if you first told me the truth about seeing Pandora in a boat."

"Fair enough." He finished his coffee, then hesitated, considering his words before he spoke. "Last night I told you I was much attracted to Pandora and I confused this attraction with love. I believe it was the third week she was here that I went to Venice with her. We stayed two days."

Abruptly he stopped speaking, then said, "What is this expression I see on your face, Catherine? Does it disturb you that Pandora and I were lovers for a brief time?"

I forced myself to look at him. "No. Why should it?"

"I can think of no reason," he said, studying me. "You are not an Esther Sullivan to be horrified so easily. I am sure Pandora had many lovers. They meant little to her, and soon she meant little to them."

"I told you it doesn't matter." My voice was unexpectedly sharp. I did not know why Pandora's love affair troubled me—it was hardly a new discovery. But I found myself unreasonably offended that she and Mario had gone to Venice together.

Mario shrugged. "In any case, we went to Venice, a city where it is almost impossible to avoid traveling by boat, unless one is born with wings."

"A gondola!" I exclaimed. "You meant she rode on a gondola! Probably on a narrow canal where she could jump to the pavement."

"No. She pleaded an upset stomach and did not want to go with me in a gondola." Mario shook his head, and his brows raised in self-mockery. "I was desolate. A gondola is the most romantic craft in the world, and I consider myself a very romantic man. But, *poverino!* We took the vaporetti, the steam-engine water buses."

"That proves how frightened she was!" I looked at Mario in astonishment. "But you gave the opposite impression last night. Why didn't you tell the exact truth?"

"Because you had already told quite enough dangerous truths for one evening," he answered slowly. "You have finished your breakfast? Then let us walk somewhere so we cannot be overheard so easily."

As we strolled toward the deer park, he said, "You realize that the newspapers are always interested in our family. Althea is still a famous diva, Konrad a millionaire, and even I am fairly well-known, at least among artists. Such a thing as you said last night, if it reached the ears of reporters, would guarantee months of vicious publicity. For what purpose? There is nothing to be gained."

"Pandora never entered that yawl of her own free will," I insisted. I would not yield the struggle.

"*Basta!* You believe this. But even if you are right, it

proves nothing. Suspicions and doubts are raised, good people are injured by scandal. For nothing! Give this up, Catherine.''

We walked for a time in silence, passing the gates of the park and the caretaker's shed, and at last reaching the stone terrace in front of the villa. My mind was in turmoil.

"Let us face the truth, Catherine," he said quietly. "If Pandora did not enter the yawl willingly, then she was forced to do so. I think that would be murder, would it not? Is that what you are claiming, Catherine? That Pandora was murdered?''

"I don't know," I answered. "I have no explanation, and I am not accusing anyone.''

"Then you accuse us all." Mario kept his voice gentle, but I felt steel behind the tone. "No one, I assure you, would have harmed Pandora. There was no reason.''

I leaned against the balustrade, gazing across the lake, wanting to believe he was right. I said, "Yet everyone quarreled with her. Everyone here, I think.''

"Yes," he agreed. "Her former husband, *Signor* Carr, was enraged enough to have done anything when he arrived here. But Althea paid him his money. I no longer thought Pandora was worth my anger, and I believe Konrad had reached the same conclusion.''

He was, I supposed, telling the truth, and even if Mario should be mistaken, I had no idea what my own next step should be. Last night I had announced the truth about Pandora, but no walls had fallen, no doors opened.

We stood for a moment in silence. "I saw you last night," he said. "You were standing at the doors of the balcony. So you, too, heard her scream.''

"Yes. It was dreadful, terrible.''

He nodded slowly. "I was restless. After I went to bed, I began to worry about the relief sculpture on the museum stairway, about how stale the idea is and how much I dislike it. I could not sleep, so I started to the museum, perhaps to work. I was not sure. Then I heard her.''

He rubbed his hand across his forehead, brushing back a

lock of dark hair. "These dreams come to her, then she is ill. For nights afterwards she is afraid to sleep, afraid the dream will return. I thought your coming here might have changed that. Then last night . . ." He paused, making a gesture of futility. "I am helpless to stop her suffering, and I feel a rage I cannot describe. It is unfair, unjust!"

"I want to talk to her today," I said. "I'll wait another hour, and then I don't care if she orders me away. She must not be alone, not alone all day shut up in her room."

"All day?" His smile was ironic. "More likely three days. I have known this to go on for a week after an attack."

As we were parting, Mario said, "I hope you will think no more of Pandora's death, Catherine. It is wrong to brood, to imagine unhappy things. You must realize that no one at the villa hated Pandora. I, for instance, certainly wished she would leave, but I did not wish her harm. Think about this. *Ciao*, Catherine."

After he left, I hesitated on the terrace, wondering if I could ever give up my doubts about Pandora's death. Just offshore Ilse Donato's fishing skiff bobbed at anchor, so close I could almost distinguish the features of the heavy face shaded by her peasant hat. Today, garbed in black and crouched in the boat, *Signora* Donato more than ever resembled a fierce water fowl—some dark, heavy bird of prey, always hovering near-by, always ready to strike.

Mario had said that no one at the villa hated Pandora, but in at least one case he was mistaken. Ilse Donato, I thought, hated us all.

An hour later I tapped on Althea's door, then entered— ignoring the forbidding handkerchief and giving her no chance to tell me to go away.

The room was darkened by closed draperies and Althea, dressed in a long yellow robe, rested on a couch heaped with pillows.

"Come in, Sullie," she said. "I'm not sleeping, unfortunately. Is it too soon for me to take another capsule?"

As she turned her head toward me, I saw that she wore a black velvet mask, eyeless, to shut out the light.

"It's not Miss Sullivan," I said. "It's Catherine."

"Catherine?" She sounded surprised but not pleased, and I felt a sudden anxiety bordering on desperation. I had to talk to her, to offer help or comfort, and I didn't know how to begin. What could I say to reach her, to keep her from sending me from the room?

"I'm not well, Catherine," she said quickly. "I'm afraid I am unable to—"

"Forgive me for bothering you, and I'm sorry you're ill," I said. Then an idea, a different way of approaching her, came to me. "I wouldn't have disturbed you except I need your help, your advice."

"My help?" She sat up, and as she began to untie the eye mask, I knew my effort had succeeded—at least for the moment. Everyone always offered her help, but I was sure no one had asked her for help in years. "Open the draperies, please," she said. "Since I won't be napping for a while, there's no reason to sit in the dark. And, my dear Catherine, the draperies *are* closed to help me sleep. You must not think I lurk in the dark from sheer morbidity."

I let light flood the room, and opened the windows to freshen the air. When I turned back to Althea, her appearance startled me. Only last night she had been a beautiful woman of late middle age; now she had suddenly become old. She blinked at me, her eyes unfocused, and her whole body seemed shrunken and somehow diminished.

Drawing up a footstool, I sat beside her. "It's about last night. I need so much to talk to you."

"Last night?" She was wary, uncertain. "About what you told us at supper?"

"No. I don't think that was very important." This, I felt, was no time to worry her about Pandora. "Long afterwards— hours later—I had a terrible nightmare. Today I'm still shaken by the dream. I think it would help me if I could tell you about it."

For an instant a trace of suspicion crossed her face, then she nodded. "Of course, my dear. You must tell me. But first, please ring the kitchen for ice. Press the button four times; the cook knows what it means. My head is rather groggy and some ice water may help."

I drew back the curtains that concealed the sliding doors of the cabinet elevator and signaled by pressing the button. Faintly, I heard a buzzer sound on the floor below.

"I suppose my grogginess comes from the sleeping tablets I have to take," she said, glancing to the bedside table where a bottle of pink and white capsules stood near a water carafe. "Usually they make me sleep soundly, but last night they failed. I took another this morning, hoping for a nap. That has also failed."

Troubled that she might be too dependent upon some drug, I asked, "Do you take them every night?"

"I sleep better when I do," she replied, avoiding my question. "They are quite harmless, and they calm my nerves wonderfully."

The ice arrived on the little elevator. I put some in a tall glass with water, she drank a bit, then dipped in a corner of her handkerchief and daubed at her temples.

"I have the wretched affliction of being cursed with nervousness," she said. "This is a new thing for me. I used to have nerves of steel, except when I was working." She chuckled, lifting a sardonic eyebrow. "Oh, at times I was a terror at rehearsals! I've kicked over music stands, hurled scores. Once I snatched a baton from Sir Lawrence Biggs, the conductor, and tried to break it over his head! They said I was a savage, the worst temper since Medea!" She paused, musing a little sadly about the past. "It was really nerves. I was always so terrified that everything would go wrong. That was why I found the concert stage easier than opera. I was a perfectionist and I demanded the love of perfection from others. Now I am more understanding."

As Althea spoke, her effort to sound light gave way and her words became tinged with faint bitterness. For a moment she appeared to drift away into her memories, her eyes closed, then she forced herself to concentrate on the present again.

"You were speaking of a nightmare, Catherine?"

"Yes. A dream I can't forget." Then I told her about it, every detail. She listened intently, tight lipped and controlled, flinching only when I spoke of the voice saying, "Lillian."

"Even now in daylight it seems real," I said at the end of the story. "But why should I dream about *Macbeth*? I've never heard the opera; I only know it as a play I studied in a literature class."

I did not tell her the actual ending of the dream—that it was her scream that awakened me—and I did not reveal what I heard from her room later.

She sat silent and motionless for a long time, eyes closed, and when at last she spoke I realized it took courage for her to tell me what had happened.

"I caused your dream," she said. "You heard me singing."

"Singing?"

"Yes. I, too, had a nightmare; the same hellish dream that comes to me again and again. How many times have I awakened screaming from it? In the dream I am singing the role of Lady Macbeth, and it is the 'Sleepwalking Scene.' I know I am really singing—I hear my own voice—although when I awake I can sing no longer." She looked away from me, again forcing herself to remain under control.

"When I am awake, I may sing three or four notes, then nothing. My voice fails; there is hardly a whisper. But last night you must have heard me and you recognized the words. Not the Italian from the Verdi opera, but in English, the version Richard Halpin wrote for me." She hesitated, her hands tense. "I have never performed that role in public, although I nearly did."

Remembering the night before, I decided that what Althea said must be true. I was probably dreaming anyway, imagining the figure beside my bed. Then I must have heard Althea, faintly, through the open doors to the balcony and, although half-asleep, recognized the familiar words. "*Yet here's the spot. Out, damned spot, out I say!*"

This had prompted my dream, just as thirst in sleep can cause a dream of a desert or a fountain. "Did you call the name Lillian?" I asked, "Or was that only my dream?"

"I don't know. Probably I cried out. My daughter Lillian, your adopted sister, comes to me in this dream, but not as the return of someone you have loved. She comes . . ." Althea shuddered, then forced the word. "Horribly! Not the good memories, but the worst moment of her life and of mine!"

Trembling, she fell silent while her gaze searched the room—lingering on the doorway, the armchair, the settee, as though discerning some presence invisible to me. Then she lay back against the pillows. "Of course, she returns with the memory of *Macbeth*. What hopes we had for it! There was a small role, the gentlewoman, and this was to be Lillian's debut as a singer. We planned to perform it first in the small theater here, then if it seemed successful, we would have arranged for full staging at Teatro la Fenice, where I sang many times. But this did not happen. Instead—" Her voice faded to silence and she turned her head away from me, tears coursing down her cheeks.

Her grief lay beyond the reach of any comfort I had to give. I sat by her side for almost an hour, then tiptoed from the room, thankful she had at last fallen into a fitful sleep.

Alone in my room that evening, I thought about my conversation with Mario Donato and his remark that while almost everyone at the villa had good reason to be angry with Pandora, no one had cause to do her injury—much less cause her death. The more I considered this, the more sensible it seemed. Mario had been a disappointed lover and Konrad a disillusioned one, but I couldn't believe their feelings had been violent enough to cause Pandora's destruction. If someone had lured or forced Pandora into the yawl during a storm, that person must have felt a powerful hatred or another deep compulsion to commit such an act. As far as I could determine, no one at the Villa Pellegrina felt such emotions. I did not know what caused Pandora to quarrel with Prince Luigi, but it was hard for me to imagine any relationship between them deep enough to lead to violence.

I stepped onto the balcony and stood quietly for a moment, gazing at the brilliant stars that seem so low in the sky during summer in the Italian lake country. Mario had urged me to let go of the past, to forget my doubts about Pandora's death. Was it possible for me to do this? Perhaps I should try. At least I must not worry forever with a riddle that seemed to have no answer.

As I was turning back into my room, there was a tap on my door and Althea's voice called, "Catherine? Are you awake?"

"Yes, of course." I hurried to open the door. "What is it?"

"Nothing at all. I just wished to chat a moment." Entering she took the small chair at the desk. "I slept away the afternoon. Oh, Catherine, I am so much better."

"You look stronger," I said, smiling. It was true. Color had returned to her cheeks and the terrible tension had vanished.

"I have been thinking, Catherine," she said. "Last night we both had bad dreams and we must do something about this. We must have a change! Tell me, how well do you know Venice?"

"Hardly at all," I answered. "I know Rome and Florence quite well, but I've only spent two days in Venice."

"Two days?" she exclaimed, almost indignant. "Not enough time to see more than the Doge's Palace! Only two days in the most enchanting city in the world. It is an outrage! Well, we shall change that. I had planned to go in a week, but why should we wait? Why remain here among these unhappy memories? We shall go to Venice tomorrow morning."

A sudden burst of enthusiastic energy carried her to her feet. "And not just the two of us to be lost in that huge palace Victor was foolish enough to buy! The whole household is to go. Everyone!"

"What about work at the museum?" I asked.

"Let it wait. What difference can a week or two make?" Taking my hand, she held it in hers. "Oh, what a wonderful time we shall have! I will be young again in Venice. I will be twenty years old!"

I think she meant to stay late, to talk far into the night about Venice and tell me about the many roles she had sung at Teatro la Fenice, but her strength proved less than she had believed. In less than an hour she seemed exhausted, but when she left me there was a glow of expectation on her face, and she held contentedly to her childlike faith that Venice would mean a new life for her.

And I think that I, too, was carried along by her assurance; I almost believed we could magically leave the past behind us, locked safely away at the Villa Pellegrina. Although I knew better than that—knew that life does not miraculously change by changing one's location—I felt that Venice held some unknown promise for me. I did not suspect then that it was a promise of death.

Chapter Ten

We did not leave for Venice the next morning. Even Althea's royal commands could not so quickly move the household, as well as Richard Halpin, who was also invited. Nor was Althea herself feeling strong enough to travel, although she refused to admit this.

But three days later a peculiar motorcade formed in the drive of the Villa Pellegrina. Althea, Konrad, Mario, and I led the procession in an ancient but gleaming Rolls Royce—a vehicle, I supposed, once mandatory for celebrated sopranos. Konrad drove because old Don Pasquale, keeper of the deer park and also family chauffeur, had to follow in another car with Rajah as his only passenger. Althea would not travel without Rajah, and no one else would travel with him, since the ocelot had an alarming way of leaping back and forth over the seats in a moving auto.

Miss Sullivan and Richard Halpin followed in a station wagon crammed with Althea's luggage—enough for a grand tour lasting six months—even though Mario, anxious to finish his work, had extracted a promise from Althea that we would not remain in Venice more than two weeks. Bringing up the rear was an antique taxi hired from the village to transport the cook, her helper, a rack of spices, and various indispensable pots.

"A safari!" said Mario, lifting his eyes heavenward. "Like Hannibal crossing the Alps. We lack only a few elephants."

Yet the procession reached Venice in good order, and the people, luggage, and ocelot were quickly transferred to a water taxi and a pair of motorboats that served Althea's house in Venice.

When Althea gave detailed instructions to the boatman about the route to follow, he looked at her in surprise.

"*Signora*, that is out of the way. Far out of the way."

"I am aware of that. But my daughter—" She beamed at me. "—does not know Venice and we must make a good impression on her."

A few minutes later I found myself transported into a world painted by Canaletto, a dream of floating palaces with domes that hung bell-like from the sky. When I had seen Venice before, it had been on a stormy weekend, sunless and bleak with cold rain. Even then it had beauty, but today the island city shimmered in the first flush of summer, bathed in that light which is tinged with both blue and gold.

I found myself exclaiming at everything. "It's the sunlight playing on those pinks and greens. Althea, it's incredible!"

Mario, sitting behind me, chuckled. "Venice is called the bride of the Adriatic, but I think the sun is her secret lover. She blooms when he smiles on her."

From the grand Canal we swept far out into Bacino de San Marco, then turned back so I could see the most famous panorama of the city: the domes of St. Mark's, the towering spire of the Campanile, and the facade of the Doge's Palace. Then we turned back into the winding waterways, where it was color everywhere—the stripes of awnings, the gay fringes of umbrellas, and the fluttering flags that marked various landings. Above the bridges I saw the sheen of blue and yellow tile, the verdigris patina of bronze.

Gondolas glided past us, their Oriental prows reminding me

that Venice was once as much of the East as of the West—Europe's link to the far-away lands of silks and spices. The boats skimmed the water as gracefully as black swans while the gondoliers shouted their centuries-old cries of *primi, stali,* and, in the old Venetian dialect, "*A-Oel!*"

We entered a narrower, quieter canal, then passed through open gates of the docking entrance to Althea's Palazzo Malaspina, a handsome five-story mansion with massive obelisks mounted on stone cornices. I had expected luxurious furnishings, but the floor at the entrance level was undecorated, the big rooms almost bare.

"This was once a warehouse," said Althea. "Most of the old palaces are like this. At one time these rooms were stacked with bales of silk, with perfumes and rugs and tapestries."

"Not to mention cages of shivering apes," Konrad added. "And every imaginable species of exotic bird."

The next floor had served as the business offices of the palazzo centuries before. Here the accounts were kept, the bargaining and trading conducted.

"Prince Luigi has an apartment on this floor," Althea told me. "It was part of the arrangement when Victor acquired the palazzo."

Another cause for princely resentment, I thought. This floor, which was called the *mezzanino,* was hardly the place for a royal suite. "Victor Donato seems to have had a strange interest in buying everything Prince Luigi owned," I said to Althea.

"Not strange," she answered carelessly. "Victor's family had worked for the Malaspinas for generations as peasants and woodcutters. Buying their property or acquiring it through their creditors was simply Victor's way of purchasing a little royalty for himself. Of course, it was to Luigi's advantage, too."

We mounted a broad marble stairway which was at least twice the size of the main stairs at the Villa Pellegrina."

"Gigantic!" I exclaimed. "How many rooms are there?"

"Thirty-two," said Konrad, smiling. "The original palazzo was larger. Years ago Luigi sold a dozen rooms that face the Grand Canal. That part is now owned by an American film director. You have heard of Howard Hutchinson?"

As a child I had been enthralled by the film epics of the much-married, highly scandalous Howard Hutchinson, who specialized in extravaganzas featuring hundreds of charging camels or elephants, or thousands of Roman chariots. Then I remembered another name, Bart Hutchinson, the man Giulia had described as Lillian's lover. He must be the son, or perhaps the grandson, of the filmmaker.

The great stairway led to a long, dim room so vast that it could serve no conceivable purpose except giving a ball or holding a convention. This room, called the *piano signorile*, rose two stories high except in the center, where the ceiling spiraled upward to an onion-shaped dome. A huge chandelier holding scores of candles hung suspended from the dome by a heavy chain.

"Is the chandelier gold leaf?" I asked.

"Worse," said Mario with contempt. "Gilt paint over bronze with a few brass trimmings. A complete fake."

I wondered how the candles could be lit and replaced. "You'd need a ladder at least twenty feet high," I said.

Althea shook her head. "No, it's lowered on a pulley from a corner of the balcony up there."

A narrow balcony, furnished with fragile plush chairs, ran around three sides of the room.

"The whole thing is overwhelming," I said.

Mario contradicted me. "Merely hideous. The palazzo is a criminal waste of fine marble. Beautiful stone squandered! Barbaric!"

Palazzo Malaspina dated back so many centuries that every part of it had undergone half a dozen restorations and remodelings. All the rooms had furniture left by various generations, creating a mad and wonderful clash of designs. In the bedroom and sitting room given me, at least three centuries were represented, and I loved it. Arched draperies framed the doors of a balcony overlooking the canal, and from the balcony the whole unreality that is Venice spread before me.

Althea, I decided, had been right to come here. This make-believe city was what we needed for a time.

That afternoon I found my way up a curious old stairway to the roof, intending to do what generations of Venetian women have done; sit on the roof where the sun would dry my newly washed hair. I took my sketch pad, since it seemed to me that ne one could be in Venice an hour without longing to paint or draw its exotic skyline.

Concentrating on the distant tower of the Frari Church, I lost myself in my work and became unaware of my immediate surroundings until a voice called, *"Ciao!* Hello, there."

Across the roof a young man sat cross-legged on the low brick wall that divided Althea's property from the Grand Canal portion belonging to Howard Hutchinson.

He was in his early twenties, and even if I had not known who lived next door, I would have suspected that he was somehow connected with Hollywood. His wind-ruffled hair, thick and curling, gleamed like pale gold in the sun, and his face, although pleasantly freckled, seemed a shade too pretty. A camera case hung from a strap around his neck and he wore the Italian male costume of the moment—a striped shirt and tailored but faded denims.

"Are you drawing the Frari Church?" he asked.

"Yes."

"I've just been photographing it." He hesitated a moment, glancing left and right as though on the watch for some unknown hazard, then swung down from the wall and came across the roof to join me. "I live next door," he said, as though this guaranteed his welcome. "I'm Bart Hutchinson."

"Hello. I'm Catherine Andrews." I instantly recognized the name of Lillian's lover and tried to remember what Giulia had said about him. Something about a "terrible film," but nothing else came back to me.

He studied my drawing a moment. "I like the way you've handled those rooftops. A nice rhythm."

"Thank you."

"Are you a friend of Konrad's or of Mario's?" he asked, putting aside the drawing and moving directly to matters that really interested him.

"They're both friends of mine," I answered, an edge to my tone. "But I don't think that's what you are really asking."

"Excuse me! Beg your pardon!" He lifted his hands in mock contrition. "You're staying in the palazzo, and if not with Mario or Konrad, you must be a friend of Madam Hoffman's. Right?"

"I only met her a short time ago," I said cautiously, suspecting that the full truth would end any chance to learn more about Lillian.

"Cigarette?" he asked, offering me one.

"No, thanks."

He inserted the cigarette in a short black holder and, lighting up, made himself comfortable, resting his back against a brick chimney. For a few minutes we chatted about Venice, and he seemed less brash and self-satisfied than I had first thought.

"Are you an actress, Catherine?" He asked me.

"No. What makes you ask that question?"

"Just that so many people who know Althea Hoffman are in the theater or are musicians, singers—people like that."

"Are you a photographer?"

"Yes. But what I really want to do is make films for television. So far I've only worked with videotape. Filming with videotape is like making home movies. No special lights, no crew to pay. That's how I became acquainted with Madam Hoffman. Videotape." He gave me a sudden look. "Maybe she told you about that?"

"She's never mentioned you," I answered truthfully.

Hutchinson's smile was grim. "No, I suppose not."

"How did you meet her?" I inquired, trying to show no more than polite interest.

"Well, I talked to this Englishman, Richard Halpin, in Harry's Bar not quite two years ago. He mentioned an opera they were going to do, and I suddenly realized that a television special about Althea Hoffman would be a great idea. Not bad in Europe and absolutely tops in the United States.''

"Why in the United States?" I asked. "She's never sung there except at the start of her career.''

"*That* was the great idea!" He leaned forward, becoming confidential. "She can't go to the United States because years ago she was involved in some crime. I don't know the details, but I heard it was kidnapping. I knew that after the film was made and all the contracts were signed, the publicity men could work up a campaign based on the scandal. It couldn't fail! An opera singer with a criminal past, the mistress of an Italian billionaire. Victor Donato had just died a few months before and the name was still news.''

I stared at Bart Hutchinson, astounded. I was shocked not so much by the cheapness of his plan as by the ease with which he talked about it. Why tell such things to me, a stranger? For a moment I thought he was trying to impress me with his cleverness, then decided it was not that at all. He was of a world I knew nothing about, a jungle with its own laws. Obviously it did not occur to him that there might be something evil exploiting Althea's tragic life to reap publicity for a television film.

"Madam Hoffman, I soon learned, has no interest in television. She refused to talk to me. But I don't give up easily. I knew her daughter, Lillian Donato, and Lillian finally persuaded Madam Hoffman to let me try some taping.''

So he had used Lillian to reach Althea. I wondered if I had ever met anyone so shameless.

"I lived at the Donato villa for a month. Then for a while Lillian and I had a house in the village across the lake. I liked Lillian. It was a terrible thing that happened to her—but you know all about that.''

"No, I don't.'' He seemed not to hear, and stared gloomily across the roofs toward the church spire and a distant dome.

"I have the most sensational videotape ever made!" he said bitterly. "And it's bottled up forever. I can't sell it; I can't even show it except in private."

He paused, brooding, and I prompted him. "Why not?"

"Because Madam Hoffman made me sign a contract. I can't do anything with the tape unless she gives her consent. I'm losing out on a fortune. I hear she can't sing anymore. Good! It serves her right."

Hutchinson stubbed out his cigarette. "I shouldn't have said that. You're a friend of Madam Hoffman, now I've offended you, when all I really wanted to do was ask you to have dinner with me tonight at the Peoceto and some dancing afterwards."

"I'm not offended, and I wish you'd tell me about this tape you made."

"Tell you? I'll show you! Do you want to see some of the most sensational television drama ever made? It's all set up in the projection room next door."

I hesitated. "What does it show?"

"Oh, not much." He smiled at me, a smile that did not reach his cold blue eyes. "Just the great Althea Hoffman getting away with murder."

The projection room was on the top floor of the Hutchinson house and resembled a wide, windowless corridor. I waited, sitting in one of the dozen leather armchairs, while Bart adjusted various dials. There was a soft whir of rewinding tape, then some ear-piercing electronic bleats.

When he had used the expression "getting away with murder," I had certainly not taken the words literally. But I knew what he was about to show must reveal Althea at her worst, and I felt a growing apprehension—a fear that I was about to witness scenes that would be painful and mortifying.

"I've taken a lot of unfair criticism because of this tape," he said. "Some people thought I was some breed of subhuman without a heart. Yes, it was horrible! But they don't understand that I felt numb while it was happening. I just automatically kept the camera turning. Afterwards, I was sick.''

None of what he said made me feel better about what lay ahead.

"None of this is final editing," he explained. "I'm just showing you a little background and buildup, then the terrific few minutes." He lowered the lights. "This starts with one of the *Macbeth* rehearsals. Most of the singers hadn't arrived at the lake yet, and they were just testing a few technical effects and costumes.''

I had never seen videotape before, and had expected it to be shown on the large projection screen at the end of the room. Instead, the images appeared on an ordinary television set he had placed near my chair; at first there were only blurs and wavering lines, then a picture of a dark-haired girl came into sharp focus. She smiled in silent approval as she inspected a long gown on a clothes hanger, holding it in front of her to check the size, showing the full winglike sleeves made with yards of shimmering net.

"Lillian Donato," said Hutchinson. "A beautiful girl, wasn't she?"

"Very," I answered, but I did not really agree with him. She had the youthful attractiveness of many girls her age—about eighteen, I guessed—but her lips, despite the smile, seemed to pout, and her strong chin was too prominent. I tried to remember where I had seen her portrait or a photograph of her at the villa. Was it in the library? I could not recall, but she seemed vaguely familiar.

The scene shifted to a half-finished stage set: gothic arches and a flight of steps. Lillian and an unfamiliar middle-aged man entered, paused down center, and after several omnious chords from an unseen piano, the man opened his mouth to sing, but changed his mind.

"Miss Sullivan!" he called toward the wings.

"Yes, Mr. Wilson?" Esther Sullivan stepped into view carrying clipboard and pencil.

"I need a quill pen and some paper, probably a scroll, for this scene. Will you tell the master of properties?"

"I am taking care of properties myself, Mr. Wilson," she told him with a crisp smile. "We have only the household crew until the production moves to Venice." She made a note and walked off stage briskly.

The scene had taken place less than two years ago, but Miss Sullivan looked a decade younger. This was not an illusion of light or photography; the difference showed in her step, in her least gesture.

Mr. Wilson, a tenor, then began to sing, and as I recognized the words, I restrained a shudder. It was the introduction to the "Sleepwalking Scene"; he was playing the doctor and Lillian had been cast in the brief part of the gentlewoman, Lady Macbeth's attendant. When she sang her responses to the doctor's questions, her voice rose with a pleasant, youthful innocence. I supposed that in a provincial opera company no one would have singled her out for either praise or criticism.

Then the music changed—four heavy and memorable chords built to the entrance of Lady Macbeth—and when Althea stepped onto the stage, the doctor and the gentlewoman, although they still sang, hardly seemed present. In rehearsal clothes, without makeup, but carrying what seemed to be a flaming oil lamp, she dominated the scene even in silence, and when she sang her first full line—*"Yet here's the spot!"*—the words rang with terror and revulsion. I sat entranced, forgetting the room, oblivious to Bart Hutchinson; Althea held me enthralled. Only once was the scene marred—and then only slightly—when Lillian, who should have been quietly listening, overreacted with gestures and sighs of sympathy, momentarily drawing attention away from Althea.

As the aria neared its climax and conclusion, the lights dimmed except for a spot on Althea and the glow of the lamp she carried. Then, with a sudden and violent gesture, she raised the lamp sharply, holding it just below her chin so her features were unnaturally illuminated from underneath, creating an effect of unearthly eeriness. Her final exit as the broken, guilt-driven queen was magnificent. I wanted to applaud.

The lights came up and Richard Halpin climbed onto the stage. "Perfect!" he shouted. "Bravo!"

Althea reappeared, charging onto the stage, ignoring him. She advanced upon Lillian, her face contorted with rage. "How dare you try to draw attention away from me! If you weren't my daughter, you'd be out of this cast in one minute!" Althea stormed, pacing the stage in a performance almost as overwhelming as her Lady Macbeth.

"It is not just for myself I am concerned," cried Althea. "You ruined the scene. You looked like a fool, an amateur!"

Lillian fled to the wings, passing Esther Sullivan, who gave her a consoling pat on the shoulder.

"Please, Althea," Miss Sullivan coaxed. "I saw it from out front. It wasn't serious, and I'm sure it wasn't intentional."

Instead of having a calming effect, Miss Sullivan drew the prima donna's wrath upon her own head. "I've had quite enough of your interference, Sullie! If you do not like the way I manage my family, you can leave. I told you that yesterday, and I'll thank you to remember it."

Then, just as the scene was fading, Althea unexpectedly burst into tears.

"Madam Hoffman's a real sweetheart, isn't she?" Hutchinson shook his head. "A witch!"

"Couldn't you see the strain she was under?" I protested. "It must have been agony to sing that aria."

He pressed a button, causing the tape to advance rapidly. "I'm skipping a lot. I had a candid-camera view of an argument backstage between Lillian and that prune-face Miss Sullivan. But I don't show that."

"Why not?"

"Because the quarrel was about me," he said drily.

But I did see a few seconds of their confrontation when he stopped the speeding tape by mistake. Lillian, chin high, shouted defiance at an angry Esther Sullivan. "Don't speak to me that way, Sullie! I'm only doing what my mother did for years!"

"Sorry, wrong spot," said Hutchinson, speeding the machine again. "And now we see the first dress rehearsal of *Macbeth*, which, as it turned out, was also the final one. But first, a candid backstage prologue with that charming lady, Althea Hoffman."

Again the girl on the screen was Lillian and again there was the elaborate dress with the huge, filmy sleeves, but this time she was wearing it. The camera was above her and she appeared unconscious of it as she took a few awkward steps, trying to manage the long and obviously unfamiliar train of flowing tulle.

Althea spoke off-camera. "Lillian, what on earth are you wearing?" Then Althea herself appeared in a simple but striking costume with a cape attached at the shoulders.

"It's perfect for the gentlewoman." Lillian's tone was rebellious. "After all, she's a lady of the court."

"You are planning to wear that onstage?" Althea looked as though she had just felt the shock of an earthquake. "It is a parody of Isadora Duncan! Change at once."

Lillian's temper flared. "Are you afraid I might be noticed?"

"I have had enough insolence from you. At least cover that ridiculous outfit with a cloak or cape if there isn't time to find anything else." Althea hesitated, then said slowly but fiercely. "I am warning you for the last time. I have reached the limit of my patience."

Hutchinson skipped a long section of tape. When the screen came once again into focus, I recognized the set for the "Sleepwalking Scene," but now it was finished. Behind the stairs and platforms, a rear wall made of gauze dimly revealed a murky landscape.

When Lillian and the bass entered, I saw that Althea had won part of the battle over the costume. Lillian still wore the filmy gown, but a hooded cloak covered most of it—although it billowed with Lillian's every movement and actually did little to improve matters. I suspected the backstage quarrel had continued, for Lillian appeared flushed and nervous.

All doubt about the quarrel vanished at Althea's entrance. She moved with a tautness that made her almost awkward, and her voice had lost the marvelous flexibility I had heard before. The mechanics of the performance were exactly the same; every gesture and pause identical. She stood center stage, and the lamp she held flickered in a draught. Lillian posed on a platform a step higher and behind Althea. To my surpise, she had still not learned her lesson and was flagrantly overreacting, edging so close that she shared a little of the spotlight intended only for Althea.

"*All the perfumes of Arabia,*" sang Althea. Then I saw her shoulders grow tense, and I knew she realized what Lillian was doing.

"Enough!" It was a cry of fury. Althea whirled toward her daughter and at that instant there came a flash of light as though the lamp Althea carried had exploded.

She dropped the lamp to the floor, a long blue and yellow flame still spurting from it, and Althea's scream blended with Lillian's as both women stood for an instant transfixed by horror, paralyzed by the sight of Lillian's burning cloak. The fire leaped from the cloak to her net gown and then the girl was swathed in flame, a screaming torch as she clawed wildly at the costume.

She fled, trailing fire, stumbling upstage, where she hurled herself against the painted gauze wall, which for a second seemed to enmesh and trap her; then it, too, became a net of fire.

I could bear no more. I ran from the room, heedless of Bart Hutchinson's surprised shout. Somehow I found the door to the roof and reached the stairway of the palazzo, scratching my arm on the rough brick of the dividing wall. Blinded by tears I could not control, I paused on a landing, unable to remember the way to my own room, still shaking with horror at what I had seen.

"Catherine!" Mario stood in the hall below me, then raced up the stairs. "What has happened?"

I tried to tell him, but choked on the words. Then I felt his

arm holding me, and I leaned against him, trying to hold back
tears and failing utterly.

Mario stayed with me more than an hour, bringing me a
glass of cognac, listening quietly when I was at last able to tell
the story of Bart Hutchinson and the television tape.

"I don't know what made me break down so completely. I
don't burst into tears this way! But it was so . . ." I
searched for a word. "Shocking, I suppose. It was like a
physical blow."

"Tears are nothing to feel shame about," he said gently. "I
do not understand why people, especially men, must apologize for weeping. I wept the night Lillian died; I wept for her
pain, and for our mother's and for my own loss. I also had
tears for Miss Sullivan, who loved Lillian as she would have
loved her own daughter."

I looked at Mario's dark, sun-bronzed face and could not
quite imagine him weeping. He seemed unbreakable, but
something in his voice told me this was not so.

"Sometimes tears are the only speech left to us," he said.
Hesitating, he moved to the window and stood a moment gazing down at the canal. "Part of our sorrow over Lillian was, I
think, a feeling of guilt. We were angry with her the last
weeks of her life because of her love affair with this worth-
less, unfeeling Hutchinson. I was angry because she had no
discretion—she flaunted her behavior. Twice I heard her tell
Sullie she was only following our mother's example. It was
bitter for everyone."

"What really happened on the stage that night?" I asked.
"I saw the lamp explode, then the fire." Now I could speak of
it without shuddering, but I did not allow myself to recall any
picture of what I had seen.

"The lamp burned out, like many cigarette lighters and
party candles. The open flame was dangerous, but Althea
took the risk because she felt any artificial light would seem
false, and a candle is blown out too easily by drafts. When she
twirled toward Lillian, she jarred the lamp and a small valve

controlling the gas came loose. That is what the police decided afterwards. Everyone agreed it was no one's fault.''

Not everyone, I thought. Althea had never forgiven herself, and even today harbored a guilt so deep it could only express itself in nightmares.

"You have finished the cognac, Catherine," he said, then took my hand lightly. "Now forget all this. It is of the past, over and done. Let it go."

"I'll try." Even as I spoke I realized that the initial force of the shock had been dissipated simply by Mario's allowing me to pour out the story. His quiet sympathy had calmed me, and the few words he had said made me realize that what I had seen was, indeed, part of the past. No feelings of mine could change it.

"You will put this aside," he told me, "because our minds create a mist that blurs the worst things we remember." He paused, and when he spoke again, his tone was light. "Besides, I intend to distract you. You cannot be sad in Venice, and tonight we shall be tourists in Piazza San Marco, drinking white wine and seeing the world stroll past. But we are not to stay late, because tomorrow I have orders to show you Venice."

"Orders?" I exclaimed. "Do you mean that Althea—"

"Yes. She ordered me to be your guide and I always obey her." Mario smiled a slow, warm smile. "Always—except when I decide not to."

After he left, I lay on the bed, eyes closed, to let the cognac work its calming effect. But after a few moments, impatient with myself, I went to the bathroom, where I splashed my face with cold water. Returning to the roof of the palazzo, I found my charcoal and the unfinished sketch of the Frari Church where I had left them near the main chimney. For the next two hours, until twilight came, I worked steadily—my mind focused completely on the church spire, then on the leaded roofs rising like foothills toward the great summit of St. Mark's—stopping only when the sunset slowly turned the Adriatic crimson.

When I closed the sketchbook and started toward the attic
stairway, I knew that the work had restored me, and in leaving the roof I was leaving at least part of the past behind.

That night lanterns twinkled on the prows of gondolas, and
the carvings of a slate facade sprang to life when blue spot-
lights shone on an ancient church.

We wandered across the decorated paving of St. Mark's
Square, and Mario paused to point high in the sky above the
bell tower. "A new moon, Catherine," he said. "You must
make a wish and say it to yourself three times. You may wish
for the things of money or for the things of love. But if you
wish for both, you will be given neither."

I did not know what to wish for, yet I had a strange feeling
of expectancy. A breeze brought the freshness of the sea to
the warm night, and then, as we passed a flower vendor, the
air was perfumed and heady. I heard the summer night music
of Venice: chimes from towers, the deep-throated horns of
ships in the harbor, and a blend of the music from the sidewalk cafés with the distant rumble of an organ. A pair of lovers, leaning close in the shadows, laughed softly.

What had Althea said? "I will be young again in Venice." I
understood her.

We found a table at the Café Florian and Mario ordered a
carafe of white, shimmering wine from Orvieto and a platter
of tiny fish—this morning's catch from the Adriatic—fried
crisp in a salty batter.

Mario told Venetian jokes and tried to teach me words of
the Venetian dialect, which is a language almost separate
from Italian. He remained a mystery to me, a mixture of so
many intense qualities. Then he would change, become almost boyish, as he was tonight.

"I have a confession to make, Catherine. A very Venetian
confession, and you must promise not to betray me."

"I promise in the Venetian way," I answered, smiling.
"Which means I can betray you at any moment."

"I am bringing up an unpleasant subject," he continued,

"but you must know that you have been avenged in a manner traditional in this city."

"Avenged?" I could think of no one who deserved my vengeance. Then I knew the name he would say. "Bart Hutchinson?"

He nodded grimly. "While you were resting this afternoon, I went to a café where he often goes. I waited in ambush, lurking behind a terrible Roman sculpture of Neptune. When he emerged from the café, I seized him; I lifted him over my head and held him while he squirmed . . ." Mario hesitated.

"And then?"

"Then I threw him into the canal. It was a shallow canal, one where the bottom is muck and slime. His hair was less golden when he poked it from the oily water. Since he did not dare emerge near me, he had to wade across. Quite a sight! He lost his shoes in the mud." Mario chuckled. "I enjoyed myself. Maybe I will do it again."

I was laughing with him, and the thought of Hutchinson puffing and blowing, covered with ooze, further diminished my unpleasant memory of the afternoon. If I saw him again, I might think of the hideous film, but at the same time I would see a picture of his slimy, bedraggled figure climbing from the canal.

The café band burst into a rollicking Venetian folksong, while a baritone sang lustily in a dialect I could not understand.

Mario lifted his glass in a salute. "To the Catherine I have discovered." He dipped his dark head in an exaggerated bow. "Like Venice, her loveliness always offers new surprises."

"How gallant, *signor*," I said. "But I know Italian men. They set no limits to flattery."

"You may know Italian men, but you do not know me." And then he was no longer smiling. I looked away, afraid to meet that clear gaze, knowing that at this moment he and I had reached a turning point. I knew him hardly at all; yet nothing could be easier, I thought, than to fall in love with this man.

But when he spoke again, his tone was bantering. "We should finish our wine. Remember, Catherine, when the wine is good, you must save a smile for the bottom of the glass. *Salute!*"

We were laughing together when a photographer stopped at our table. "A souvenir of the evening, *signor*?" he asked with a wheedling smile. "A picture in the most beautiful colors?"

Mario started to wave the man away, then smiled broadly. "*Si.* We will have a picture. Catherine, your loveliest pose."

A strong, unexpected aversion arose in me. "No, I—" But then the flashbulb blazed.

Mario paid the photographer, who gave him the picture a moment later. "You seem not to be filled with happiness, Catherine." He studied the photo, then turned it face down on the table. "Perhaps you consider café photographs childish, but I do not understand why it disturbs you so."

"I'm sorry," I said. "I was reminded of Pandora. There was a picture among her things. Pandora and you sitting at a table—this same table for all I know. The memory made me uncomfortable for a moment, that's all."

Mario shook his head in disbelief. "There is no such picture. You have imagined this, Catherine. I know because I have always thought these street photographers are a nuisance. But tonight I felt this foolishness had its value."

"But I—" Then suddenly the truth came to me. "You're right—it was not you in the picture, but Konrad." But even as I spoke I realized it didn't matter who was in the photograph. I had been reminded that Mario had once brought Pandora to Venice, that he had believed himself in love with her. My resentment was completely unreasonable, but I could not help it.

Mario's face darkened, a sharper note came into his voice. "Are you foolish enough to believe that my brief affair with Pandora was a time of lingering in cafés and grinning at a camera as I found myself doing tonight? With Pandora, I assure you, I did not think of walking hand in hand across Piazza San Marco to feed the pigeons! She was not that kind of woman."

"And you think I am?" I demanded.

"*Si*. And I am just foolish enough to join you in such things."

Then, for no reason, we were both laughing. Mario ordered a final glass of wine, the new moon stood at the tip of the great bell tower that guards St. Mark's, and I could not remember a night so beautiful.

Chapter Eleven

The next morning pale sunshine poured through the curtains to the balcony. Outside, a thousand bells seemed to be ringing at once, although it was not Sunday, and I realized this must be the festival of some major saint.

Putting on my robe, I went to the balcony and looked out at the island city. The bells had sent thousands of pigeons wheeling in the air above the piazzas and canals, the birds crying out in noisy protest while the ancient leaded roofs and carved facades echoed the great paen. Early boats were already on the narrow canal below, gliding under its humpbacked stone bridge. On the cornices of the palazzo across the way, stone dolphins preened in the sunlight, and it was, as I had hoped, a cloudless day.

Half an hour later I was in the kitchen helping the astonished cook prepare breakfast, simply because I was so filled with energy and well-being that I had to do something. I bustled about the huge room, brewing what the servants contemptuously called "that thin English coffee" or even worse, "American ditch water."

Mario joined me for breakfast a few minutes later. Dressed in one of his striped, sleeveless shirts, jeans, and sandals, and carrying a floppy Venetian boatman's cap, he looked ready for a day on the canals. "A perfect morning," he said, then tasted the coffee I had made and his smile withered. "The cook has at last decided to poison us. I knew it would happen." He rang the service bell.

"I'm guilty," I confessed. "I wanted a taste of New England."

"Sullie does the same terrible thing, but she calls it a taste of her native Canada. It is in her blood, although she has not been in Canada for almost twenty years."

"She has no family?"

"We are all her family as far as she will allow us to be," he said with a slight frown. "Her father died long ago, just after I was adopted by Althea and Don Victor. There couldn't have been other family because Sullie had to go to Canada to take care of her father in his final illness. She was gone weeks, maybe months. I remember how desperate everyone was for her return because she managed our lives."

"You're very devoted to her, aren't you?" I asked.

He hesitated, then spoke carefully. "No, not devoted. I admire her, I am grateful to Sullie. But my devotion, if you mean my love, was something she never wanted."

Mario glanced at his watch and said, "We should start if we are to see anything. I have a business appointment at four this afternoon with the manager of a gallery who shows smaller works of mine, bronze castings. We have until then. And you must allow time to rest and to dress for tonight."

"What happens?"

"Did not Sullie tell you? Tonight we attend the opera. I warn you, it is a state occasion when La Dama Hoffman arrives in splendor at Teatro la Fenice, whose stage—as the newspapers say—she has graced so often."

"I suppose everyone recognizes her?"

Mario grinned. "Everyone. And to make doubly sure, she takes Rajah with her wearing one of his famous collars. A prima donna might be forgotten, but not a jeweled ocelot. You may be certain La Hoffman will be recognized!''

We used the smaller of the motorboats, and for Mario the procedure of poling out of the docking entrance, turning into the little canal and then the Grand, seemed as natural as taking out the family car. He felt at home in the confusing water traffic of the canals, shouting "*A-Oel!*" to claim the right of way. He had not only the accent but also the aggressiveness of the native Venetian boatmen.

"First, we will take a moment to see the most delicate designs and colors in the city," he said, leaning back and steering with one hand while the other rested lightly on my shoulder.

"The Academy?" I asked, supposing he was talking about paintings. "The Guggenheim collection?"

Mario chuckled. "No. The most beautiful fish market in the world is near the Rialto Bridge. Everybody else goes there to buy, but I, being crazy, go to look at the silvers and pinks and aquamarines. Fish may not be perfume, but colors are where you find them."

The market *was* beautiful, and was probably the right introduction for what followed. I quickly learned that Mario's eye was keen but unconventional.

"The most graceful sculpture in Venice is not the fat horses at St. Mark's or those dead lions at the Arsenal. It is any gondola in the city." We stopped to inspect one, inch by inch. "So many woods go into these. Oak, walnut, cherry, elm," he explained. "They are perfect down to the smallest brass fitting. And the shape! I think of a wasp—graceful but sinister. Or a black water bird, smooth as a swan, but the steel prow makes a fiercer beak. It took more than a thousand years to arrive at this final design."

We visited none of the celebrated monuments and museums that day. I had seen the Doge's Palace and St. Mark's and Ca' d'Oro. "They are magnificent," Mario remarked, "but they are of another Venice, the public city."

Our route wound through backwaters, and in some places

the canals were so shallow that Mario shipped the motor and used a pole.

"Look at that studded door and the grills on those windows! We are not in Italy—this is the Orient."

So the morning passed and when the hour came for the long, leisurely lunch, Mario led me to a shadowy tavern that seemed to be a haunt of Arabs and lascars. But behind the tavern lay a concealed garden that might have been created for a sultan.

After our meal, Mario frowned and said, "The time has gone too quickly for me."

I nodded agreement and my smile concealed a sudden sense of loss. The day had been too precious to last, and several times I had asked myself if this was what it meant to be falling in love—this reckless surge of emotion that made the consequences seem so unimportant. Looking at him now, across the table in the garden, I could almost hear my prudent New England ancestors whisper warnings to me. He was intense and mercurial, and giving my affection to him was giving him the power to hurt me. Not only was he a stranger, but he was a storm, a torrent.

I thought I could read in his eyes that he cared for me. But how deeply? Soon, I supposed, I would lose him; his interest would fade. That I would face when the time came, but meanwhile I'd live from day to day, pretending he loved me and it was forever.

Mario rose. "One last stop," he said, "then I must take you back to the palazzo."

"What stop is that?"

"Not very interesting. A small shop where I will buy a gift for Konrad. It is difficult to give him anything, because he immediately buys anything he wants. So when I hear of something special, I buy it and keep it until the proper time."

"And you have heard of something special? What is it?" I asked.

"A pistol. Konrad is fond of guns."

* * *

There was no sign on the shop, only a tarnished nameplate tacked to the door saying, "J. Rossi." The window was chalky with dust and so curtained by cobwebs that it gave no clue about the room that lay behind it.

A wizened man with a pointed beard answered Mario's ring, peering at us through thick lenses. "*Ah, Don Mario,*" he murmured, bobbing his head in greeting. His voice was dry, breathy.

The dim room behind the door was stacked with curios of every variety: a rhino's head, ivory tusks, fans, canes, ancient locks and lanterns. More disturbing was the rear of the room, where a witchlike crone muffled in shawls presided over a cracked glass counter, on top of which sat a skull dotted with colored stones—Aztec, I supposed—and a collection of hideous masks. Seeing her reminded me that the first memories of Casanova, who was born in Venice, were of a witch chanting incantations while black cats slithered about and powders blazed.

"I'll wait outside," I whispered to Mario, and stepped to the door. The light breeze on the pavement felt heaven-sent after the mustiness of the shop.

On the other side of the canal at a short distance, I caught sight of the familiar figure of Esther Sullivan. But she was not, as usual, moving quickly and surely along with her head erect. Instead, she walked with slow steps, her eyes downcast. Just before Mario emerged from the shop, she disappeared into an arcade where a large sign with an arrow directed passersby to a flower market.

Mario carried a velvet-covered box, which he snapped open to reveal an antique pistol, double barreled and, to me at least, incredibly bulky and ugly. "He'll like it," said Mario. "It is different."

"You're already late for your appointment," I said, "and I just saw Miss Sullivan go into that flower market. You go on, and I'll come home with her."

"I am late," he agreed, "but let me at least take you across the canal."

"No, I'd really like to cross that stone bridge just ahead. I'll see you later." Then, keeping my tone light, I added, "Thank you for a wonderful day."

Drawing me to him, he pressed his lips against my hair. "*Ciao*, Catherine. Until tonight." Then he was gone.

I stood still, eyes closed, holding that moment in my memory, determined to always remember it exactly—his touch, his quiet breathing, the sound of his voice.

As I crossed the bridge, I felt like singing, and perhaps I did sing aloud, for several staid Venetian businessmen gave me puzzled looks. Or perhaps the radiance I felt inside showed. I hurried to the arcade, found the flower market, but didn't see Esther Sullivan. Then I realized that the arcade became a passage to another canal and lagoon.

When I reached the docking area, she was already seated in a gondola, moving swiftly away toward an island that was unfamiliar to me.

A little shell of a boat was moored nearby, and its owner, seeing my hesitation, called in English, "Taxi, lady?"

"Can you overtake that gondola?" I asked—an absurd question, for there lived no boatman in Venice who did not believe he could outdistance a battleship. My answer from this oarsman was a pitying look and a gesture to come aboard.

At the outset there seemed a remote hope of catching the swift gondola, but it vanished when a fleet of craft swept in from the mouth of the Grand Canal, preempting the lagoon between my boat and Miss Sullivan's gondola. The oarsman stopped rowing, doffed his cap, and crossed himself.

"They are bound for San Michele," said the boatman mournfully.

Then I realized the fleet was a funeral cortege and the island ahead was the huge San Michele cemetery. Leading the procession was a gilded barge propelled by men in black tam-o'-shanters. A figure of a lion weeping into a handkerchief decorated the bows, and at the stern stood an angel with a beard, a strangely winged St. Peter.

The fleet was decked with funereal crepe and tangled

plumes and sprays of flowers—fresh blossoms, as well as dusty ones made of paper. Jutting from the dark array of mourners and decorations, I saw a startling ensemble of brass instruments: a tuba, trumpets, and a French horn. A man in a black silk hat practiced silently on a trombone.

Our arrival at the San Michele landing was chaos and caco-phony—trumpets vying with trombones and the entire brass band struggling to drown out the groans of a portable electric organ that had arrived with an earlier cortege. I escaped from the crowd, mumbling apologies as I pushed my way among the milling people, and at last reached a quieter corner of the island. It was entirely an accident that I glanced through broad, open gates and saw Esther Sullivan.

She did not realize I was there, and I felt thankful when I saw her face. She looked waxen, and her steps were unnatu-ral, almost mechanical, as she moved along an overgrown path. I wouldn't have dreamed of intruding on her, and when I saw her halt to kneel at a large, marble tomb, I went quietly to the thicket of gnarled yew trees to wait, concealed, until she left.

As I followed the path she had taken, I realized what a strange cemetery this was. It held the feeling of an old, aban-doned New England graveyard, untended and run to weeds. Yet there was a richness in the thick grass, and the foliage softened the harsh outlines of granite and marble monuments. It was an old cemetery, but the tomb where Esther Sullivan had knelt still had the sheen of new marble. I slowly read the inscription.

LILLIAN ELSPETH DONATO

There was no epitaph except the dates of her birth and death. Only seventeen when she died; so young, I thought. She had not quite reached her birthday—March 19, according to the inscription. On the tomb lay a single white rose, Miss Sullivan's reason for pausing at the flower market.

Rising above the marble of the tomb was a sweep of

bronze—a flaring, winglike sculpture that could only be Mario's final gift to his sister. I turned away, following the path back toward the landing.

I was outside the gates when a thought came to me, and I said, half-aloud, "March nineteenth? Her birthday was March nineteenth?" Pandora had drowned on the twentieth of March, just one day after Lillian's birthday. A double measure of grief for Althea, for on the day before Pandora's death she must have thought of a celebration that was not held.

I found a gondola and gave the boatman the address of the palazzo. As we crossed the basin toward the city, I remembered what Mario had said about Esther Sullivan—that she had never wanted his devotion. Perhaps not, but today I knew she had loved Lillian Donato and would never cease mourning her death.

Chapter Twelve

Althea planned our arrival at the Teatro la Fenice that night with her infallible sense of timing.

Our party—the same group that had shared supper at the Villa Pellegrina only last week—appeared when the lobby was crowded, but not so close to curtain time that the audience was rushing to its seats. Althea swept through the entrance with Rajah, on a golden chain, padding a little ahead and the rest of us trailing like small craft in the wake of a liner.

The management, four men in evening dress, awaited her with a great sheaf of roses; not only a tribute to her past performances in this theatre, but a stratagem to delay her, to make sure she was observed and recognized. It did not harm business to have it told that La Hoffman was present for the opening of a *Carmen* by an almost unknown cast.

The lobby rang with applause for Althea. We were ogled at, inspected, and I realized Althea had been right in urging me to wear one of her flowing, theatrical cloaks. We couldn't avoid being part of a show, so we might as well live up to the public's expectations. Even the cloak's outrageous clips of counterfeit diamonds seemed appropriate, and I loved the brilliance of the solitaire—also on loan from Althea—that flashed at my throat, hanging on an all but invisible silver chain. "Anything, anything I own, to prevent you from wearing those unlucky opals," she had said.

When we were ushered into our box, a spotlight scanned the theatre for a moment, then settled on Althea, cueing more applause and shouts of adulation. She gestured, she threw delicate, graceful kisses, she clasped the roses as though moved to a deluge of tears. I heard Mario's dry chuckle. "All a *lemonade!*" he whispered, using the Italian slang word for a farce or pretense. "Both the star and the audience are playing a game, and they both love it."

Prince Luigi, grand in a silver pompadour tonight, served as Althea's escort. I was on Althea's left, next to Konrad and Giulia.

"Mario, you are to sit at the rear of the box," she said, banishing him. "Stay out of sight as much as possible. You never sit through *Carmen* and it is insulting to the artists when you constantly leave and return."

"I managed my first hundred *Carmens* with love and patience," he said. "I expect to be spared the dull parts of the second hundred."

Althea leaned toward me. "In the old days everyone wore masks at the opera in Venice. I should have loved that!"

I wondered how she could have endured not being instantly recognized, then realized that a mask would have changed nothing. She would have devised some banner for identification, some trademark—like Rajah, who now lay dozing at her feet, his tail occasionally swishing against my ankles.

Then the orchestra struck up the overture of the world's most popular opera, and from the first crescendo, the performance was enchantment for me. I loved the flaring zarzuela skirts, the chatter of the castanets, and the young mezzo who sang Carmen captured the audience with her verve and audacity.

In our box Prince Luigi kept one eye on the stage and the

other on Giulia—watching, I was sure, what headway she might be making with Konrad. Konrad himself appeared to enjoy her adoring gaze, yet seemed not fully captivated, which caused her to pout at moments—and she pouted very prettily. I avoided glancing at Esther Sullivan, who sat pale and silent in the shadows.

Althea, after keeping herself aloof at the beginning, gradually allowed her natural enthusiasm to carry her away. During the second act she rose to her feet to applaud the "Toreador Song." Clutching my arm, she exclaimed, "That young man gave it new life! Imagine! That old chestnut was exciting again! *Bravo!*"

When the act ended, she was breathless from cheering and applauding, but aglow. "These are wonderful young artists! We will give them a party, a celebration for their opening in Venice. Sullie, telephone the palazzo and tell the servants to expect the whole cast. Tell them to order food—those singers will be hungry as tigers. I always was! Send someone to San Marco to hire a band and waiters and—"

"I know what will be needed," Miss Sullivan said, and left.

Althea turned to Konrad. "My dear, go backstage and invite the cast and orchestra. Tell them I shall come back myself after the final curtain. We will make it like Carnival!"

During the dozen curtain calls after the last act, Althea created a sensation by hurling her bouquet of roses to the stage, where it landed at the feet of the surprised young mezzo who had sung Carmen. A few minutes later we went backstage, where Althea embraced the singers and urged them to come to the palazzo. "We are calling it a carnival, so wear your costumes if you like."

In little more than an hour, the servants at the palazzo had transformed the great ballroom. A hundred candles sparkled in the chandelier, broad ribbons of gaily colored silk streamed from the balcony railings, and someone must have bought the entire cargo of a flower barge. Miss Sullivan had found a basket filled with masks, leftovers from a Mardi Gras celebration.

After doing some quick flower arrangements, I helped Althea greet the singers and musicians—speaking Italian, English, and trying to summon my schoolgirl French. In a few minutes the party had turned into a costume ball, and not all the costumes were Spanish. The star of the evening, Carmen, appeared dressed for *Samson et Dalila,* her assignment the following week. The singer's entrance caused a burst of applause, led by Althea.

It was when dancing began that I realized Mario had disappeared. Konrad, deserting Giulia for the moment, was passing and I asked if he had seen Mario.

"No, and do not bother to search for him. He is known to vanish from large parties." Konrad took my hand. "How lovely you look, Catherine. I have never seen you wear red before. You must buy three more dresses that color."

"Thank you. Everything I'm wearing is borrowed from Althea," I said.

"And fits you perfectly—which is no small compliment to Althea. Come, let us dance."

"Will Giulia permit that?" I asked with mock innocence.

Konrad's eyes twinkled. "She is already cross with me and trying to make me jealous by flirting with the baritone who sang Escamillo tonight."

"And are you jealous?"

"Of a baritone from Teatro la Fenice? This is a game Giulia plays, nothing more."

I could not remember when I had last danced, but with Konrad as a partner I quickly gained confidence. Moving smoothly and gracefully himself, he somehow made me feel that I, too, had such talent. When the orchestra paused, someone from the *Carmen* company began to play a concertina, a boisterous Sicilian tarantella which I had once learned in a college folk dance group.

"This is an Italian dance," Konrad explained. "It comes from Naples and Sicily. Watch me, I will teach you."

"Thank you," I said.

A moment later Konrad was laughing as he clapped his hands. "*Prodigioso!* You are secretly a Sicilian!"

Afterwards, breathless, we took glasses of champagne to a quieter corner of the room. "To my dear Catherine," he said, toasting me. "We will run away to Paris and become Sicilian dancers in Montmartre."

I did not see Prince Luigi approaching until he interrupted us. "You seem to be enjoying yourselves," he remarked, with a smile as patently false as his wig.

"How could I not enjoy myself with Konrad present?" I replied, baiting him.

A waiter came through the crowd and said to Konrad, "A telephone call for you, *signor.*"

"At this hour?" Konrad was irritated. "And no telephone on this floor. Tell the person to call tomorrow."

"The operator spoke of an emergency," replied the waiter.

"Very well." Konrad shrugged and excused himself.

"The emergency is doubtless some lonely lady in Paris or Rome," Prince Luigi said. "Konrad's small intrigues span several oceans."

"Such fascinating gossip," I said. Italians of Prince Luigi's age and rank were reputedly insidious, but these efforts to steer me away from Konrad could hardly have been more obvious.

"As an old friend of Althea's, I warned your sister not to take Konrad seriously. I felt desolate later when he dropped her so coldly."

"I am a little older than Pandora and much wiser," I said. "For instance, tonight when Konrad asked me to go to Paris with him, I understood his intentions completely."

The outraged expression of Prince Luigi's face was well worth the small deception. His reply, however, was drowned out by a loud thunderclap that reverberated over the city, and at that moment the skies began to pour—one of those sudden nocturnal storms that seem to drown Venice in a matter of minutes.

The rain signaled the breaking up of the party. Guests hurried to catch covered launches or gondolas, and I left Prince Luigi for the ballroom doors, where Althea was bidding the *Carmen* singers goodnight. Seeing Konrad, I asked, "Was the telephone call a major emergency?"

"Apparently not. The caller had hung up by the time I answered."

Giulia approached, smiling brilliantly at Konrad, obviously ready for a warm reconciliation. I wondered if Prince Luigi might be more clever than I'd believed. Probably he had bribed the waiter to bring a false telephone message, thus neatly ending my conversation with Konrad.

A few minutes later, the last guest having departed, I started up the stairs toward my bedroom, tired but not sleepy. Just off the first landing was a huge, rather dusty room with bookshelves from floor to ceiling; a forbidding library with its stacks of yellowed manuscripts, but I supposed it must contain some readable book. The room was dark when I entered except for a single pool of light from a hooded desk lamp. Mario, his face in the shadows, sat at a table spread with papers and folios, most of them yellow with age. Nearby stood a decanter and a half-filled brandy glass. He still wore the dinner jacket he had put on for the opera, but the tie had been removed and his shirt was open at the collar.

"Buona sera," he said. "The party has ended?"

"Yes. We missed you."

He shrugged. "I have attended too many of these tribal entertainments for singers. Too many people and all of them chattering about themselves." Mario lifted his hands in a gesture of dismissal. "No, that is not completely true. At times I enjoy such things. Tonight my mood was wrong."

"I hope I'm not interrupting," I said, indicating the papers on the table. "I came for something to read."

"It is no interruption. I was looking through old records of the Castle Malaspina for details about the pilgrim legend—old maps, and plans. Such work needs a Latin scholar. Besides, tonight my mind wanders; I cannot concentrate." He turned on a dim overhead light. "If you want a book, the newer ones are on the shelves beside the door."

As I searched for a book in English, I was conscious of his gaze upon me and of the silence in the library. There was no sound except a patter of rain against the shutters. I selected a thin volume of short stories. "These seem to be cheerful," I said.

"Will you join me for a brandy?" He gestured toward a fan-back chair near him at the table.

"I'll join you, but not for brandy. They were serving champagne at the party. The combination might be dangerous."

"Ah, yes! Dangerous!" he smiled and there was light mockery in his voice. "You must not do anything dangerous. Pandora told me how cautious you are. I have always thought caution was a dull virtue, but today and tonight I find that I myself am trying to be cautious."

I looked at him, saying nothing, trying to understand this change of mood. At the opera he had been quiet, but had seemed to enjoy the performance; now restlessness was upon him—I could sense indecision, a conflict of emotions.

"Pandora has been in my thoughts tonight," he murmured, lifting his glass. "I must tell you something honestly, Catherine. I believe I am responsible for Pandora's death."

"What do you mean?" I asked sharply.

"I was angry with Pandora that last morning. The night before, I had talked with the man she had been married to, the American who was staying at the villa until the next day."

"Gordon Carr," I said.

"*Si*. He told me many things—how he had expected to marry you, Catherine, but was blinded by Pandora. He expected to find you again when he returned to America. Do you know he is still in love with you?"

"I doubt that," I said. "Probably he's imagining the past as he wishes to see it." There had been a time when the words Mario had just spoken about Gordon would have set my heart racing. Now I only wondered if they might be true.

"I felt this *Signor* Carr was a good man, and Pandora had

treated him badly. The next morning Pandora irritated me by trying to play some mysterious game. She seemed to be accusing me—I don't know what she meant, but I think she meant I had been stealing from the kitchen at night. Some childish nonsense like that to attract attention to herself. Then she began to talk about wanting to go sailing, and I lost my temper. I remembered how she behaved about boats in Venice, so I challenged her, dared her. I taunted her by saying she had never sailed in her life—that she'd been lying. And so I think I drove her to sail out in the yawl. I have been haunted by that worry."

"You're mistaken, I'm sure of it," I told him. "Believe me, no words on earth could have driven her." Again Mario had surprised me. I had not thought of him as a man who would look back and examine his own conduct, who would be concerned long afterwards about his harshness toward Pandora.

Mario rose, moved to the window, and opened the shutters. The rain had slackened; he stood gazing into the darkness.

"Have you thought of your future, Catherine?" he asked. "I do not suppose you will stay forever at the villa."

"No, I suppose not," I said carefully.

"You should go back to America," he said abruptly. "Find this professor who loves you and marry him."

My voice seemed to choke in my throat. I thought of Mario this morning, face glowing as he found a favorite canal. I remembered his hand brushing against mine, and a certain smile I had hoped was for me alone. Then my pride came to my rescue, and I said calmly, "Is that what you would like me to do?"

"No, not what I would like." He still did not face me. "It is what I think is best for you. This American is—what is the word I want? Reasonable. *Si*, he is reasonable. And if not him, there are other men like him who would love you. He would never hurt you, never cause you alarm. He would have no black, impossible days—times when he had to be alone. Life for you would be orderly, calm."

"Thank you," I said, rising to leave. "But my future need not concern you."

He turned sharply toward me, a flash of anger in his eyes. "Concern? Do you think this has cost me nothing? Since this morning, I have been struggling to understand myself, trying to know what I am able to give and what is impossible for me. Catherine, I have no interest in a pale summertime love affair."

"Nor have I." My eyes returned his challenge.

He went to the table, refilled his glass. "I am going to finish my work at the museum quickly. Then I will travel to Switzerland for a few days, perhaps for a week."

"Why Switzerland?"

"I have a *capanna*—in English I think you call it a hut—on a mountain lake. It is a wild, deserted place. The mountains tower around it and when I am there, my own problems seem small. I want to think about what is important in my life." He moved nearer, took my hand. "And I hope that you, too, will think."

"A moment ago you told me I was cautious," I said. "Now it seems you are the one who is frightened of risks."

"Frightened?" He smiled slowly. "*Si.* I did not expect to fall in love with you, Catherine. We saw each other at the villa, but it is only yesterday we really met. I do not want you to give your love to a stranger. Let us be sure—sure enough for a lifetime."

Then suddenly he was holding me in his arms, gazing into my eyes. "Catherine," he whispered, "Catherine!"

When I entered my room that night, I was not filled with the wild elation people attempt to describe when they talk of finding themselves in love and believe that their love will be returned. My happiness was warm and deep, but quietly certain. With Mario I felt so many things: excitement, a sense of mysterious promise, and a glow of affection ready to burst into flame. He had been right when he said, just before I left him, "We will be friends before we are lovers."

I found myself smiling and humming a melody from *Carmen* as I stood at the long mirror, taking off the solitaire borrowed from Althea. I was putting it safely away in a drawer that locked when I realized I'd left Althea's cloak on a downstairs coatrack. For a moment I considered going to retrieve it, then decided there was no need. I prepared for bed, thinking again of Mario and of how suddenly and unexpectedly we had found each other—had discovered feelings that would become, I was sure, a deepening love.

The palazzo had been built in the days before anyone thought of clothes closets, and every bedchamber was furnished with a tall standing wardrobe chest—those spacious cabinets that lovers and sometimes husbands use for concealment in Italian farces and folk tales. I opened the doors of mine to hang up Althea's red dress, and my eyes widened.

On the inside of one of the doors, where I could not fail to notice it, was the opera cloak, its hanger attached to a hook. Just as obvious as the cloak itself was the absence of one of the star-shaped diamond clips Althea had put on the high collar to give bolder decoration.

Alarmed, I dropped to my knees, searching the floor of the wardrobe. I remembered stories of jewel thieves haunting parties given by the rich, and felt thankful that the solitaire, at least, was secure. But how valuable was the clip?

"Counterfeit diamonds and a few real chips," Althea had said. "But the trick is in the settings. They're set in silver like real stones." In other words, the star clip was expensive.

Then I realized that a thief would have taken both clips, not just one. This was an accident; somehow the star had fallen off and a maid, who must have brought the cloak upstairs, hadn't noticed. Putting on a robe, I began to retrace my steps, certain that both the stars had been in place when I'd arrived home from the opera.

The storm had resumed, and just as I touched the knob of my door, a bolt of lightning followed by a thunderclap made the lights flicker ominously. I took a candle and matches from the dresser—a wise precaution, not because the electricity failed, but because all the lights had been turned out by servants and the switches seemed placed in the most unlikely locations.

The winding corridors of the palazzo were eerie in the darkness; the wind seemed to breathe and whisper in the stairwells, while torrents gushed from the eave spouts outside with a muffled roar. A sudden icy draft extinguished the candle, and I stood midway on the stairs, almost holding my breath, telling myself I was not a child to be afraid of the dark. My matches would not strike on the slick, damp marble of the balustrade or on the wall, and the stairs themselves were covered with thick carpet.

Then, as I groped in the darkness, I had a strange sensation that I was not alone, that someone else moved quietly near me. Apprehensive now, I listened without making the least sound, then moved downward a step, then another, still straining to catch any unnatural noise.

By the time I reached a landing, I had almost decided it was nothing more than the gloomy atmosphere playing upon my imagination; then I heard an unmistakable rustle, a stealthy movement. Summoning up my courage, I called, "Who is it? *Quién vive?*"

No answer came but the mocking echo of my own voice. Then lightning flashed and just ahead I saw a landing and a doorway that I thought led to the balcony of the ballroom. I went quickly forward and a match flamed when I struck it on the wood of the door.

The gleam of the candle restored my confidence. Light, even a small flickering light, meant safety, because no one could approach without my knowing. Including the servants, there were more than a dozen people sleeping in the palazzo. If threatened, I had only to cry out. But why should I even think of being threatened? I reproached myself. The drafty palazzo in the dark of a thunderstorm was dismal, the strangled breath of the wind in the corridors could unnerve anyone; but I had no real reason for fear.

In the entrance hall at the bottom of the stairs, I found a line of light switches set in the wall just above the wainscoting, and a moment later a pair of bracket lamps dispelled the darkness. Another switch turned on the light in the cloakroom to my left. Still holding the lighted candle, I entered the long, narrow room and inspected the empty rack of hangers. Nothing had fallen to the floor. As I turned to leave, an explosion of thunder so violent it seemed to shake the walls burst overhead.

Where else had I worn the cape? Where, in fact, had I taken it off?—for I remembered carrying it to the cloakroom. Then it came back to me that immediately upon arriving at the palazzo from the opera, I had gone into the pantry to see if Esther Sullivan needed help in arranging the huge bouquets of flowers. I'd removed the cape, and Miss Sullivan had taken it from me and draped it neatly over the back of a chair. That must have been when the clip had come loose, and I hadn't noticed when I took it to the cloakroom later.

In the hall, I tried every light switch before remembering that the ballroom was illuminated only by the huge chandelier with its hundred candles and by a dozen or so wall sconces.

Holding my own candle high, I crossed the threshold of the ballroom—hesitant, moving cautiously, although I'd heard no other strange sounds. But the room, yawning like an enormous black cavern, seemed to hold an unknown threat—a feeling of menace I could neither define nor identify. Unlike the rest of the palazzo, the ballroom was floored with wood; hard, thin strips of board set in a way to make the surface springy for dancing. Now it felt unsteady, and it creaked at every step.

Above, in pitch darkness, rain pelted the slates and lantern glass of the high ballroom dome. In the lower part of the room, a hall lamp, set low in the wall, cast a long, narrow patch of light through the open doors and dimly illuminated the floor almost to the center. Even so, the violence of the storm and the unaccountable atmosphere of danger were enough to make me abandon my search. I had no intention of crossing the long room to reach the pantry.

But then I caught sight of something sparkling brilliantly ahead of me. I stretched out my arm so the beam of the candle was cast forward, then sighed audibly with relief. It was all so easy to explain; there was no cause for alarm, and there had been no jewel thief.

In the center of the ballroom, where it could not possibly be missed, stood the chair from the pantry, and on the top rung of its back, the star clip twinkled in the candlelight.

I could easily understand what must have happened. While cleaning after the party, a servant must have found it near the chair and, not recognizing it, placed it where it was certain to be found. Now the clip was waiting for me, an inviting twinkle in the gloom. I moved quickly toward it, and started to reach out. I had at that moment no feeling of alarm, not the least sense of impending danger.

I can never be sure of exactly what happened. I think I heard a sound, a faint clank of metal above me or perhaps from the balcony. I only know that some noise warned me. I remember a flash of lightning and an almost simultaneous roar of thunder as Rajah bounded out of the darkness, startling me so that I leaped back with a cry as he brushed silently past. I tripped, fell to the floor, twisting my ankle painfully and dropping the candle, which sputtered out.

Then I thought the dome of the ballroom had been struck by lightning. A deafening crash rang in my ears, the floor buckled, and I thought it was going to give way as a piece of splintered wood struck my shoulder and cheek. My head throbbed, and I seemed to remember striking it on the floor when I fell. There was stillness then, until a voice far away in the house shouted something.

For a moment I lay numb, shocked, not understanding what had happened. Light still spilled in from the hall, but it was dim; I could make out nothing. Very clearly I heard a creaking of metal, as though a rusty hinge had closed. Fumbling for the extinguished candle, my hand touched cold metal—something thick and round like a pipe. But that was impossible; there was nothing made of metal in the center of the ballroom.

Suddenly the numbness vanished. I realized a huge shape loomed beside me in the darkness, and searching wildly, I found a match in the pocket of my robe. There were voices and footsteps approaching as I struck the match on the floor, and in the flaring light I saw what had happened.

The huge chandelier had crashed down from the ceiling, crushing the pantry chair, its points and sharp edges slashing through the surface of the floor in the exact spot where I had been standing—only inches away from where I now lay.

It was then I screamed.

Chapter Thirteen

It was afternoon when I awakened, and at first the room was blurred, out of focus. My head ached, and my eyes so resisted the light that it took a conscious effort to force them open. When I did, and the haze cleared, I found myself lying in a bed gazing up at a tapestry used as a canopy. Although I was too groggy to wonder where I was, I foolishly kept trying to remember which Titian painting was copied in the tapestry's figures.

A voice said softly, "Catherine?"

"Yes," I answered, turning my face toward it.

Althea sat in a great winged chair beside the bed, a book in her lap, and I had the impression she'd been sitting there a very long time. Had I awakened before?

Her smile was gentle—suddenly she seemed very young, and I could not tell why this should be, because her face was drawn and her eyes were rimmed with red. She left the chair, went away, then returned with towels, a face cloth, and a basin of wonderfully cool water.

"I don't understand," I said. "I don't remember what happened, how I came here."

"You're not quite awake, dear. We gave you two of my sleeping pills last night to calm you. You're not used to them, and they're quite strong."

"Lightning," I said. "Now I remember. I was in the ballroom when it was struck by lightning. The chandelier fell."

Slowly my memory was returning. I realized there was a small bandage on my cheek where I had been cut by the splintering floor, and I shuddered.

"No, it was not lightning," said Althea. "The chandelier was on a chain so it could be lowered to light the candles. The hook where the chain is attached on the balcony somehow came loose. We think it was jarred by the thunder."

Lighting a spirit lamp, she made me a steaming cup of strong tea, and as I gratefully drank it, the details of the night gradually came back.

"What we don't understand, Catherine," she said, "is how you came to be alone in the ballroom at such an hour. Were you walking in your sleep?"

"No, I was looking for a clip." And I told her about my search, and how Rajah's alarming dash across the room had saved me from being crushed by the falling chandelier. "But I must have told you all this last night," I said.

She shook her head. "Don't you remember? Mario went into one of his classic rages and insisted you were too weak to answer questions."

I nodded, vaguely remembering, then fell asleep again.

Dr. Tasso, a neighbor, made an inventory of my injuries early that evening after I'd been moved back to my own room. "As I thought last night," he said. "Mild concussion from the fall, a twisted ankle that will be troublesome for a little while, and a scratched cheek. What has made you ill today, besides shock, is the sleeping drug given you last night. Much too strong! I would have forbidden it." He left, clicking his tongue at the follies of people with sedatives.

A few minutes after the doctor had gone, there was a tap on

the door and Mario entered. "What did the doctor say, my dear Catherine?"

"Only a mild concussion."

He moved a chair near the bed, but instead of sitting, paced the length of the room. "Althea told me about the missing clip. I found it this afternoon beneath the chandelier. Like the chair, it was smashed to bits." Mario leaned against the wardrobe, his face grave. "A strange thing. Sullie is the one who brought the cloak to your room. During the party she thought it might not be safe downstairs with so many strangers in the house. She is sure both clips were in place when she left it in this room."

"But that's impossible!" I exclaimed. "That would mean someone entered my room and—"

"*Si*. That is exactly what it would mean. Now tell me the story again. You must remember every detail."

When I had finished, he said, "It is peculiar. All the servants deny placing the clip on the chair in the ballroom. The entire thing seems to have been arranged, arranged so carefully."

"But that doesn't make sense," I protested. "There was a good chance I might not have noticed the clip was missing, and an even better chance that I wouldn't have searched for it until morning."

He shrugged his shoulders. "If some person was arranging an accident, he had nothing to lose. If you had not gone downstairs, you would have found the clip today in the cloakroom. Then a new lure would have been tried." Mario sat in the bedside chair, leaning forward, intent. "Catherine, have there been other things like this? Accidents or narrow escapes?"

"No," I said, then corrected myself. "Yes. When I was exploring near the museum, someone had taken away the warning signs from the chapel. If it hadn't been for Miss Sullivan, I don't know what might have happened." I clearly remembered her strength, her quiet voice urging me to safety.

For a moment we were both silent, both of us searching for answers we could not find.

"I think if someone wanted to harm me, I'd know it," I

said. "I don't feel that from anyone here except Prince Luigi. When I'm near him, I have a sense of evil. I'm afraid of him. But, of course, he wasn't in the palazzo after the party."

"There is a door that goes to his apartment," said Mario. "It is supposed to be locked on both sides, but you can be sure he has keys to everything." He rose, seeming to have reached a sudden decision. "I am taking you back to the lake. I do not like these connecting doors. There are too many empty rooms, too many stairways no one uses."

"You are serious about this!" I said, surprised. "You really think it was planned?"

"On the contrary, I feel almost sure what happened was quite accidental. But to be almost sure is not sure enough."

"How will you explain our leaving to Althea?"

Mario smiled. "I will not explain. I will only say we wish to return to the lake. Who knows? Perhaps the idea will please her."

As it turned out, the next morning when Mario mentioned the Villa Pellegrina, Althea announced her own intention of returning there. "The accident has unnerved me," she said. "I will be happy not to be here when the remains of the chandelier are hauled away and electricity is installed in that room."

We were a smaller party leaving than we had been arriving. Konrad decided to remain in Venice a few days, and seemed to have rather indefinite plans about sailing in a forthcoming regatta.

As the launch, piled high with luggage, drew away from the palazzo, Althea took my hand and said, "I am sorry this terrible accident spoiled your holiday in Venice, Catherine. I had hoped everything would be perfect."

"Venice was good for me," I answered. "I want to come back soon."

"We will," said Mario.

During the first few days after our return to the Villa Pellegrina, disturbing memories of those few minutes in the dark ballroom in Venice would suddenly force their way into my memory. I recalled the metallic sound I had heard just before the chandelier crashed down. The creak of a hinge on the balcony door? Someone entering or leaving? Perhaps the sound of a hook being twisted and loosened.

I did not welcome such disturbing thoughts, but as the peaceful days at the villa continued, they came to me less frequently.

During those quiet days, I learned what Mario had meant the night he told me he was "not reasonable." Absorbed in finishing his work, he practically lived in the entrance hall of the museum. I saw little of him that week, and when he did emerge from the castle, he seemed distant and preoccupied. But then he would suddenly smile, aware of me and of the world again.

Now I had a regular visitor; the child Lisa, who came almost daily for a drawing lesson. I remember particularly the morning I learned she knew no fairy tales. It was unthinkable to me that a child should grow up without Cinderella and Snow White, so that day I decided to tell a story and draw simple illustrations. I chose *Hansel and Gretel* as the first story—inspired, I suppose, by the music box in my room upstairs.

". . . And so Hansel filled his pockets with white pebbles, and every few steps he would drop one. That night, when the moon rose over the forest, the shining stones marked the way home."

"*Bella!*" said Lisa, wide-eyed. "What a clever boy. Also, it is a pretty picture, the stones in the moonlight. When I learn more, I am going to draw that."

Our lesson over for the day and the story to be continued, Lisa left me. I opened my own sketchbook and again studied the project Althea had asked me to do for the museum.

It was, of course, impossible not to have a statue of Althea herself displayed in one of those minitheaters in the part of the museum that Mario and I now irreverently called "the waxworks." But which of her many operatic roles should be shown? *Tosca* was the popular favorite, but her greatest critical acclaim had been won in *La Gioconda*. Althea shrewdly decided to choose neither. She would not be shown in an opera, but as herself, younger, giving a song recital. The display would also score a professional point for Althea: Only a few singers have been equally successful in opera and on the recital platform. Althea was one of them.

"But what for a background?" Althea demanded. "I know plain draperies, velour or the like, would be correct. Oh, so dull!" The next day she proposed a solution. I was to attempt a backdrop of clouds and mists based on the portrait of Althea in the living room.

During the past three days I'd been making sketches, and now, as I added a little more shading, I felt ready to begin on the canvas itself.

I heard the slap of espadrilles on the terrace and looked up to see Mario approaching. Clearly, he had just come from working; there was a streak of white marble dust in his hair and a white patch on his left forearm.

"*Buon giorno, cara.*" He seemed full of energy and good spirits as he took a deck chair next to mine.

"You're taking a few minutes from your work? I can't believe it," I said.

"I am so close to finishing that a few minutes will not matter. How good it is to be close to my liberation from that musty building! I am so happy about it that even the annoyances of the morning have not bothered me."

"What annoyances?"

"Some of my tools were missing. Four very good chisels that will bring good money in a pawnshop." He shrugged. "I will charge the museum for them—let Konrad pay, he can afford it. Have you seen him today?"

"No. I didn't know he'd returned from Venice."

"*Si.* Late last night. He brought some interesting news. Before we left Venice I hired a young man, a Latin scholar, to study the documents about Castle Malaspina. He told Konrad he has already found ancient accounts of the pilgrim legend that mention dungeons and tunnels. He wants us to search the villa, because he has found clues that the entrances are not from the castle but from the 'outer building'—which must be the villa.''

"Does the villa have cellars? I'd never thought of it.''

"Only a small wine cellar off the kitchen. It is kept locked, but Miss Sullivan and the cook have keys. And I have a key because if I am working late at night, sometimes I go to get a bottle of wine. A glass or two before going to bed calms me after—'' Mario broke off speaking, sat for a moment lost in thought, and then murmured, "Pandora. That must have been what she meant. But how strange!''

"What is it?'' I asked.

"Remember I told you that Pandora, just before she disappeared from the villa, said something puzzling to me? I paid little attention, and her exact words still do not come back to me. She said she was the only one who knew what I was doing in the kitchen at night. Something about knowing the truth.'' Mario frowned, concentrating. "I thought it was nonsense because I never go into the kitchen except early in the morning. But I do go through the kitchen for wine. Not often, perhaps once a month. No, it still makes no sense.''

"What makes no sense?'' It was Konrad who spoke, entering from the open doors of the villa. He wore a blazer with a club's insignia and a floppy bow tie.

When Mario repeated what Pandora had told him, Konrad's face showed surprise. "How peculiar! She said almost the same words to me. It seemed to be a warning, or even a threat. Since I did not understand at all, I took it for an American joke. American jokes are seldom clear to me.''

None of us could find an explanation, and after a few minutes of futile cross-questioning, Mario left, saying he intended to examine the wine cellar for any concealed entrance.

"That's an attractive blazer you're wearing,'' I remarked to Konrad. "What club is it?''

"A target-shooting group. I am interested in handguns, are you?''

"I'm afraid not."

Konrad leaned against the marble balustrade, his back to the blue of the lake. Behind him the broad expanse of water was choppy, touched with foam as a breeze stirred it. "I am sorry you are not fond of pistols." Konrad fussed with his necktie. "I hoped to lure you with an offer of seeing my collection."

"I wouldn't know what I was seeing," I told him.

He smiled. "Very well. But can I lure you to retie this bow for me? I am awkward at such things, especially without a mirror."

"Of course."

I stepped close to him and began reknotting the silk. His gray eyes had a twinkle in them. "Every man should have a beautiful woman to manage his bow ties."

"What a fulfilling career, Konrad!"

He leaned closer to me. "You could do worse."

"Maybe I can do better," I said, turning away. I gathered up my sketch book and the pastels I had been working with.

"Are you starting the backdrop today?" he asked.

"Yes, I believe I'm ready."

"Good. This afternoon I will come to the museum."

I shook my head. "Don't bother. You'll see nothing but some charcoal lines."

"Nevertheless, I intend to be present at the creation." Then the lightness vanished from his tone as he added, "Everything in the museum is of great concern to me. After all, it *is* a monument to my father—although at moments that fact seems forgotten."

Progress on the backdrop was more rapid than I had dared hope, and I was proud of the composition that was emerging, although I realized that for the most part I was merely copying and enlarging another artist's work. But what I did was skillful—and skill, I knew, was no small matter.

Late that afternoon I left the long corridor housing the showcase stages, crossed the large hall devoted to curious and historic musical instruments, and climbed the stairway to the offices. No one was at the desks, but I heard voices in the studio next door and found Esther Sullivan there with Konrad and Mario. They were gathered at a workbench, examining a crude map. Mario was speaking Italian.

"The walls of the wine cellar are solid," he told his listeners. "Perhaps something lies behind them, but there are no doors. I tested carefully."

Miss Sullivan noticed me. "Good afternoon, Catherine. What may I do for you?" Always, I thought, that polite formality.

"Tomorrow morning I'll begin working with color," I said. "I need a swatch of the actual material of the dress for the figure of Althea. I want to have the exact tint."

"Of course. By the way," she reached into the pocket of her smock and produced an envelope. "One of the maids brought this from the villa a few minutes ago. It's for you."

Mario glanced at it and smiled. "From your young drawing student, Lisa, I would guess. I am surprised she knows any letters at all."

My name was printed in large, awkward capitals with red crayon, and spelled with a "K" instead of a "C." I knew it could not be from Lisa, who always addressed me as "*Signorina.*" Inside I found a smudged scrap of paper and gasped as I read the words.

GO AWAY OR YOU WILL BE *KILLED* LIKE I SAW YOUR SISTER BE KILLED.

Silently I handed the message to Mario. "*Per l'amore di Dio!* What madness is this?"

Miss Sullivan glanced at it and paled.

Konrad took the note from Mario, read it, and said, "It is nonsense. You should not give this a serious thought."

He started to crumple the paper, but I caught his hand in time. "No, this is serious. It should go to the police."

"The police?" He looked thunderstruck. "But that is impossible! You cannot do such a thing."

"Why not?" I demanded.

"Listen to me, Catherine!" He spoke quietly, but with an intensity I'd never realized he possessed. "We are friends and I am fond of you. But now I warn you; if you take that paper to the police, you will lose a friend and gain an enemy." He still held the note, and before I could prevent it, he twisted the paper and thrust it into his pocket. Ignoring my protest, Konrad strode from the room.

Mario caught my arm. "Catherine, don't you understand? He thinks this note was written by his mother."

"Of course she wrote it," said Miss Sullivan. "Ilse has sent many insane messages like this to Althea. You must remember she is only a pathetic madwoman."

"It says Pandora was killed," I reminded her. "Ilse, or whoever wrote it, claims to be a witness."

"I am sorry, Catherine, but this was written by Ilse. I have seen such notes before," said Mario. "She is Konrad's mother, and we can do nothing." There was no mistaking the finality of his tone.

I looked from Mario to Miss Sullivan. Both of them were shaken, but when it came to protecting Konrad they would be unyielding, and I knew that for the moment there was nothing I could do. But this, I promised myself, was not the end of the matter.

That evening Althea gave an informal supper for the Wilsons, an American couple who lived in Rome but had taken a lakeside house for the summer, hoping to escape the heat. George and Alice Wilson, Althea told me, were both musicians; she a violinist, he a very successful teacher of voice.

When they arrived at the villa, I instantly recognized George Wilson as the singer who had performed the role of the doctor in the ill-fated *Macbeth*. His features, as grave and fatherly in life as on the television tape, brought unwelcome memories of Bart Hutchinson and that terrible hour in Venice. Nor was I especially happy to see Prince Luigi and Giulia again. The other guests were two German couples who spoke neither Italian nor English and a tenor from La Scala who seemed not to speak at all.

Because of the warm weather, supper was served on the terrace at a cluster of café tables. Seated next to George Wilson, I tried to make conversation, but my mind kept returning to the anonymous message of the afternoon and my apparent inability to do anything about it. Mario, at another table, caught my eye and smiled, but shook his head in sympathy as though to say, "I know, it has upset you, but we can do nothing."

I realized Mr. Wilson was speaking and I forced myself to pay attention.

"As a vocal coach I helped your mother prepare many a recital and recording," he said. "And in opera, I sang several supporting roles in Hoffman vehicles. Besides a great voice, she had an unusual acting ability."

"Why speak of me in the past tense, George," said Althea, and it was less a question than an accusation. "Schumann-Heink was magnificent at the Metroplitan when she was sixty-eight! Then there was Melba, superb at the age I am now. Why put me in the past?"

Mario spoke quietly. "But why not, Mother? In the past is where you have chosen to live.

"*Touché.*" Althea's smile was thin.

To fill an embarrassed silence, George Wilson quickly said, "One remarkable thing about Althea onstage is that she never, never varies. Of course, there are always certain emotional or vocal changes, but once a movement or a gesture is established in rehearsal, you can count on her. There are no surprises to confuse you; once a thing is set, it remains set."

Wilson's determined stress on the present tense did not help, and again conversation died. The four Germans suddenly burst into laughter about some German matter.

"We'll have coffee and cognac inside," said Althea, rising. "The night is cool enough now."

As we moved toward the living room, Mario said to me softly, "Please, *cara*. I know it was disturbing to you, but think how much worse for Konrad."

"Of course." But Konrad was not the one who had been threatened, and I could not understand why everyone insisted upon Ilse as author of the note. There was no proof at all.

Richard Halpin had seated himself at the piano and was quietly playing music from *The Thirteenth Pilgrim*; I recognized the overture, then the processional chorus. No one was paying attention until suddenly a clear, bell-like soprano began an aria.

> I am a stranger in this land,
> A pilgrim on a lonely road . . .

The room fell silent but for the quiet piano and Althea's unfaltering voice, silver and crystal—that of a young girl, a youthful pilgrim singing of Alpine lakes and forests. I listened transfixed and spellbound, understanding her true greatness for the first time.

When the last note had faded and we stood around her applauding and cheering, I saw tears course down her cheeks. Then I realized that I, too, was weeping—and so was Mario. I remembered he had said there are times when we have no speech but tears, and this was such a time.

"I have been working in secret," Althea said, when finally she could be heard. "I did not intend to sing tonight, but they—" She flashed Mario a smile of triumph. "—I have never been one to ignore a challenge."

Miss Sullivan had gone to the kitchen to order champagne for a toast to Althea. I was just giving Althea my own congratulations when she returned, her expression troubled, and spoke so that only Althea and I could hear. "I'm sorry to tell you I've discovered something unpleasant. In the kitchen I caught sight of Angela, the girl who helps the cook, using the pantry telephone. She seemed furtive, so I went to the hall and listened on the extension.''

Althea clicked her tongue. "And you heard a wicked, sizzling chat with her boyfriend. Really, Sullie, you cannot purify everyone's morals.''

"Not immorality, but treachery," replied Miss Sullivan. "She was reporting to Ilse Donato. She described the sudden recovery of your voice, and gave a list of our guests. Ilse thanked her and told her to come for her money on Saturday evening as usual.''

I expected Althea to explode in rage, but apparently she would let nothing mar the evening. "How irritating!" She shook her head. "But do not discharge the girl. Ilse would simply bribe whoever replaced her, and this way we know who is the spy. Now let us enjoy our celebration!" And she whirled into the room, laughing.

Sleep would not come to me that night. Perhaps it was the excitement of Althea's recovery, of her being able to sing for the first time since Lillian's death; but more likely it was that I could not put the note, with its blunt threat of death, from my mind. I was not alarmed by it, for I doubted that anyone seriously bent on harming me would sound so clear a warning. But the hatred conveyed in the few words seemed so brutal and the reference to Pandora's death so disturbing.

The doors to the balcony stood open, and although there was no hint of a breeze, I decided I might find it cooler outside.

The Villa Pellegrina lay in silent darkness, the moon obscured by clouds whose promise of cooling rain rain seemed unkept tonight. I leaned back in my chair, watching the flicker of fireflies, trying to convince myself that I was growing drowsy. And I succeeded, for I was on the point of dozing when I heard the music.

It was faint, so faint that at first I thought I might be imagining the sound. Then I decided a radio was playing far away, possibly on the mountain road. But it grew slightly louder—a piano intoning chords in a minor key. Someone in the house, also unable to sleep, had turned on a record player or radio, I thought.

Suddenly a man began to sing, words I recognized too well—words that brought me from my chair in surprise and apprehension.

I have two nights watched with you, but can perceive no truth in your report. When was it she last walked?

Those were the opening words of the "Sleepwalking Scene," sung by George Wilson. But the Wilsons had left the villa at least two hours ago, so it seemed impossible.

Then the gentlewoman replied to the doctor, and I realized I was again hearing the voice of Lillian Donato; a recording *was* being played. Quietly I crossed the balcony, moving toward Althea's open windows until I reached the balustrade and could go no farther. Only a little space, not more than two yards, separated my balcony from from hers, and now I was sure that the music came from Althea's room. But the thought of her lying in the darkness torturing herself with that particular music struck me as inconceivable—a mad notion. As I stood listening, it came to me that I might have lived this scene before, on the night when Althea's screams had jolted me from my own dream.

Now the voice was Althea's own, coming softly, eerily from the dark room. *"One . . . two . . . Why then 'tis time to do it! Hell is murky . . ."*

"Althea!" I called, but no answer came; only the inexorable recording going on and on. *"So much blood in him . . ."*

Running through my own room to the corridor, I dashed to Althea's door, but there I hesitated, not knowing what to do. I could shout, pound on the door, but I dared not do it. If Althea had chosen to play this music as an atonement—a self-inflicted punishment—then I had no right to disturb the house, to summon witnesses.

I tapped softly on the door and waited. There was no sound

in the corridor, and I thought the music had ceased playing until I pressed my ear to the panel. For a few seconds, silence; then the scene began again with the voice of the doctor.

Cautiously I turned the knob, my anxiety increasing. The dimness of the corridor, with only the small night-light at the head of the stairs, had suddenly become sinister. To my surprise, the door was not locked; it swung open silently, and I stepped forward, holding my breath. The music was louder, yet still soft and far away, surrounding me in the darkness. I stood listening, fascinated and horrified, as the scene moved on mechanically.

Unable to find a wall switch beside the door, I moved carefully ahead and to the left, where I knew a small lamp stood on a table. There was no music now, but from the darkness came a sound of heavy, labored breathing.

The lamp held only a dim bulb, but when I turned it on the large room was illuminated well enough for me to see at once that nothing was obviously amiss; there was no intruder, no sign of a record player or a tape casette. Althea lay in the broad bed, head propped up by pillows resting against the headboard of the carved, gilded swan. The black velvet eyeshade bound around her head made her appear helpless and vulnerable, a woman blindfolded.

Then, as I stood gazing at her, the familiar piano chords sounded again, and my eyes searched the room as I tried to determine the source of the music, so diffused and echoing that it seemed to come from everywhere and yet from nowhere at all. As I moved closer to the bed, the volume seemed to increase slightly.

Then I looked toward the wall, and understood what was happening. The music was being played in the little elevator that Althea called a kitchen lift. Its curtains were closed, but the sliding door behind them must have been opened. Some sort of equipment must be hidden there. I made not the least sound as I moved toward the curtains and parted them slightly.

There was nothing behind the curtains—no shelves, no cabinetlike elevator; only a hollow shaft dropping to the kitchen and, floating up through that dark well, the words of the doctor as the scene began its endless repetition.

I have two nights watched with you . . .

I had not yet fully grasped what was happening—what had been taking place for months—but I went swiftly to Althea and touched her shoulder, hoping to awaken her quietly. But her eyelids did not flutter and her heavy breathing did not change, even when I put my hand to her cheek. For a terrible moment I thought she'd fallen into a deep, dangerous coma, then I noticed the bottle of sleeping tablets and the carafe of water on the bedside chest. She had told me she took one—at least one—every night, and I remembered well that two of the pills, given to me in Venice, had left me numb and drugged for hours afterwards.

I shook Althea's shoulder, chafed her wrist, but she only mumbled and tried to push me away. The hateful music continued behind me while Althea, fitful now, still slept. But I could see that its sound tugged at the edges of her consciousness; she moaned softly, tried to bury her head deeper in the pillow as though to shut out the sound.

Turning, I looked at the closed curtains of the shaft, and suddenly whatever fear I had felt was replaced by anger. Without thought, spurred by ourtage, I ran to the corridor and toward the stairs, turning on lights as I passed switches.

"Mario!" I shouted. "Mario! Konrad!"

Confident I had aroused the house, I paused only a second at the door to the kitchen, but at least some sense of caution remained, for I pushed it open slowly and did not venture ahead until I had turned on bright lights. The long room stretched before me empty, tiles gleaming on the floor and walls, and at my right was the series of cupboards, their wooden doors closed—all except one, and that deep cupboard, set into the wall, housed the kitchen elevator. It gaped open, but there was nothing on either of its small shelves.

At the far end the room the door to the service area stood open, and in the spill of light I could see a corner of the garden. Whoever had been here had heard my shouting, my steps on the stairs, and had fled swiftly and silently into the darkness outside—where I dared not follow.

It was then I realized I was alone in the villa; no one had answered my cries of alarm.

Controlling my panic, I went quickly through the deserted living room and up the stairs to Althea's room. She still slept heavily, and my frantic search for a key to the door did not awaken her. In the end, I barricaded the door with chairs, then lay down on the couch, sleepless until after dawn. I returned to my own room only after hearing sounds of the servants' arrival in the kitchen.

Chapter Fourteen

That morning I asked Mario to join me on the terrace, and there told him what had happened the night before.

"It is my fault," he said when I had finished. "I should have realized that Konrad might spend the night elsewhere. Sullie's room is at the end of the north wing, past Konrad's rooms. She would not have heard you, and I was at the museum. Last night I was standing at my window, and I thought I saw a lantern or a flashlight in the castle. I went to search; perhaps I could surprise the thief who has given us so much trouble. I was there more than an hour and I found no one." Rising, he moved to the balustrade, struck his palm with his fist in anger. "That I should let this happen! I had forgotten **t**hat you do not know about the bells."

"Bells? What bells?" I asked.

"There are two buttons in Althea's room. One rings a bell beside Sullie's bed; the other is a loud alarm. They were installed after Ilse Donato was discovered wandering in the villa one night."

"Ilse!" I exclaimed. "Of course she must be in back of it. What a horrible way to take revenge, through nightmares."

"Nightmares?" Mario returned to his chair, frowning.

"Althea has had the same terrible dream over and over: a reliving of the "Sleepwalking Scene" when Lillian died. But now we know it's caused, or at least prompted. The nightmares are suggested! Someone plays a recording—it must be a tape—very softly, and this brings the dream to Althea's mind. Or perhaps she isn't dreaming at all, she just hears the music and because of the sleeping tablets doesn't know what's happening, only that she's terrified. She told me it was more like a haunting than a nightmare. Now I understand what she meant."

Mario considered this carefully. "There is a flaw in this, Catherine. Last night there was no reaction at all, you said. No nightmare came, even though the music played."

Last night, huddled on the couch in Althea's room, I had thought out the problem step by step. "Remember what you told me about the attempt to lure me to the ballroom in Venice? Such an attempt doesn't have to work the first time, or the second or third. It's the same with the music. Last night Althea was so deeply asleep that it couldn't affect her. So there's another attempt the next night. If it only works once in a dozen times, it's enough to destroy her."

For a moment we were silent, and against my will I once again imagined the scene that must have taken place so many times in Althea's room. A figure moving silently in the dark, sure that the drugged sleeper would not awaken; the door of the kitchen lift slid open, but the curtains left closed, so if Althea ever awakened fully nothing would appear amiss in the room.

A sudden realization came to me. "We should have expected something to happen last night!"

I quickly told Mario about Angela, the girl who worked in the kitchen, and her call to Ilse Donato.

"We know Ilse hates Althea, and probably couldn't bear

the idea of Althea's recovering her voice. Of course! Ilse, or someone in her pay, would attempt to harm Althea." I paused, troubled by one problem. "But I don't understand how Ilse—if it was Ilse—obtained the tape recording. Probably from Bart Hutchinson."

Mario shook his head. "A dozen tapes were made; not for television, but ordinary recordings so the singers could study their own performances." He thought for a moment. "Catherine, I want you to promise me not to tell Althea of this. Today I will change my room; I will move across the corridor from you. The museum has a collection of sound equipment and Richard can easily install a device so I will hear the next time this is attempted. And I will take no chances—I am borrowing one of Konrad's revolvers."

"Shouldn't we warn Althea?"

"No! I will not tell her that some sinister person—someone who hates her—slips in and out of her room at night, and that whoever it is is still at large! Besides, there seems to be no physical danger. This is emotional torture. A planned torment."

After Mario left to go to the museum, I went to Althea's room, where I found her having a late breakfast. She had heard nothing during the night, but complained of troubled sleep. I congratulated her again on the return of her voice.

"It's as though I've come to life again, Catherine!" Her eyes sparkled. "If all goes well, I'll be doing some recitals this winter. I wish you would think about going on a short tour with me. You could be enormously helpful."

I smiled. "I imagine Miss Sullivan takes care of everything."

"She used to." Althea looked troubled. "But I am worried about her health. There is something wrong."

I agreed. Esther Sullivan grew more haggard with every passing day. I had noticed it first in her hands. One day when she was helping in the studio in the museum, skillfully restoring an antique music stand that had been broken, I had noticed that the fine, strong bones almost showed through the taut skin of her knuckles. The hollows beneath her eyes had deepened and her cheeks had lost the last trace of color.

"It is difficult for me to think of Sullie being ill," said Althea. "In all these years she has suffered bad health only once, and that was long ago. Even then it was more emotional than physical."

"Emotionally ill? With her iron control?"

"Such people often suffer the most. She was in love, you see." Seeing my look of surprise, Althea said, "Oh, yes. Sullie fell in love twice. The first time was with Victor Donato—my Victor."

"But how did you manage that?" I asked, astonished.

"By doing nothing. I doubt Victor ever realized how she felt, but naturally I knew. Nothing could have come of it, even if Victor had responded. In Sullie's eyes he was a married man, Ilse's husband for life. So she worshiped him silently. Later there was Paul Sheldon, who was my concert accompanist for a time. That was less than twenty years ago, but not much less. He was rather spiritual looking—he had a poet's face. For a while I thought he and Sullie might marry, but Paul was not so innocent as he appeared. He met a Swedish divorcée ten years older than he was. They eloped, and he retired on her money. That was a small loss to music, but a terrible blow to Sullie."

"She took it badly?" I asked.

"Oh, it was dreadful! Then, before she was at all recovered, she had news that her father in Canada had a terminal illness. She was forced to go to take care of him—there was no one else. It must have been torture for her, watching him slowly die. When she came back, she looked like a ghost."

"Emotional or physical, I'm sure she's ill," I said.

"I'll try to get her to a doctor," Althea said with a sigh. "She probably will not listen to me. She thinks of illness as divine punishment, a sort of terrible justice. Perhaps she's merely upset because we have been quarreling lately. Do not look so startled, Catherine. We have quarreled for twenty years, and it means nothing." She chuckled. "Two strong-minded, middle-aged women could hardly live together without clawing each other now and then, could they?"

A little later in my own room, I tried to rest but it was impossible. Memories of the night before nagged me, and I felt surrounded and stifled by questions I could not answer.

On my desk lay several letters from America, minor business matters requiring no immediate replies. I gathered them up and opened the center drawer to put them away. It was then my glance fell on the play program I had found among Pandora's things. The trunk with her clothing had been returned to a storeroom, but I had kept the snapshots and the program because she had been so proud of having her name in print as an actress.

Then, when I looked at the title of the mystery drama, a message came to me as clearly as if Pandora herself had spoken. The play was called *I Saw You*, and Pandora had appeared as a foolhardy girl who tells a group of suspects, speaking privately to each one, that she has witnessed a crime—a murder. She implies she knows the identity of the criminal, and the idea is that the guilty one will then attempt to silence the witness, thus walking into a trap.

Now, remembering the plot, I thought of the puzzling things Pandora had said to Mario. She had told him she'd seen him in the kitchen at night; he thought she was making some accusation, but hadn't understood. And Konrad also had professed to be baffled when Pandora, again privately, said the same things to him. I saw the truth now; she was acting out the play in real life.

And why did the accusation involve the kitchen? It had to be that Pandora had discovered what I myself had learned last night. After all, Pandora had occupied this room next to Althea's, and I'd wondered earlier if Pandora had heard the outcries when a nightmare came upon Althea. Clearly, she had not only heard, but also investigated. Then, instead of telling Althea, she had tried to be clever, tried to trap someone in a dramatic way, and that had been her undoing.

Now I could understand her quarrel with Prince Luigi, and realized she might have enraged others as well. Poor, foolish Pandora—playing, as she so often did, with unpredictable fire that blazed beyond her control.

I felt a need to be outdoors; I would think more clearly outside these confining walls. Putting on a sweater, for the day was now overcast, I went across the lawns toward the lake, not sure where I was going. It was the familiar sight of Ilse Donato's skiff standing far out on the lake that made me decide. Why not simply ask her if she wrote the note to me yesterday, and if so, what she had seen?

Because the water was choppy, I chose the *Thais*, the heavier of the two speedboats. Racing toward the center of the lake, the breeze whipping my hair, I forgot myself for a moment and enjoyed the power and balance of the boat as it skimmed the water, almost flying.

Ilse Donato had seen the boat at a distance and, apparently thinking Konrad was approaching, waved her hand in greeting. Then, as I slowed to draw alongside, she realized her mistake, and the hand balled into a fist.

"*Fuori!* Go away!" she shrieked at me, then burst into a tirade of German punctuated by an amazing repertoire of Italian gestures I took to be obscene. Standing up in the skiff, she threatened me with her fishing pole.

"Please, *signora,* I wish to talk with you!"

"You have frightened the fish," she screamed in heavily accented English. "A look at you would frighten them, you devil's child. *Váttene in malora!*"

It was no use. Mario had been right—she was mad, and any conversation was impossible.

Not ready to return, I gave vent to my frustration by plunging toward the far shore at full speed. Just as I docked at the village quay, I realized there were no other craft on the lake; the gaily striped sails were missing and not even the fishermen had put out. A large, single drop of rain splashed on my hand, and I looked apprehensively at the sky. To the north, lowering clouds had gathered ominously, threatening a squall, and without hesitating I swung the speedboat back toward the western shore.

I felt no fear of anything worse than being rain drenched. The speedboat was heavy and strong; I was confident I'd reach the villa before the lake became seriously roiled by the storm. But a moment later I learned my first lesson about the treachery of Alpine winds. Heavy gusts and powerful cross-currents came from every direction at once—winds that peaked the water first one way, then another—and I found the speedboat pitching. In a less sturdy craft I would have been alarmed, but the speedboat was built to withstand pounding and it responded to my least touch.

Then, at a distance, I saw Ilse Donato's boat, and at first did not understand what was happening. Instead of running before the northwest wind, she seemed to be drifting. She turned, floated into a trough, and a high wave broke against her, spinning her so the next wave broke at her stern and she took on water.

Ilse crouched over the outboard motor, jerking futilely at a length of rope to crank the motor to life. There was no question about the seriousness of her plight; a heavy wave could capsize the boat, and if she kept taking on water, she'd be swamped in a very few minutes. Drawing as near as I dared, I shouted, "Do you need help?"

She stared at me, her heavy face white with fear. "*Ja! Ja!*"

Stooping low, she found a weighted line and tossed it—gesturing that she wanted to be towed to the village shore—and on the third attempt, the rope landed in the speedboat. I made it fast to a cleat, tying a simple knot that I could instantly loosen with a jerk at the short end. I did not like the idea of towing her, for my own situation had suddenly turned dangerous.

The skiff was about twenty feet behind me, and if it were suddenly hurled forward by a wave, it could ram the speedboat—and what happened then depended on fate. I felt at the mercy of the whims of the wind and water as spray, now mixed with rain, whipped across my face.

I headed for Ilse Donato's dock, which was closer than the village. The last five hundred yards were nerve-racking, but the real peril was over. A hulking man—a gardener—ran out to help moor the boats as I helped the unsteady Ilse to her door and entered behind her, unasked.

"Thank you for bringing me to shore," she said, fumbling with the buttons of her rain-soaked sweater. A spark of truculence appeared in her face. "But I would have reached home without you, nevertheless."

Seeing that I was shivering, she grudgingly offered me a cup of tea.

"Thank you, yes. And I'd like to telephone the villa. They may be worried about me."

"I regret there is no telephone," she told me, and the hint of craftiness in her voice convinced me this was a lie.

The tea came tepid, a cracked cup on a chipped saucer, and looking at the squat, coarse woman sitting opposite me, I wondered how she had ever produced such an attractive son as Konrad.

"I wanted to see you because of the note you sent me," I said.

"What note? Who says I sent you a note?"

"It was kind of you to warn me," I continued quietly. "But I wish you would explain. Tell me more."

"There is no reason for me to do you a kindness. You try to lure my son! You stand on the terrace kissing him in public. Have you no shame?"

"I have never kissed Konrad in private or in public," I told her, and was rewarded with a contemptuous look. Then a picture came to my mind—Konrad leaning against the balustrade with me standing close to him knotting his tie. She had watched, misunderstood, and this had triggered her rage. The threatening note arrived only a few hours later. I started to explain, but her disbelief was so obvious that I gave up.

"I've wasted my time in trying to see you," I said. "From the note, I thought you really knew something. But you were pretending, weren't you?"

"So it is pretending now I do!" She bridled, as I knew she would. "Nothing goes on in that evil house I do not know. Come, I will show you—then you can tell that evil woman how my eyes are always on her!"

Excited, she led me up an iron spiral stairway. In a room unfurnished except for a chair stood an old brass telescope facing a window toward the lake.

"Look for yourself, so you can tell her. It is a powerful glass; I see everything that happens. From me, nothing can be hidden."

I said slowly, "You were watching the day Pandora died. You saw what happened." I gazed into her face, trying to force an answer by sheer willpower.

But she remained defiant. "So? Why should I speak?"

"Because it was murder."

"I admit nothing!" The small eyes were opaque, impenetrable. "Like you, your sister tried to lure my son away from me. She flaunted herself before him, she flattered and cajoled him. Am I then sorry she dies? Pleased I am and happy!"

I had to escape, to get away from this madwoman and the evil she generated. But at the head of the stairs I turned back to say, "You make me sorry I helped you on the lake. You do not deserve help."

"It would not be your nature to leave me there," she replied. "But I owe you a favor and I will pay my debt. My memory is long, as you have cause to know."

I hurried down the stairs, out of her house, and almost ran to the speedboat. The rain had stopped and the wind was dying, and a few minutes later, as I crossed the lake, I did not mind the long rollers the storm had left behind.

Thinking of Konrad, I felt a surge of pity and an admiration for him I had not known before. Genial and cheerful, he never betrayed a hint of the scenes he must endure with Ilse. I remembered his face, the look of desperation when I had said I would take the note to the police. He felt compelled to protect her, and no one could know what it must cost him.

Then, as the cliffs of the villa loomed before me, I thought of myself. Certainly I had never been like Ilse Donato; but I had once allowed the past to poison my life, and my unwillingness to forgive or understand had been like a frost, keeping me from new growth.

Mario was waiting for me at the dock, an electric lantern in his hand, and in the gathering darkness the light glowed a welcome.

"I was not really worried," he told me, as we moored the *Thais*. "But I called the inn, and they told me the boat was moored at the village."

We climbed the stairs, and I was about to tell him what had happened with Ilse Donato when we found Lisa huddled on the steps of the terrace sound asleep, her cheeks streaked with tears. She threw herself into my arms, stammering out a story so broken by sobs that Mario had to translate the confused Italian for me.

Her mother, Mario explained, had fallen ill. When she was taken to a nearby hospital, the children were placed with an aunt, who ridiculed Lisa without mercy for coming to the villa, attempting to learn to draw, and, in general, trying to be above her own family. Lisa had fled and was waiting for me to return.

We took her in, washed her face, gave her a snack of oranges and milk, then found her a small, cheerful room near Althea's. Since she was still trembling and on the verge of tears, I brought her my music box and let her play it, reminding her of Hansel and Gretel.

She nodded. "The path of stones shining in the moonlight. That is what you told me."

"Yes, Lisa. And this box plays the song about the fourteen angels who watched over their sleep in the forest."

When finally I was able to turn out the light and leave her, I was surprised to find Mario waiting for me in the doorway of his new room across the hallway from Althea.

"Soon, Catherine, we must find time for each other. There is much we must talk about."

"Yes?" I waited, wondering.

"Our lives will change with the end of summer," he said. "Althea will leave here soon to try to resume her career. Konrad, too, will go. I think he will go with Giulia."

"With Giulia? You believe things are serious between them?"

"What an odd way to speak of love—to call it 'serious.'" He was laughing at me, but gently. "Is that how Americans think? I could be in love my whole life and never have a serious moment."

"Stop teasing me, Mario. You know what I mean."

"Yes, I know. I think Konrad will marry her. He is over thirty; he feels it is time to become a responsible husband and father. That is natural—it is how a man becomes complete in life."

"To become complete in life?" I said. "I hadn't thought of marriage that way. Of course, you're right."

"And since we are talking of love, Catherine—but not becoming too serious—I should tell you that I already love you more than I love bronze, and by next week I may love you even more than I love marble."

His eyes met mine, held them, and now he was not laughing. "So we, too, must make plans. We must decide where we will live, or whether we will wander for a time. You must learn to manage this wild Italian peasant."

"What are you saying, Mario?"

"I am saying that we, too, must be complete in life."

And holding me close, he kissed me.

Chapter Fifteen

At some hour long after midnight, the storm that had abated returned in fury to lash the villa and the cliffs below it. I awoke suddenly when the doors to my balcony were slammed violently shut by the wind. When I went to lock them, I saw a jagged bolt of lightning slash down the sky and strike somewhere high on the mountain near the ruins of the monastery.

Worried that Lisa might be frightened by the storm, I went quietly to her room and looked in. She slept peacefully, but by now I myself was thoroughly awakened and lay awake listening to the rolling thunder and torrents of rain until the storm ended at dawn.

In the morning I went to the museum to work on the background painting for the Althea Hoffman exhibit—arriving early, but not so early that Mario was not there before me. He sat on a scaffolding, glaring at the relief of *Pan Discovering Music*—his expression so black that I was happy to slip into the waxworks section without his noticing me. The surest way to make marble come first with him, I thought, was to interrupt him while he was working with it. Especially when he thought the work was going badly.

During the first hour I found it difficult to concentrate. Not only was I weary from a sleepless night, but the curtains of the other exhibits in the corridor were open and the life-size, eerily realistic figures disturbed me. Directly across the way a triumphant Tosca raised a dagger to plunge into the heart of an unsuspecting Scarpia. On the next small stage an evil-looking spy lurked near La Gioconda and her blind mother. I felt uneasy watched by so many unseeing eyes, but eventually lost myself in my work, and when a real watcher approached, I did not even hear him until he spoke.

"Good morning, dear Catherine," said Prince Luigi, and I turned, brush in hand. He was elegant in summer white, and the ebony cane he carried gave him a dapper air.

"Catherine, in that paint-streaked smock and bandana, you look quite like a professional artist."

"I *am* a professional artist," I informed him. "I have made my living that way for several years. Were you looking for someone in particular?"

"No. I am here as a tourist. In my mail this morning was an announcement that the museum will be open to the public in two weeks. So I am indulging in a last look while the castle is still private."

"I'm sure you'll find it interesting. The collection of ancient instruments on the next level is fascinating."

I turned back to my work, but he showed no sign of departing. "This is to be the Althea Hoffman display?" he asked.

"Yes. As a concert artist."

"Very unfortunate, all these displays. They remind me of stalls in a market."

The bitterness in his voice was strong enough to make me turn and listen.

"*Si.* For more than a thousand years this was the seat of a splendid family. As noble and ancient a family as can be found in all Italy. In all Europe, for that matter!" His eyes roved the walls, the stone vaults of the ceiling. "And it ended in the hands of a man who was the son of one of my peasants. And this peasant's son bequeaths it as a museum, a public curiosity, where every lout and pig-eyed tourist can enter its doors. *Osceno!*''

I drew back a step, watching him carefully, wondering why he was so indiscreet. Before, he had always conveyed his contempt for Victor Donato by veiled allusions—the tilt of an eyebrow, the twist of a smile. Now, his eyes had an expression so fiercely possessive that I realized he felt Castle Malaspina still belonged to him. Then a smile crossed his masklike face. "But for a thousand years we have survived and won in the end. I think we will win this game, too."

"I don't understand," I said.

"No, my dear Catherine. You do not understand—but you will." And with that he left me.

I finished my work and returned to the villa for a very late lunch, meeting Miss Sullivan at the dining room door.

"I have a message for you," she said, "from Mario."

"Isn't he here?"

"No. He raced off half an hour ago to drive to Milan."

"All the way to Milan!" I exclaimed. "Is there some emergency?"

"Indeed there is," Miss Sullivan's tone was dry. "He broke a chisel blade, and you'd think it was the last one on earth. He said he had to replace it today if he's to finish his work tomorrow. That, however, is not the message. He is expecting a call from Venice, from a Professor Folin. If he hasn't returned, he would like you to take the call. He said it is important and that you would understand."

There was a faint look of annoyance on Miss Sullivan's face, and it struck me that even in taking a small telephone message for Mario, I was impinging upon territory she had claimed years ago.

"I do not know what it's about," she said stiffly. "Mario did not explain."

"Thank you," I said.

Professor Folin was surely the scholar studying the ancient documents of the castle—but if Mario chose to say nothing about this, it was not my place to explain.

An hour later I was in the library when the telephone rang. I picked it up, and heard nothing but an ear-shattering racket of pops, roars, and electronic screeches. I realized then that this was another of those days when the Italian telephone system was in chaos. After two more futile attempts, a man's voice, asking for Mario, emerged amid the uproar. "Professor Folin?" I shouted into the telephone.

"*Si, si.*"

The telephne emitted a series of buzzes. Suddenly I could overhear a Venetian lady shouting at a fishmonger about short weight on a flounder. Then the professor was again on the line, and I managed to understand that he would call on the telephone in the museum in half an hour, that perhaps there would be a better connection there.

As I crossed the lawns to the museum, I noticed that the day had brightened, had become almost cheerful. In the entrance hall I met Richard Halpin, who appeared to be leaving for the day.

"Is the museum open?" I asked him. "I'm expecting a telephone call here."

"Oh, yes. It's open except for my office." He took an extra key from a large ring. "You can return this to me tomorrow. There's still an hour before the workmen lock the main doors and turn on the alarm system."

The castle seemed not the least forbidding as I mounted the stairs to the office. From the lower floor I heard the laughter of two workmen, a joke about using so much red paint—that opera wasn't worth seeing unless there was plenty of gore.

Inside Halpin's office, I leaned back in the deep leather desk chair and opened a copy of *Handbook of Modern Composers* to read while awaiting the call. I remember wishing the professor would hurry, because I was tired and at moments the type on the page seemed to blur.

* * *

I awoke startled in the dim office, for a second not remembering where I was. The windows were pale, luminous rectangles against the dying twilight and my watch said almost seven o'clock. As I turned on Richard Halpin's desk lamp, I wondered why Folin had not called, and picked up the telephone. There was no sound at all; the line was dead.

The men who had been working downstairs must have left by now. I went quickly to the office door, opened it, took half a step forward, then halted abruptly. The corridor was utterly black; no night-light glowed, not a gleam of twilight penetrated the windowless passage.

Several times I had heard Richard Halpin speak of the electronic wonders of the museum, how everything operated automatically from a control panel with a computer; certain lights went off or came on at set hours, gates closed or opened, alarm systems were activated. But I hadn't the least idea about the location of this control panel or how to manage such a simple thing as getting light in the corridor.

For a moment I stood in the doorway, hesitant, undecided. I could remain in the office, locking the door, until someone from the villa came looking for me. As I peered into the darkness, this seemed an appealing idea. But I felt it foolish to skulk for an hour or two behind a locked door because I was too timid to find my way through a few yards of corridor and down a flight of steps to the doors, where I could no doubt open some sort of bolt or bar. I made up my mind to leave, first making the way easier by turning on the overhead lights in the office and leaving the doors open wide to the corridor.

I found I could see quite well by the light spilling from the doorways, and I walked quickly to the stairwell. But with every step down, the light grew dimmer, visibility more difficult. On the landing, the top of Mario's nearly finished relief panel seemed only a surface of broken shadows. Then, to my relief, I saw that a very dim lamp burned in the entry hall below.

The lamp was too dim and too distant to light the stairs, but its small flicker was consoling, a reassuring beacon to move toward. Using the marble balustrade as a guide, I descended, trying to make out the outlines of the risers at my feet. I reached the hall, where the balustrades on either side flared outward to give a generous, welcoming effect, and there I looked to my right, toward the place where I had seen the lamp.

It was gone. I clutched the marble bannister, confused, trying to remember clearly about the lamp. Could it have been a reflection, that tiny gleam? I supposed so. It must have been a trick of light, an illusion. At any rate, now I had only to cross the entrance hall, being careful to avoid the tall Roman statue of the muse of choral song. Then I saw a tiny thread of light, very faint, and decided it was the line where the double doors met.

Suddenly that line was blotted out, as though some shape had moved in front of it, and in the darkness nearby I heard the unmistakable sound of a suppressed cough. Someone stood near the doors waiting for me to move toward them.

While my heart pounded, I resisted my first, terrified impulse to cry out, to demand who was there. Such a cry I knew would be useless and, worse, would reveal that I knew about the intruder's presence. I could turn back—try to flee by running up the stairs, hoping to reach the office—but that involved the risk of stumbling in the darkness and being overtaken before I gained even the landing.

Holding my breath, I took a quiet step to my left, away from the doors and away from the invisible figure lurking there, then another step, and another. If I remembered correctly, I would shortly be in the Hall of the Composers. A feeling of panic came to me as I thought of finding my way among those cases and cabinets of mementos, the antique music stands and ancient instruments.

I brushed against something, perhaps a chair, and then behind me, not far away, I heard muffled footsteps.

Terror welled in me; heedless now of making noise—aware only that I was being pursued, hunted—I blundered ahead, and a metallic crash rang in my ears as I knocked a heavy object to the marble floor. I nearly stumbled on the slope of the ramp leading to the opera exhibits.

At the end of the ramp the floor became level again, and my hand touched a velvet curtain at one of the display stages. I halted, leaning against the wall to steady myself, my breath coming in short, jerky gasps. A tinkling sound, light and silvery, came from the hall above, telling me that my pursuer had touched the chimes that stood near the head of the ramp. I had lost him for a moment at least.

But my blood pounded more quickly when I saw a glimmer of light and realized that the lamp I had seen earlier had been a small flashlight. If my pursuer dispensed with secrecy and used the light, I had small hope of escaping.

Compelled to move ahead, I kept a hand on the curtains and reached the far side of the display; when my fingers touched the edge of a control button, a sudden thought came to me. If the sound system had not been turned off by the main panel that controlled the lights, there was a chance I could attract the attention of someone outside. To attempt this would reveal my hiding place, and for a moment I considered slipping behind the curtains in hopes that I'd remain hidden. But then, summoning my resolve, I pressed hard on the button under my hand and groped my way toward the next exhibit without waiting.

Cymbals clashed, there was a stir of strings and flutes, but before the aria began, I pressed a second control button. Someone would hear, I thought wildly, someone would have to hear!

Then, just as music blared on the second stage, I heard a shout. "Catherine! Catherine!"

The small beam of a penlight appeared at the top of the ramp, and I retreated into the nearest exhibit, pulling back as I stumbled against some scenery, recoiling when my hand touched a cold arm made of wax.

A brilliant white beam like a spotlight flashed on at the head of the ramp, and only a few steps away from me I saw Prince

Luigi pinned against the wall by the light. He raised his hands to shield his eyes from its brilliance.

The music from the two displays ended. Into the silence Luigi Malaspina spoke calmly, addressing himself toward the flashlight. "Good evening, Mario, my boy. I confess I hardly expected to find you here at this hour."

We were in Richard Halpin's office—Prince Luigi leaning back comfortably on the visitors' couch, Mario and I standing beside the desk. Mario still held the heavy, powerful electric torch he had used in searching for me.

"I do wish you would refrain from wielding that flashlight like a weapon, Mario," he said. "I am not likely to attack you or attempt to flee. I never reveal my age, but I assure you it is far more than twice yours, and you know from searching me that I am not armed."

There had been nothing in his trouser pockets except a ring of keys and a billfold with very little money. More damning evidence turned up in the rumpled trench coat he wore; besides the penlight, he carried tools for picking small locks, such as those of the display cases. In another pocket were two autographed programs stolen from the museum.

"Not much of a haul," he commented. "I don't suppose Wagner's signature is worth selling, and Verdi's is not valuable. Still, small sums add up, I have learned."

"Added together, these thefts will indeed amount to a serious crime," said Mario. "You do not seem to realize your position."

"You won't alarm me with charges you cannot prove," he remarked, brushing away a spot of dried mud from the lapel of his coat. "I admit only one thing: my mortification at being surprised wigless and hatless. I am not really as egg bald as I now appear. I shave my head so my wigs fit better."

Mario glared at him. "Fortunately for you, you did not actually harm Catherine tonight, or despite your age I would—"

"Yes, dear boy. I know what you would do." The prince

heaved a long sigh. "But I had no intention of harming her. I wanted only to escape, to flee without being recognized. How should I know it was Catherine? I supposed it was a watchman, some muscular bully like yourself. I wished only to take my small bit of loot and leave the way I entered."

"And how was that?" Mario demanded.

Prince Luigi waggled a long finger at him. "I reveal no secrets."

"When you change your mind, you may write me from prison," replied Mario pleasantly.

Sitting very straight, Luigi studied him with narrowed eyes. "Let us understand each other at once. You can charge me with trespassing and perhaps with the theft of those autographed programs, although I will concoct a good story to explain everything. But Althea, not you, would have to bring such charges, and you know very well she would not. Also, there is a high card in my hand—you might say the ace of trumps." He looked at his watch. "Right now I imagine Konrad and my lovely niece are crossing the French frontier. Tomorrow morning they will be married, probably in Monte Carlo."

I glanced at Mario, who nodded. "I know. Konrad called Althea an hour ago."

"Giulia, a poor orphan girl, regards me as her father," he continued smugly. "She does not know of my activities here, my small business with the museum, and learning about it would distress her greatly. That in turn would distress Konrad. Since there is so little you can prove, is it worth trying? Of course not! Let us be reasonable."

While Prince Luigi spoke, Mario had been examining the keys on the ring. "The kitchen door of the villa," he remarked, pointing to one. "So that is how you entered and managed your torments of Althea."

Prince Luigi spread his fingers in a gesture of futility. "I merely forgot to turn over a key to Miss Sullivan years ago. And what is this about the kitchen of the villa?" He looked at

me, frowning. "Your sister made an unpleasant scene in public about my supposedly slipping into the kitchen of the villa
at night. Ridiculous! I had no idea what she meant."

"I think you did know," I said, my anger rising. "Pandora
discovered what you were doing and—"

"*Per favore!* You can prove nothing, and you are wasting
time. Now let me tell you the bargain I will make." His face
hardened and his eyes turned shrewd. "I no longer need the
extra income I have earned here. Giulia will see to my welfare. If you agree to say nothing, I will agree to go away, to
vanish from your lives. The pleasures of Rome have long appealed to me, and now I can afford them. I am even prepared
to forgive your family its low origins now that I shall live off a
fraction of the Donato millions. Is this not better than a scandal, Mario? Be reasonable."

He smiled—his hooded, reptilian eyes searching us, wary,
ready to spring or strike in any direction open to him.

The brief look Mario and I exchanged said many things: anger, frustration, unwillingness to accept this defeat. It was
easy to see how he had engineered the torment of Althea. He
had needed only a tape stolen from the museum's sound library and a key to the villa; he already had full knowledge of
the operation of the household.

I even understood his hatred. Althea owned the villa in
which he had held court as a young man; she was queen of his
Venetian palace. Althea even held sway here in the castle—
the stronghold of the Malaspina family, his pride, his heritage.
And Pandora had foolishly revealed her suspicions to a man
whose cruelty had no limit.

Mario's eyes held understanding—he knew what I felt—but
he shook his head slowly. "We accept the bargain," he told
Prince Luigi, "but with conditions. First, I want you to leave
this neighborhood now, tonight."

"I am already packed," he answered with a smile I found
almost unbearable. "I was on my way when I made this unlucky detour."

"You have a lifetime right to the apartment in Venice."

Mario's voice was like steel. "It was given to you because of my father's generosity. You will lease that apartment to someone else and never return to it. Understand also that if we find evidence of other crimes you have committed or attempted, we will accuse you."

"Of course you would," said Luigi. "You are a man of honor. We agree completely." He started to rise.

"A moment!" Mario seized him by the shoulders, almost lifting him into the air, and his voice, although soft, was deadly. "If you come near anyone I love—any member of my family—and do them harm, I will not wait for the law, I will not wait to prove matters. I will kill you."

We returned to the villa. Prince Luigi, his hands trembling and his face ashen, had departed through the gates to the road—never, he assured us, to be seen at the lake again. I believed him; he was terrified.

"He is brave enough creeping about in the darkness," said Mario. "Not quite so brave when dragged into the light."

"I suppose we will never know for sure what happened to Pandora, will we? It seems wrong, unfinished."

He nodded, and his arm encircled me. "Let us try to believe it was truly an accident, that Prince Luigi was not responsible. How strange it is that I do not feel vengeful. I detest Luigi Malaspina—I have loathed him for years. But I want to be left in peace with you, Catherine. I want to forget what has happened more than I want vengeance."

"What made you come to the museum tonight?" I asked.

"Professor Folin reached me on the telephone. He said he could not get through to the museum. When I found you were not in your room, I came searching."

In the dining room Althea and Richard Halpin sat side by side, finishing their supper and going over the score of *The Thirteenth Pilgrim*.

"The cook put your young friend Lisa to bed," Althea said. She smiled at me. "I know Mario has told you the news about Konrad." She lowered her voice. "Sullie is in her room. I gave her to understand that Konrad and Giulia were married this afternoon. I did not lie. I was merely ambiguous."

"Why?" I asked.

"It is ridiculous, but the idea of their traveling together—overnight—would upset her. She is so fond of Konrad. Poor Sullie! I am afraid the modern world has gone beyond her understanding. Worse, it has gone beyond her charity—which is sad."

"I also have some news," said Mario. "Professor Folin has found evidence that the castle was founded at the site of a Roman tin mine, and there are references to dungeons and tunnels as late as the eighteenth century." He smiled at Richard Halpin. "He has not proved the pilgrim legend, but he has shown it may be true. The professor now needs a modern map of the buildings and grounds."

"I'll be happy to send him one," said Halpin.

"It will be faster for me to take it to Venice myself. Tomorrow I expect to finish my work at the museum. The next day, Sunday, I will see the professor. I will return in the evening, and I think we should all four have supper across the lake at the inn to celebrate."

"Of course. We must celebrate Konrad's marriage," Althea said with no great enthusiasm.

"To celebrate everything!" Now that the tension of what had happened in the museum was over, Mario was suddenly in high spirits. "We will drink to the end of my work at the museum. And to the future. *Si*, to the future!"

Later, Mario and I strolled across the broad lawns, past the rose garden, and sat on a bench near the deer park.

"You are serious, Catherine," he said. "Is it difficult to realize there is now no reason for fear?"

I hesitated. "Yes, I suppose so. But I do believe Prince Luigi has gone forever. You know, he was the first person connected with the villa that I saw when I arrived. Somehow I knew then that he meant trouble and bad luck."

"When I went into the museum tonight searching for you, I

was afraid. I have been worried since that night in the ball-room in Venice. Now we will think only of the future."

He looked toward the sky, into the troubled moonlight, at the great, slow moving clouds. His face was strong and serene in the pale light. He said, "*E quindi uscimmo a riveder le stelle.*"

"I've read that, Mario. I can't remember where."

"In Dante. It is the last line when the poets come from darkness and once more see the sky." He repeated it, this time in English. "From there we came forth to see once more the stars."

I heard a faint rustling, a cautious sound of branches part-ing. A deer, silver in the shadows, had approached the fence and stood gazing at us with great, unblinking eyes, beautiful and shy. When I stirred, his head lifted; he quivered as at a scent of danger, then plunged into the tangle of the thicket to hide in the darkness beyond the reach of the moonlight.

Chapter Sixteen

Sunday always brought a pleasant change of routine at the Villa Pellegrina: No servants reported for work; there was no intimidating cook to prevent my padding about the big kitchen in a comfortable robe and slippers, brewing my shockingly weak American coffee, moving happily at my own pace.

In college, when I had been studying Italian, the class had read a story about a saint. He worked in a kitchen at a humble job, but at times the pots and pans took on a radiance for him and an iron spoon would shine like the brightest gold. This morning I expected no visits from angels, no heavenly halo above the toaster, but I smiled to myself as I recalled the story, for the sun poured through the open windows, making the tile counters gleam and lending a cheerful glow to the copper bottoms of the hanging pans.

Mario had left for Venice early, taking with him the maps Professor Folin needed, and as I entered the kitchen I saw Esther Sullivan driving away, going to the Sunday religious service she never failed to attend. A few minutes later Lisa came downstairs and I gave her a quick kiss, thanking her for the drawing she had slipped under my door the previous night—a charming picture of Hansel and Gretel following the pebbles.

I prepared a breakfast tray for her, which she took to the garden. It was nine o'clock and I was still sipping coffee at the kitchen table when, to my surprise, Althea appeared in the doorway.

"The world is ending," I said. "I've never seen you before noon except on the day we left for Venice."

"Put it another way," she replied, chuckling. "You have never seen me in training before. I have exercises to do; the body and the voice. I have returned to work, and you will find I am well disciplined." She poured a glass of orange juice and took the chair opposite me. "I took no sleeping tablet last night—partly because I shall be working, partly because Mario threatens to beat me if I continue using them. Catherine, you must save me from him. I suspect you have influence with him."

"Really?"

She put her hand on mine, her touch firm and assuring. "Are you happy, Catherine?"

"Yes." I hesitated, then said, "Yes . . . Mother."

For a moment we were silent, until she looked away, blinking rapidly. "It is apparent, of course, how matters stand between you and Mario. Nothing could make me so content, so pleased with life. Mario is very special—but all of my children have been special." Her eyes wandered to the window, and she saw Lisa playing outside. "I hope the child's mother recovers quickly. I like this little girl. Yesterday I heard her singing the *Hansel and Gretel* prayer. She did not know the words, so she had made up new ones."

"She learned the tune from the music box."

"This morning I'm going through the score of Richard's *The Thirteenth Pilgrim*," Althea said, finishing her glass of orange juice. "I think it might be perfect for the young soprano we heard in *Carmen*. Not the mezzo, but the lyric who sang Micaela. A sweet voice! We might stage it here at the museum. We had once planned to have living opera an important activity at the museum. Now we will do it."

She saw my look of surprise, and smiled. "Yes, Catherine, I am entering life again, fully. I have felt my faith in myself returning, and I began to face Lillian's death. That was the beginning of forgiving myself. Not entirely, of course; never entirely. I am responsible for what I did in impatience and rage. Still, it was an accident. I could as well have been the one burned. Such a thing is beyond human control."

A few minutes later, when she left me to begin work, I lingered over her words. Going out to the terrace, I stood gazing at the grim walls of the castle. I thought of Prince Luigi and his hatred of Althea, the resentment that had burned beneath the surface for years. Althea had just said, "I could as well have been the one burned." Remembering those words, I recalled the scene on the television, forcing myself to think of the details. I again saw Althea suddenly lifting the lamp, its light just below her face, the flame wavering, flickering on her features. I remembered the strength of her gesture, the violence of the effect.

I knew that once a movement was set in rehearsal, Althea always repeated it exactly, and on the night of the accident the valve controlling the flame of the lamp was loose. If Althea had not whirled on Lillian, then a moment later when she gestured suddenly with the lamp, a tongue of fire would have seared her own face, inflicting a cruel and horrible wound— perhaps even blindness, I thought. Had Prince Luigi been in the wings that night? Had he tampered with the lamp, arranging a painful accident not for Lillian but for Althea?

Again I felt the frustration of having no evidence, no proof. Surely there was a way to convict him of this and, in so doing, to relieve Althea's burden of guilt. But what could we do? I could think of nothing, nothing at all.

My brooding was interrupted by Althea's calling. "Catherine? Where are you?"

"Coming!" I answered, and went to the living room.

She was holding a clipboard and pencil in one hand, the score of *The Thirteenth Pilgrim* in the other. "Richard has changed the ending," she complained. "The girl who avenges her sister is thrown into a dungeon to starve. Just the way Luigi told the story—an Italian ending! Also, I suspect Richard has misquoted the *Bible*. Do you recognize this?"

She read some lines that were unfamiliar to me but seemed Biblical. "I don't recognize the passage," I said.

"It was too much to hope you would. I have searched the library, and with all those books there is no *Bible*!" She paused, considering something. "Of course. There is a *Bible* in Sullie's room. Would you get it for me, Catherine? I do not dare, because Sullie is a tigress about her privacy. But she has never actually told *you* not to enter."

I didn't like this errand, and as I walked the length of the corridor in the north wing I regretted not having refused Althea. But now the only thing was to complete the mission as quickly as possible.

If the door had been locked, I would have had an indisputable reason for not fulfilling Althea's request—but it opened when I turned the knob.

I had never seen Esther Sullivan's room before, and I wondered if anyone had, except perhaps one of the maids. Since her life was totally occupied with serving people who were not her own family, I supposed she kept her room as a place of retreat, a private sanctuary. But what I now saw astonished me.

It was a large room—much larger than mine—but almost unfurnished, containing only a narrow bed, a bureau, and a writing desk with a straight, wooden chair. There was nothing else except the inevitable standing wardrobe. No reading lamp, no bedside rug to give protection from cold tiles, no hint of comfort or beauty. Nothing hung on the stark, white walls but a small mirror above the bureau; nor were there any photographs, except one—Lillian. It stood on the writing desk in a silver frame. Beside it rested a large, leather-bound *Bible*.

Returning to the living room, I gave the heavy book to Althea. "Please finish with it quickly," I told her. "I feel like a thief who has just robbed a nun's cell."

"Nonsense, Catherine. What does it matter? I will take full responsibility if this hideous crime is discovered."

We both went to our rooms upstairs; she to check the opera libretto and I to get out watercolors and brushes. I felt no particular inspiration to paint, but I needed some task to divert my mind from Lillian's death and my bitterness that Prince Luigi was escaping justice. I did not dare think about Pandora.

I took the fire opals from their case and put them in the pocket of the fresh smock I was wearing. The clasp, I had noticed a few days ago, was loose. I would repair it later in the museum studio, if either Miss Sullivan or Richard Halpin opened their office this afternoon. I had no intention of working alone in the museum, but Halpin often was in his office at odd hours on Sundays.

I was about to go downstairs when I heard the sound of a car entering the driveway and, from the balcony, saw Miss Sullivan returning.

She was dressed as I had seen her on the cemetery island in Venice—black dress and gloves, and the round black hat that reminded me of a bonnet. Instead of entering the house, she went toward the museum, moving with her usual strong, erect carriage. Perhaps she was ill, as Althea believed, but certainly not ill enough to miss her religious meeting. She never missed a Sunday, Althea had told me.

No, Althea was mistaken. Pandora had died on a Sunday morning, and Miss Sullivan had been in the villa, so she must have been too ill to have gone out.

I carried paints and paper to the terrace, the opals still in my pocket, and began working quickly, as one must with watercolor. A girl's face emerged on the paper, and a white mantle with the red cross of a pilgrim. Then I found myself painting shadows converging upon the girl's figure, although I did not know their meaning and simply painted as feelings came to me.

Inside the villa a door slammed, and Althea shouted, "Sullie! Where are you?"

Startled by her tone of anger and outrage, I hurried to the living room. Althea furiously paced the floor, clutching Miss Sullivan's *Bible*. "The treachery! And that she should have thought me incapable of kindness, incapable of understanding!" She flung the *Bible* onto a table and whirled toward me. "Have you seen Esther Sullivan?"

Althea had never used that name. Always it was "Sullie," and usually there was affection in her voice; now her tone conveyed fury.

"I saw her go toward the museum," I said. "What is it?"

"I'll explain after I've dealt with her!" Althea picked up the *Bible*, then slammed it down again. "No, I won't need it."

She stormed from the room, rushing toward the museum, and her golden robe with its great full sleeves flowed behind her like a train.

Puzzled, I opened the *Bible*, since it seemed to be the cause of her rage. First I discovered two photographs: one of a handsome, middle-aged man—a stronger version of Konrad—whom I recognized as Victor Donato. It had been autographed, "From Victor, with love to his darling—" The lower right corner had been off, but I suppose it said "Althea." The edges of the photograph were worn from handling.

The second picture showed a young man whose rather weak good looks were apparent despite a huge "X" in india ink slashed across the surface. He was seated at a piano, and on the back of the photo I found the name Paul Sheldon and the address of a London booking agency for concert artists. So this was the man Althea had believed was Esther Sullivan's lover—the man who'd deserted her for a wealthy divorcée. The desertion would certainly explain the childish crossing out of the face, but why had she kept the picture?

Returning the photos to the back of the *Bible,* I turned to the flyleaf and saw a handwritten record of the Sullivan family. There were dates of births, deaths, and marriages in different styles of handwriting—a harmless list, of no interest to an outsider. I was about to close the cover when something caught my attention. Esther Sullivan's father, Henry, had died thirty years ago. But that was impossible. Miss Sullivan, I had been told, went to Canada to nurse her father in his final illness more than ten years after that date.

So she had lied when she asked for that leave of absence. Why? There could be only one answer; I knew the truth before I saw that Esther Sullivan's mother was named Elspeth, and I remembered the tomb in Venice. Lillian Elspeth Donato.

Her daughter. Lillian was Miss Sullivan's daughter, born during her long absence and later reclaimed—adopted by Althea. But selected, of course, by Esther Sullivan, since Althea could not bear to visit an orphanage.

When I had seen Lillian on the television screen, I had thought she was somehow familiar, perhaps from a portrait. Of course, I had noticed the line of the jaw and cheekbones, the resemblance to Esther Sullivan. I supposed no one in the family had ever thought of it.

Esther Sullivan! I could have wept for her—a life of loneliness and deception created by her own guilt, her own foolish shame. No one, least of all Althea, would have been unkind to her or to the child. It was wasteful and foolish. To use one of Esther Sullivan's own words, the deception had been wicked.

I closed the *Bible* and turned my head to find Miss Sullivan standing just behind me, although I had not heard a sound. Her eyes were unnaturally bright, the pupils dilated.

"I'm sorry. So very sorry," I said.

She inclined her head and, without a word, held out her hands. I gave her the *Bible.* She still wore the black gloves and hat.

"I'm going to my room to pack a few things for tonight. I'll send for my other possessions tomorrow. Will you wait for me here, then take me across to the village in the *Thais?* I can manage the boat, of course, but someone must bring it back."

"Of course," I said. "But this can't be necessary. You must not leave like this—whatever Althea feels now."

"I am doing what I must do." She drew herself up, a slender but commanding figure. "This is a day I have longed for. I have waited for it."

She moved toward the corridor of the north wing, walking slowly and with dignity.

Turning to the window, I watched the bobbing of striped sails on the lake, still feeling pity for Esther Sullivan; but other thoughts were forming in my mind. I remembered her bitter quarrels with Althea just before Lillian's death, and I thought of her dexterity, her cleverness with wood or glue or metal. And she had been in charge of the stage properties for *Macbeth;* she had prepared the gas lamp, she had—

A voice behind me said, "Turn around very slowly, Catherine. You are not going across the lake today. You are to keep another engagement."

Miss Sullivan stood near me; in her gloved hand, held very steadily, was a pistol taken from Konrad's room.

"Do not attempt anything foolhardy," she said, her voice calm but higher pitched than usual. "I am quite capable of using this pistol. You may count on it."

"Althea!" I exclaimed, still too shocked to feel my danger. "Where is my mother?"

"Waiting for you, Catherine. Shall we go to her now?"

Then the reality of what was happening broke through to me; a moment before it had seemed a dream, but now I knew real fear. Measuring the distance between us, I decided to try to wrest the pistol from her. If she could only be distracted, made to glance away for a second! Praying I had inherited a little of Althea's gift for drama, I looked past Miss Sullivan— over her shoulder—and cried, "Mario! You're here!"

She did not turn away and her expression held contempt. "A miraculous arrival, since I spoke to him not ten minutes ago on the museum telephone. He was ready to leave Venice, but now he will stay there to wait for you and Althea. A long wait, I think.'' The twist of her lips was not a smile. "Now move slowly ahead of me. We are going to the museum.''

Outside, the sunlight was blinding, and as I walked along the terrace, the pistol a few feet from my back, the terrible incongruity of what was taking place struck me. Black and yellow butterflies flitted among the flower pots on the parapet; far out on the water the lake was gay with patterned sails. Danger and fear ought to be qualities of darkness, not part of bright, beautiful daylight. But I trembled in the hot sun.

Someone would appear at any second, I thought desperately. A car would enter the gates, Richard Halpin would cross the lawn. Someone had to arrive.

We reached the castle gates, and involuntarily I balked, my feet refusing to move.

"No, Catherine. Go ahead, turn left to the museum entrance. I told you, I am taking you to your mother.''

She did not prod the pistol barrel into my back, yet the effect of her voice was chilly and metallic. She is feeling nothing, I thought—nothing. I went on slowly, step after step— then, on the far side of the courtyard, standing near the ruined chapel with his back toward us, I saw Richard Halpin.

"If you make a sound, you will only endanger him.'' It was a thin whisper. "I have nothing to lose, remember.''

Even so, I might have cried out, but my voice froze in my throat. Trembling, I went toward the museum's open doors, praying Halpin would turn, willing him by the force of my mind to turn.

Mounting the stairs, one faint hope came to me. Richard Halpin's presence had surprised her; he must have arrived only a few minutes earlier, and whatever plans she had made would have to be changed. I clung to that hope, although I had seen madness in Esther Sullivan's eyes.

She ordered me to enter the office and again I heard that peculiar pitch of her voice, strange and distorted. When had her mind broken? Today, when Althea accused her? Then I realized I had seen this expression before; in Venice at Lillian's tomb, and earlier on my first day at the villa when a funeral procession had passed on the road.

"Stand still, Catherine. Stand where you are and do not turn around." I halted beside the desk, my eyes searching its surface for anything—a weapon, a way to call for help. I saw nothing except Prince Luigi's little flashlight, forgotten from the night of his questioning here. As I heard a cupboard door open behind me, I slipped it into the pocket of my smock. There was a faint noise as it fell against the opals.

"Go ahead now, through the studio."

"You won't succeed with this, you know." I forced the edge of hysteria from my voice. "Whatever you're planning, you'll be found out."

"Probably not. No one found out about Pandora. No one even suspected until you came here."

"Then you . . . you . . ." At last I managed to form the words. "You killed her."

"Pandora paid for Lillian. A daughter for a daughter. But it was not fair. She had other children—she had everything in the world. I had only Lillian."

We passed a mirror near the sewing area, and I caught a quick glimpse of her—right hand slightly extended, holding the pistol. She carried something in her left hand, but I could not see what it was.

"Open the door to the storeroom. Althea is there, Catherine."

The door to the small room that contained studio supplies had a faulty catch and did not close tightly. I pulled the knob and the door opened; I took one step forward, then held back a scream at what I saw.

Althea was on the floor in a slumped sitting position, her back against the wall. Glazed eyes, open, stared at me sightlessly. "You've killed her! No, no!" My hoarse whisper seemed wrenched from me—I gasped for breath—and as I started to turn to face Esther Sullivan, something needle sharp pierced my shoulder, penetrating my smock and blouse.

I clawed at the spot, pulled the object from my skin, then looked down at my hand. I was holding a device like a miniature syringe.

Esther Sullivan's brilliant stare met my eyes as a sudden wave of burning pain swept from my shoulder through my body. As my knees gave way and I felt paralysis spreading over me, I remembered the terrified fawn at the deer park and recognized what Miss Sullivan held in her left hand.

It was the tranquilizing gun. I stumbled helplessly across the storeroom to collapse in a corner opposite Althea.

In the first few minutes of panic and horror, I thought I would die of suffocation. Then, quite suddenly, I was calm and detached, inhaling easily. As Miss Sullivan left, shutting the door behind her, I felt my eyelids blink involuntarily. I could not have moved an eyelid of my own will, could not have stirred a finger or made a sound; yet my body had its own control—breathing, blinking, even swallowing from time to time. I saw and heard everything with complete clarity— Miss Sullivan's retreating footsteps, a creak of the floor. I felt the slight draft that moved a disheveled lock of Althea's hair.

I could not turn my head toward Althea, but she was partly in my line of vision and for a moment I dared let myself believe her chest moved, as if drawing breath. But I could not be sure; no matter how hard I willed my eyes to move, my gaze remained riveted straight ahead.

My sense of hearing had sharpened. Voices, Esther Sullivan's and Richard Halpin's, echoed far away in the corridor. Time passed—perhaps an hour, I could not tell. Something lightly touched my ear. A spider? The insect moved down my cheek, then I heard a buzz as it flew away—a common fly.

Without thinking or reasoning, I suddenly knew how Pandora had died. The hypodermic gun, of course. Miss Sullivan had lured her to the boathouse, paralyzed her as I was now paralyzed, then placed her in the yawl and let the boat drift into the stormy lake, knowing wind and water would do the rest. I forced my mind away from the horror of it.

Gradually the light from the window became tinged with sunset, then faded. After another interval, the window paled with the rising of the moon, and it came to me that I had raised my eyes a bit to see it. I commanded my arm to move, but it would not. I found, though, that I could turn my foot—only a little, but it meant I was recovering. The drug was wearing off.

Then, from the corner, I heard a sound—a deep sigh—and I knew Althea was alive and she, too, must be regaining some power of movement. But the drug had another effect I had not yet learned about. Just as I began to anticipate freedom, thinking I could stagger to the door and perhaps reach the telephone, I found myself floating, drifting, then sinking into a deep sleep.

Light blazed in my eyes. "Wake up! You can hear me, wake up!"

Esther Sullivan stood over me, the pistol as steady as before. Althea was struggling to her feet, and our eyes met, a wordless expression of hope.

Whatever pain and shock Althea had felt at discovering Miss Sullivan's madness, it had now passed. She spoke calmly, reasonably. "Sullie, be sensible. You have nothing to gain."

"You murdered Lillian." She said it with quiet, dangerous finality.

"That's not true," I told her. "You yourself loosened the valve of the lamp. Lillian died because you wanted to harm Althea."

"Be quiet!" Miss Sullivan's voice rose, and I knew I had touched a nerve: her own guilt in destroying Lillian.

"Yes, I meant to punish Althea. She had to be punished. My own daughter was contaminated, lost, because she followed Althea's example. All her life she had Althea's indecency before her." Then Miss Sullivan's strange eyes seemed blurred for a moment. "You never loved Lillian," she said to Althea, but speaking more quietly now. "On her birthday this year—her first birthday after you had killed her—you laughed and chattered with Pandora, your new daughter. Lillian's replacement! I watched you."

I remember the date on the tomb in Venice. In Miss Sullivan's unbalanced mind, a death sentence had been passed upon Pandora on Lillian's birthday. A life for a life, she had said.

"Besides, Pandora had to be destroyed. She found out; she knew how you were being punished and she accused me! It was only suspicion—she wasn't sure who was in the kitchen that night. I learned that from her diary. Oh, I burned the diary, Catherine. I know how you've searched for it."

I knew Althea did not understand—still did not know about the music played in the night. She shook her head, but said nothing.

"Enough talking. Walk ahead of me," Miss Sullivan commanded. "We are going to the museum entrance."

We were almost at the office door when Esther Sullivan began to speak again; a rambling monologue, both a confession and a boasting of her own cleverness. How easy it had been, she said, to lure me into the ballroom in Venice and to release the catch of the chandelier. Now I understood the click of metal I had heard that night.

As we crossed the office I saw that Mario's powerful electric torch had been placed on the desk. Miss Sullivan picked it up; I knew we were being taken into darkness.

Behind us, the mad litany continued. She spoke of Althea's stealing Victor Donato's love, and poured out the imagined injustices of the years. "You even gave away Lillian's music box after she was dead. Even that!"

When she mentioned the music box, I thought of Hansel and Gretel and of pebbles in the darkness. The opals gently weighted the pocket of my smock. I slipped my hand in, trying not to fumble obviously as I began to detach the stones from one another, carefully spearating the links.

We were almost at the landing when Rajah bounded out of the darkness into the beam of light. In a stubborn but playful mood, he ignored Miss Sullivan's sharp command and refused to leave us—rubbing against Althea, then preening himself beside me, padding along like a pet dog.

"Good boy," I said, touching him and, as I did so, covertly attaching one of the opal links to his collar, praying it would hold and Miss Sullivan would not see it.

At the museum entrance, I deliberately stumbled, and managed to leave another stone there.

"My ankle," I moaned. "I've sprained it."

"Walk, Catherine!"

But under the guise of the sprained ankle, I succeeded in placing two more opals to indicate a path across the courtyard of the castle.

We reached the abandoned chapel, and I saw that the boards barring the way had been pushed to one side and the danger sign removed.

"Don't hang back, Catherine," she said. "It's quite safe. I myself believed Luigi's story about the building being dangerous until I followed him and discovered his secret entrance to the castle courtyard."

Rajah, not liking the building, trotted away. I pretended to steady myself against the wooden doorjamb, and found a small nail that would hold another stone.

"You were quite frightened that day, weren't you, Catherine? I don't know who took away the danger sign. I suppose it was some workman who couldn't read. But I couldn't have you exploring here. I kept this secret for myself."

We passed through the nave and crossing. At Miss Sullivan's order, Althea pulled at the edge of the retablo screen of martyred saints, and it swung open—a heavy but well-balanced door concealed by the paintings and their frames. Beyond the door a flight of stone steps descended, vanishing in blackness. A musty draft chilled my arms, and far away I heard the sound of falling water. Grasping the door, pretending to need support, I left a stone on the deep framing of a pilgrim portrait.

Soon, I knew, the end would come. She had planned death for us and to believe anything else was an illusion. I resolved then that I would fight back; I would not go meekly. But what moment to choose? Not on these stairs, I thought. They were too steep, too narrow.

We reached a stone landing, and on the right an ancient, iron-studded door stood open. As we entered the chamber beyond, I glanced back, saw Esther Sullivan touch the pocket of her dress, and heard a metallic clink of keys. This, I knew, was our destination; here we must fight for our lives or lose them. We stood on another narrow landing several yards long. On the left, a wall of granite blocks rose to a low ceiling; on the right, the unrailed landing fell away to emptiness, water gushing somewhere far below. We could not let Esther Sullivan close that heavy door behind us—we must make our stand now. Althea gave me a glance, her eyes flashing, and I knew we were together.

"My ankle!" I cried, slowly sinking toward the floor and turning back as I did so.

"It does not matter now," said Miss Sullivan. "We have reached the place where—"

I sprang at her, leaping, seizing her right wrist—and the gun exploded, spitting fire near my face. She stumbled back, falling against the door, which swung shut with a heavy thud. I had hold of the pistol now, deflecting its aim, but I could not pry it from her grip. The fingers of her other hand twisted in my hair, forcing my head back. The pistol fired again, the barrel hot in my hands.

Suddenly the pistol was jerked from me; Esther Sullivan fell backward and, with a terrible, slowly diminishing cry, plunged from the landing into the dark void—downward toward the unseen spate of water dashing over rocks in the depths of the cavern.

Althea was sitting on the top step when I returned from exploring our prison. "I'm afraid there's no way out the bottom of the stairs," I told her. "It's a long corridor with small rooms opening off it. A prison, I suppose."

I had used Mario's electric torch, which Miss Sullivan had

dropped during our struggle, and I did not tell Althea what else its beam had revealed. Below us lay a charnel house; I knew now that the grim legends about Castle Malaspina were all too true. I had followed the route of the thirteenth pilgrim to its end.

"I think we should ration the flashlight batteries, Catherine," she said. "It may be several hours before they find us."

Several hours? I turned off the light. Several days, several weeks . . . a hundred years? We both knew this, although it remained unsaid between us. The door was solid oak with iron studding. We could not rattle it, much less force its spring lock open.

"Do you know any poems, Catherine?"

"A few. And some scattered lines."

"Very well. I shall sing, then you will recite or tell a story," she said. "We will use the time to know each other better. You know, we were a long time finding ourselves, but it has been worth the waiting."

I do not know when at last we fell asleep. I refused to look at my watch, knowing that if I began to count the hours, they would become endless.

But I did sleep, and when I awakened, my body aching, I realized that Althea was no longer beside me. She stood near the door, pressing her ear against it, the flashlight in her hand.

"What is it?" I rose, and discovered the ankle injury I had pretended had, in the struggle, become a reality. I could hardly stand.

"There are voices, perhaps," said Althea, trying to contain her excitement. "Yes, voices." Taking off her slipper, she pounded on the oak boards with its heel.

And then, slowly, the door of our prison opened. Beams of light—brilliant, glorious light—flooded the landing. Mario was there, and with him other men.

"Thank God," he said as he moved toward me. "Thank God!"

Later we would learn what had happened—that our lives had been saved by Ilse Donato, who had been watching with the ship's spyglass when Esther Sullivan forced me, at gunpoint, to walk from the villa to the castle.

She realized the fate planned for me, because she had also watched Esther Sullivan on the day of Pandora's death, although she never quite admitted this.

At first Ilse delayed, then—deciding she owed her life to me—finally reached Konrad by telephone, after hours of calling hotel after hotel in Monte Carlo. Konrad then spoke to Mario, who was awaiting us in Venice, unconcerned because Miss Sullivan had told him we would arrive "very late."

But we owed our final rescue not to historical detective work, as I first supposed, but to Lisa. She followed the men searching for us and at the door of the museum cried out, "Look! A stone shining in the moonlight." They had then followed the trail to the chapel.

Later, too, the men who searched found underground passages that emerged far away, near an ancient shrine once owned by Prince Luigi.

But at the moment of our rescue, no explanations mattered; I did not care how Mario found me, only that he had come. We said no words except, "I love you," and even those were unneeded.

When he saw me hobbling, he lifted me and carried me in his arms up the stone stairway, through its ancient darkness into the shadows of the chapel. The courtyard of Castle Malaspina lay in the first pale silver of dawn, but beyond the gates the eastern sky glowed with a bright promise.